# MONSTER

# MONSTER

c j skuse

MIRA Ink is a registered trademark of Harlequin Enterprises Limited, used under licence.

Published in Great Britain 2015
by MIRA Ink, an imprint of Harlequin (UK) Limited,
Eton House, 18-24 Paradise Road,
Richmond, Surrey, TW9 1SR

© 2015 CJ Skuse

ISBN: 978-1-848-45389-0
eISBN: 978-1-474-03098-4

47-0915

Harlequin (UK) Limited's policy is to use papers that are natural, renewable and recyclable products and made from wood grown in sustainable forests. The logging and manufacturing processes conform to the legal environmental regulations of the country of origin.

Printed and bound by
CPI Group (UK) Ltd, Croydon, CR0 4YY

**C.J. Skuse** is the author of the YA novels PRETTY BAD THINGS, ROCKOHOLIC and DEAD ROMANTIC. She was born in 1980 in Weston-super-Mare, England. She has First Class degrees in Creative Writing and Writing for Children and, aside from writing novels, lectures in Writing for Children at Bath Spa University where she is planning to do her PhD. C.J's fifth novel THE DEVIANTS will be published by Mira Ink in 2016.

For Jamie, he is my brother
I said there is no other

*'Hell is empty. All the devils are here.'*

*The Tempest,*
William Shakespeare

# 1
## I, Monster

That last week at school before the Christmas holidays, death was in everything.

In Geography, the sea was eating away the coasts. In English, Juliet was stabbing herself with Romeo's dagger. Even the school gerbil, Rafferty, was found stiff in his water bowl on Tuesday lunchtime. The skies above us bore a foreboding grey gloom, telling us snow was on its way to suffocate the land. In the dorms, everyone was packing up their trunks for the coming break and preparing to say goodbye to the year.

And in our last floodlit netball practice that Friday evening, I saw the monster.

The thing generations of Bathory girls had nightmares about. The Beast of Bathory.

I watched it in the fading light through the wire mesh

of our netball court fencing. A black mass, stalking quietly across the playing fields, its two yellow eyes turning to stare at me every so often as it walked, unchecked. Unafraid.

*Pheeeeeeeeeeeeeeeeeeeeeeeeeeeeeeeeee!* went the whistle.

'Nash, pass! Pass! I'm free! I'm free!'

I was watching it as much as it was watching me.

*Pheeeeee!* 'Natasha, are you playing netball today? Or are *we* playing netball and *you* playing Musical Statues?'

I tried to get my head back in the game. 'Sorry, Mrs Scott.'

'Rebound, pink team,' she called, marching back up the court, whistle ready in her mouth. I sneaked a look behind me to the playing fields, but there was no sign of it. It must have dashed into the hedge. I put my trainer to the yellow line and clutched the ball firmly, looking for a free pink-bib to throw to.

'Aaaaaaand…' *Pheee!*

'Nash! Nash! Overhead! Here! Here!' Maggie Zappa was calling for it. Wing Attack, socks at half-mast, hair a mass of black curls. School rebel. I wasn't throwing to her.

'Nash! Here!' Clarice Hoon, Goal Attack, too much make-up, bedmate of half the Lower Sixth St Anthony's boys. We had a history. I wasn't throwing to her.

Dianna Pfaff, my opposition Centre, was using every-thing she had. She wasn't as fast as me, but she was tall, with a ballerina's balance, and had several times marked me out of the game. Her thick blonde curls bounced and flew as she darted left to right in front of me, shadowing my every movement with her hands. I had to throw.

I saw Regan. Wing Defence, black plaits hanging down and thick, clear-framed glasses. Way back on the line. She had arrived in the Lower Fifth with a subtle smell of wrongness about her and the appearance of a spinster in her late fifties. She wasn't even calling for it. I threw to her.

It bounced high off the ground in front of her, and she fumbled it offside.

*Pheeeeeeee!* 'Foul ball. Advantage blue team.'

Regan bit her lip. Clarice rolled her eyes.

Maggie Zappa puffed and blew her fringe curls up from her face. 'Da fuq didn't you throw it to me? I was free. I had acres!'

'Margaret Zappa!' yelled Mrs Scott.

'But I was free!' She turned back to me, slapping her hands to her sides. 'What did you throw to her for? You might as well have thrown it over the fence.'

The blues scored a goal before Mrs Scott had finished dressing down Maggie for a string of ensuing bad language. We all went back to the centre. Dianna Pfaff had the ball.

*Pheeeeeeeee!*

'Dianna, here! Here!'

I marked Dianna's movements like a shadow. She couldn't pass, couldn't get to anyone. Frustration screamed from her.

*Pheeeeeeee!* 'Possession. Advantage pinks.' Mrs Scott's fat thighs smacked together as she marched over to us and pointed to the spot, handing me the ball. I spotted a free pink and lobbed it across the court.

'Aw, hospital pass!' cried Mrs Scott, as the ball bounced away from Jenny. 'Rebound! Advantage pinks. Rebound. Advantage blues. Come on, you're not nailed to the ground, reach for the ball! Jump for it!' Goal Attack to Goal Shooter. Score. *Pheeeeeee!* 'Pinks lead two to one.'

Dianna threw me a look as the ball was lobbed back in my direction.

*Pheeeeeee!*

'Nash, pass! Over here, over here! I'm free!'

'Nash, for God's sake!'

'Natasha! What are you…'

It had stopped there, just in front of the hedge, a black shape moving in the falling darkness across the playing fields. The huge black shape. It was waiting for me to go over to it. I went across the gravel, across the grass of the playing fields to the swings.

'Natasha, come back here! What on earth…'

I had to see it more clearly. I had to know if it was there for sure, the thing I'd been seeing for weeks now, darting across fields, hiding around corners, vanishing behind trees. The killer of dozens of sheep and chickens. And possibly humans.

But, in a second, it had gone, vanished into the hedge with barely the rustle of a leaf.

Someone was behind me, walking quickly to catch up. I turned. Regan Matsumoto.

'That was it, wasn't it?' she said breathlessly. 'You saw it, didn't you, Nash?'

I didn't answer. Our PE teacher was marching up the grass behind us, face as red as her Aertex shirt. I was going to be punished. The only punishment Mrs Scott ever doled out: the thing no one wanted to do.

'Just what the hell…'

'I'll collect the balls, Mrs Scott.' I walked past her back towards the court.

There were many bad things about Bathory School for Girls—the rules, the staff, the food, the beds, the home-sickness and the spooky legends including the Beast of Bathory—but some things about it were truly wonderful.

For a start, there was the amount of time we were expected to be outside. We were always playing sports—netball, hockey, tennis in the summer, swimming when it was hot enough in the outdoor pool.

Then there were the Hidey Holes, secret doorways and passages all over the main house, which had been there since Elizabethan times. Apparently their original purpose was to conceal Catholic priests who'd visited South Devon and taken refuge there—according to legend, one priest had hidden in a Hidey Hole for so long that he suffocated and died. Bathory girls had found four main Hidey Holes—two linking the Fiction and Reference Libraries, one in the Laundry room behind the towel rails and one in the wall behind the stage at the back of the gym—but there were more. The house itself was this huge, imposing grey building, surveying the remote South Devon moors like some buxom grey nursemaid with shining black eyes. It had a long flat roof and large turrets at either end. One turret was the Observatory where we had telescopes for stargazing, and in the other was the Weather Station where we took readings for science.

We had Hogwartsy-style Houses—Plantagenet, Tudor, Hanover and Windsor—and there was an unwritten rule that girls seemed to get picked for them according to their status, which was kind of like Hogwarts too. All the bad girls went in Plantagenet, all the ones good at sport went into Hanover, all the brainy ones went to Tudor and all the, well, the ones who weren't really good at anything went in Windsor.

Another wonderful thing about Bathory was its setting. It was literally in the middle of nowhere, surrounded by fields and woods and acres of land in which to get lost. We were miles away from any form of civilisation, but we were quite self-sufficient. We had tennis courts, netball courts, playing fields, hockey pitches and formal and kitchen gardens where the cooks grew herbs and vegetables. Behind the house was a huge wooded valley with two large ponds and five beautiful follies in the upper sections of the woods. These were called the Birdcage, the Temple, the Wendy House, the Tree House and the Chapel. If you stood at the bottom of the valley by Edward's Pond and looked up, you could see all of them, dotted around at regular intervals, like ornaments on a giant cake.

Back in the mists of time, before it became a school in the 1930s, Bathory House was the private home of the Duke and Duchess of Bathory and their twins, Edward and Grace, who were incredibly spoilt. When the little boy had asked for a pond to keep some fish, the little girl asked for a lake. Then the boy had asked for a tree house in the woods, but the girl had asked for a life-size version of her doll's house, and so on and so forth. So basically, the Follies were monuments to the tantrums of two greedy little brats.

The wonderful really did outweigh the not-so-wonderful at Bathory and I loved it there. Especially at Christmas. The week before Christmas hols was usually the most magical time—full of parties, log fires, tobogganing down the hillsides in the snow, making sugarplums and traditional decorations for the end of term concert. It normally left me with the feeling of complete and utter happiness. Of safety. Of certainty that this was perfection.

But this Christmas, everything was different. There was no squidgy feeling. There was no safety. For me, Christmas was cancelled.

And Dianna Pfaff was making the most of my misery.

She sidled up to me as I was collecting up the balls after netball practice that evening.

'Your head's not really in it at the moment, is it?'

'Oh, it's okay, you don't have to help. Mrs Scott asked me to…'

'I want to help,' she said, and set the bibs down on the ground to help me pick up balls. 'I heard about your brother…'

'What about my brother?'

'About him being missing. Everyone knows.'

'He's not missing. He just hasn't been in touch with my parents for a few days. They're a bit worried. He'll be okay. How does everyone know?'

'Penny Marriott heard it from Kezzie Wood who got it from a Pup with chickenpox who was waiting outside Mrs Saul-Hudson's office when you went in this morning.'

'So the whole school knows?'

Dianna's lips thinned. 'What's the latest?'

She said it like you'd ask for a weather update. 'He went on some whale-watching expedition at a national park on the northern coast of Colombia. He was supposed to ring home two days ago but he didn't. Probably just out of range.'

Dianna nodded. 'Do you think you'll be staying here for Christmas then? If your parents have to fly out to Cambodia?'

The thought was acid in my mouth. 'It's Colombia. And no, it won't come to that. He'll be fine, I'm sure.'

But still Dianna looked twitchy. 'Mum said there's a chance I might be staying. Hope not though. Christmas here would be a nightmare. She's still in Spain. New boyfriend. Such a leech… Anyway, if you want a hand with any of Mrs Saul-Hudson's stuff…'

'What do you mean?'

'Well, I don't know, just, like, the diary or making her tea or organising anything, you know, just give me a shout. I'm here if you want the help.'

She'd been like this for months, ever since she found out I was the front runner for Head Girl. The final week she had really ramped up the helpful bit.

'I know you want Head Girl as well, Dianna.'

'No, no, it's not that at all,' she said with a nervous laugh, eyebrows up in her hairline, trying to come across completely blasé. She bounced a white netball between her fingers. 'But you're under a lot of stress at the moment, getting everything ready for end of term and the Christmas Fayre and the concert and what with your brother...'

'My brother will be fine,' I said, measuring every word so it didn't come out as loudly as I wanted it to. So many other words teetered on my tongue, from 'I can manage perfectly well without your help, you endless parasitic worm' to 'Get lost and die a slow lingering death in a ditch.' But none of those things were ever going to come out of my mouth. In the end I simply said, 'Thanks.'

In the changing rooms, the school matron and Maggie Zappa were arguing like two alley cats over a fish bone.

'I didn't take it, all right? Stupid old fart. Why do you always assume it's me?'

'Because it usually is!' screeched Matron, hands on hips, her tight blue uniform dotted with melting ice flecks. She'd apparently been head first in the chest freezer, looking for some lost meat.

'I haven't touched your stupid turkeys. Get your hands off me!'

Eventually, Mrs Scott and Matron grabbed Maggie's arms

and led her bodily up the corridor towards the Head's office, a string of expletives dancing along the air behind her.

'Margaret, the more you struggle the harder you're going to make this for yourself.'

'I didn't take them! Am I speaking another language? Have I woken up Chinese like that woman in the science video? I'm not responsible for your stupid turkey theft, *capiche*?'

'You're a liar,' said Matron, teeth gritted, a huge bunch of keys jangling violently against her hip and strands of her black hair coming loose from her tight bun. 'This has got your name written all over it, Maggie.'

'Where? Where's my name? Where? Tell me. Where's the proof? I haven't done anything. Nash, tell them I didn't take them!'

I said nothing as they came past me, just did that very British thing of averting my eyes, cleaning a smudge on a nearby door frame. I made my way into the changing rooms and got washed and dressed for Prep.

I couldn't associate with Maggie Zappa this week. Not this week of all weeks. I'd already blotted my clean copybook in netball by going into some kind of trance and walking off court. I couldn't defend Public School Enemy Number 1 as well. Maggie had earned over twenty Blue Tickets for Plantagenet House this month alone. This week was just too important to even be seen talking to her. That badge was too important.

All I'd wanted since I'd arrived at Bathory was the Head Girl badge. The previous Head Girl had left the school suddenly at the start of the autumn term and ever since then Mrs Saul-Hudson had been vetting potential prefects. I was the front runner, there was no doubt. I'd made sure of it. I only had one more week to wait for the announcement and then all my deportment badges, my 349 Gold Tickets, my academic awards, my staying up late to help the Headmistress with the diary, all my sycophancy would be rewarded. Just one more week.

After changing, I did my hair in the sink mirrors and found myself standing next to Clarice Hoon. 'They found your brother yet?' she said, applying a thick layer of concealer to her under-eyes.

A dark cloud descended across my vision. I covered my accelerating heartbeat and shortness of breath by combing down my honey bob until my hair looked like the two sides of a golden apple. 'Sorry?'

'He's quite fit, isn't he?' she continued, turning to look at me. She had so much mascara on she could barely lift her eyelids.

*Don't give her the oxygen of attention,* came the voice in my head. *She wants you to respond.* I checked the pleats of my raspberry tunic and plucked a lint ball from my navy cardigan, ensuring my netball, hockey, tennis and athletics badges were all equidistant down the side of the V; my prefect's badge in alignment with the base of my tie. One space remained on the V—the one right on my heart. Head Girl.

Clarice didn't like my lack of reaction. 'What will you do if he's dead?'

'Clarice Hoon, you're on your way to Prep, not the Oscars.' Mrs Scott had returned from helping Matron, complete with reddened cheeks, blown pupils and a torn shell-suit sleeve. 'Enough with the make-up.'

Clarice waited for Mrs Scott to move away before she leaned in to me. I felt her hot breath on my ear. 'I think he is dead.' She slung her kitbag over one shoulder, smiled at our teacher, and slunk out of the room like a pedigree Persian who'd won Best in Show.

I had tried to keep the thought from my mind for the past two days but hearing it from someone else—hearing it from *her*—was too much to bear. I thought the room was empty when I collapsed against the cold porcelain basin, my forehead in my hands, my sobs echoing around the white walls. But, moments later, she appeared, standing over me.

Regan Matsumoto helped me to my feet.

# 2
## The Devil Inside

Sebastian, my good-looking big brother with the shaggy blond hair. At twenty-two, he was six years older than me and he was good at it too. He'd taught me how to ride a bike, defend myself, drive a car and tie my shoelaces. Seb had tried to make me unafraid of life. Now, the only thing that made me afraid was not knowing where he was. If he was still alive.

Was. *Is*, I meant to say. He *is* still alive. His heart *is* still beating. I couldn't begin to think of him in the past tense.

Saturday came, Saturday went. Sunday came with a screaming headache, and went with more crying, this time into the Che Guevara t-shirt that I'd nicked from his room at exeat.

Sunday lunchtime, Mum called—still no word.

I found myself volunteering to do things away from everyone so I wouldn't have to look at the pitying faces, deal with the questions, talk to anyone about anything. I offered to clean the storage sheds in the Pig Yard at the back of the tennis courts, pull up weeds in the formal gardens, salt the drive, walk to Bathory village for provisions, just so I could sob without some infuriating arm coming round my shoulder. I wanted to work and walk until I was too tired to think. But it was impossible not to think.

I had looked up Colombia in the Reference Library. It had over 1.14 million square miles of land. Two thousand miles of coastline. Rainforests. Deserts. I found encyclopedia entries about tribal tales: mythical beasts that ate backpackers whole. Drug cartels who hacked off human heads with swords. Tourists going missing and never being found. Paranoia set in like bacteria and mutated over everything. I clung on to the one thing I knew—that I didn't know anything.

*I'm all right. Stop worrying. Worrying gets you nowhere.* I heard him in my mind. I wanted to believe it.

I was in the field at the top of the drive, walking the school Newfoundland, Brody, when I saw it again. And again, all was silent. The birds had stopped.

The monster.

It was three fields away, a large black shape stalking through the long grass. Definitely too big to be a farm cat. I waited. In a couple of blinks, it had disappeared into a thicket of trees.

No one alive had seen this thing for decades. There had been sightings, scratch marks on tree trunks. Blood on the odd rocky outcrop on the moor. The odd fruit-loop venturing onto the moors, trying to track it, to no avail. I had seen it twice inside of a week. Why me?

Each night since my netball meltdown, I dreamed about my brother. I'd call for him and hear nothing but growls in the distance. A burning shack in a thick forest. Running up an endless staircase, feeling my skin burn as I screamed for him. A jungle of trees. An endless landscape of greenery and strange noises and dark places. In one dream, I parted some leaves and saw the monster, the huge black Beast, its head bent over Seb's body. It looked up at me, orange eyes gleaming, my brother's beating heart clamped between its jaws.

Regan Matsumoto wasn't helping. She kept appearing silently in doorways, right in front of me. Never saying anything, just looking at me with black eyes like a ghost. One night I swore I saw her on the landing by the toilet. But the next moment she was gone.

Dianna Pfaff was shadowing everything I did like a very persistent blonde stain—offering to wake up the Pups for me, insisting on monitoring Prep with me, catching the post before I could get there, giving teachers messages I was supposed to give them. All to 'give me a break'. All in the name of 'help'. I didn't need her help. I especially didn't need the kind of help she wanted to give me. I could have screamed the roof tiles down. But I simply said, 'Thanks,' every time. Because Head Girl doesn't scream the roof tiles down. Or rather, *wannabe* Head Girl doesn't. The rumours from the village weren't helping either. More and more began to swirl around: Mr Pellett had been attacked on his own doorstep in the middle of the night. There was blood spray on his hallway ceiling. A large shape had been seen stalking across his garden. Mrs Saul-Hudson told me to 'play down the rumours' and 'say it was a burglary that had gone wrong'. I wanted to say no, say, *You don't know that for sure and neither do the police. It could be the monster.* But I did the same as I always did. I said, 'Yes, Mrs Saul-Hudson.'

The more I tried to clear my mind, the more it would fog till it felt like Head Girl was a rope dangling off a cliff face and I was barely clinging on. But cling on I did. I bottled and I clung. Everything I wanted to say, I kept to myself. Everything I wanted to answer her back about—the comments about my 'scrawny wrists' as I wrote in the diary, my 'distinctly miserable face of late' that might put off prospective parents at the Christmas Fayre—I held back. I swallowed it all down with a glass of tepid tap water and left it at that.

By Monday morning, Seb had been missing for exactly five days and I was losing it rapidly. I felt like a fish on the end of an unending reel.

French:

*'Natasha, est ce qu'il ya une piscine près d'ici?'*

Something about swimming pools. *'Er, non.'*

*'Non?'*

*'Non, Madame.'*

*'Ah oui. Maintenant, nous sommes aimerons aller au la plage.'*

*Plage* was beach. I think. Or plague. *'Oui, la plage.'*

*'Pouvez-vous me donner des directives à la plage, s'il vous plaît?'*

Something about medicines to take when you had the plague? Or was she asking for cafés near the beach? My mind was a blank page. I had nothing. *'Uh, non?'*

*'Non?'*

*'Oui. Er, non.'*

*Le grand* sigh.

Maths:

'With that in mind, Natasha, what is the value of n?'

'The value of n?'

'Yes, on the board. See where it says n? What is the value of n, if we know that x = 40 and y is 203?'

'I don't know.'

'You don't know?'

'No. What was y again?'

English Lit :

'So, studying these passages in *Jane Eyre* and *A Tale of Two Cities*, how do we begin to compare and contrast some of the ways in which Victorian novelists use landscape to lend resonance to their work? Natasha?'

'What?'

'Didn't you hear what I just said?'

'Uh, no, sorry, miss.'

Big sigh. 'The landscape in these two books. How does it lend resonance?'

'I have no idea.' Sniggers from the back.

*It's not like you, Natasha. It's not like you. It's not like you, not like you, not like you.*

The only light that shone onto that day was when I saw the little white Bathory Basics van coming up the drive just before sunset. It pulled up on the gravel driveway just to the left of the front entrance, near the side door to the kitchens. I passed Mrs Saul-Hudson in the front porch.

'It's all right, ma'am. It's just Bathory Basics with the turkeys for Christmas lunch.'

'Oh wonderful, Natasha. I'll leave you to deal with it. I've got the police on their way. Do you know where Dianna is?'

I stopped in my tracks. 'The police? Is everything all right, ma'am?'

'Yes yes yes,' she said, all flustered and hair-flicky, looking all about her for something. 'They come every year around this time. Just checking on who is staying over Christmas. Making sure we've done our safety checks, that's all. All quite routine. Have you seen my handbag? Oh, I must have left it upstairs.'

'Do you need me to talk to the police with you, ma'am?'

'No, I need Dianna. You've got enough to deal with.'

'Is it about the man in the village who was killed, ma'am?'

'Yes,' she said and minced off upstairs without another word.

Bloody Dianna, I thought. Bloody bloody bloody Dianna. Why was *she* the one to help her talk to the police about it? What about me?

I tried to shake the image of the blonde assassin from my mind as I stepped out onto the front mosaic to greet Charlie Gossard from the shop and try to be happy. I'd had a substantial crush on Charlie for a while now. His dad ran Bathory Basics and he worked there, serving customers and 'out the back' though I never really knew what went on 'out the back'. It had started with the odd flirty comment about what I was buying whenever I walked there on a Saturday morning for provisions, then it progressed to long looks across the freezer in the summer. Now, we were into conversations and every now and again he'd give me some sell-by pies or sweets if there were any due for chucking out. I hadn't told him about Seb being missing or anything serious like that—our conversations mostly ran to school or what Xbox game he'd recently bought and what his top score was.

He caught sight of me as he got out the driver's door. 'Hi, Nash.'

'Hi, Charlie,' I said.

'How are you?'

'Yeah, fine thanks.'

He was big into gaming, and even though I wasn't at all, I enjoyed listening to him talk. He could have been reciting the phone book and I'd listen to him. Charlie had short blond hair, blue eyes and always wore tight t-shirts, even in winter, which you could see his nipples through. Maggie said he was a '*un renard chaud*', which meant a hot fox, but I just thought he was lovely. There was always a long white apron tied around his waist, usually smeared with grubby fingermarks.

'Do you need any help?'

'Yeah, if you don't mind. Thanks.'

His smile cut a diamond into the early evening light and he went to the back doors of the refrigerated van to unlock them, then reached in to get one of three humungous turkeys out for me to carry.

'She's a heavy one, mind. You got it?'

'Yeah,' I said, straining to hold it in both hands and making my way towards the kitchen door. He grasped the other two, one in each hand.

'Dad said make sure your cook knows they're premium birds. KellyBronze. Free range, the lot.'

'Oh, great,' I said, struggling a little with the weight of mine as he edged past me and opened the side door to allow me inside. Cook was delighted and, as she and Charlie settled the invoice, I hung around, even though I knew I had no business being there. I was just waiting. For anything. For some little shred of Charlie that I could think about for the rest of the day. Something to send me to sleep smiling tonight instead of crying.

When the invoice was settled and he and Cook had talked about cooking times and types of stuffing and 'succulence', he walked back out with me to the annoyingly nearby van.

'So,' he said. 'I guess you go home for the holidays tomorrow then?'

'Yeah. I guess so.'

'Not looking forward to it?'

I shrugged. 'It'll be nice to see my parents. Yeah. Yeah, it'll be nice. Presents and Midnight Mass and everything.'

'Oh, we went one year. Pretty boring really.'

'It's tradition though, isn't it? My mum and dad enjoy it.'

'Yeah, it is. Gotta keep the old folks happy.'

'Yeah.'

We both laughed, a nervous sort of laugh that went on as long as it could because it was obvious neither of us knew what to say next. We'd run out of conversation so quickly, I hadn't seen it coming. I had nothing in reserve to impress him with. I did a bit of subtle eye-batting and leaning in the hope of… What was I hoping for? For him to take me in his arms and ravish me right there in the school driveway? I didn't know. I just knew I needed something from him. Something more.

'What are you getting for Christmas then?' I asked, hopelessly. Desperately.

He laughed. 'Probably some Boxing Day overtime and a thick ear.' He smiled, wringing his hands like they were cold. I did the same, mirroring his movements.

'Are yours freezing too?' he asked, reaching for them and taking them in his. They were warmer than mine, but at that moment I didn't care if he'd been lying about having cold hands just so he could hold mine. I didn't want him to let go. 'Yeah, they are.' That tiny moment, with him holding my hands in his, made the day seem finally worth getting up for.

'I'm all right now,' I said, regrettably pulling them away and looking down to hide the flames in my cheeks.

'Listen, you better get in and warm up before they fall off. I've got another twelve of these to deliver before the end of the day. Have a great Christmas, all right? And I'll see you next term.'

'Yeah,' I said, as I watched him make his way back to the van. 'Charlie?' I called, when he was almost in.

'Yeah?' He looked back.

'You have a great Christmas too.' And we both smiled at each other. For now, that would have to be enough.

Monday night after Prep and monitoring the Pups' bedtime, I bathed and wrapped myself in my school-approved navy dressing gown and raspberry slippers with the school crest on and went down to Mrs Saul-Hudson's office for our usual routine of cocoa and diary. She was sitting at her desk when I knocked and went in, closing the door behind me.

'Oh, Natasha, is it that time already?' she said, already in her pyjamas and dressing gown herself and looking more flustered than normal. 'Sorry, I've got *such* a lot to do before tomorrow.'

'Good evening, ma'am.' I placed her cocoa mug down in front of her, my tap water down in front of me, and opened the diary to tomorrow's page so she could see it. 'It's all done for you to check.'

'Wonderful. Before we go through tomorrow's notes, have a seat. I wanted to talk to you about something.'

'Yes, ma'am?'

She took a sip of her cocoa and I took a sip of my water. Then she settled down the mug. 'Lovely. Just right as usual. Right, last day of term tomorrow, we've got lots of visitors coming. Who is supervising Pups all day?'

I opened my notebook and clicked on my pen. 'The usual staff, ma'am, plus I've allocated three prefects from Tudor, Hanover and Windsor House to the three groups as well. No lessons means lots of extra hands on deck, which is great.'

'Excellent. And how about the Tenderfoots?'

I checked my notes. 'Two prefects, three members of staff and two TAs. That should be quite enough, ma'am. A lot of the Tenderfoots have gone home early.'

'Good, and the Christmas Fayre?'

'Stallholders will be arriving from ten a.m. and the Years Nine and Ten have been briefed by their form tutors about helping set up stalls and—'

'What about the play?'

'Years Nine and Ten will be setting out the chairs once they've helped with the stalls.'

Mrs Saul-Hudson smiled and sat back in her large leather chair, like a queen testing out a new throne. 'Where would I be without you, Natasha?'

I smiled and blushed at the same time, taking a large sip of my water.

'So how are you bearing up? It must be very hard on you and your parents with Sebastian still not found.'

She'd sucker-punched me, bringing Seb into the conversation so quickly, but in a way I was glad she'd found time to care.

'I'm trying not to think about it really, ma'am,' I said. 'Not much I can do by worrying.'

'That's the stuff,' she said proudly. 'Keep busy, that's always the best way. No sense in worrying. Worrying, I always say, does not empty tomorrow of its troubles, just empties today of its strength. You bear that in mind, won't you?'

'I will, ma'am,' I said, once I'd figured it out.

'And you're doing a marvellous job here so it would be a shame if…well, if things started to slip.'

I didn't know what she meant by that at that exact moment, but I didn't have time to figure it out because the next demand came swiftly round the next corner.

'Oh, and in the morning I want you to arrange some signage to go up once the choral procession through the woods is over. I've asked Mr Munday to…well, we've taken steps anyway, just in case anything grisly is about. I'm sure there isn't but, well, best to be safe.'

'Yes, ma'am. Just regulation "Keep Out" signs, was it?'

'Yes. Nobody will be going up there over Christmas anyway, but we need signs keeping anyone out of the woods and away from the ponds in case they freeze over.'

I made a note in my book. 'Yes, ma'am. Is this what the police suggested we do?'

'Hmm?' she said, looking up from her papers in alarm as if I'd just asked her what method she suggested I hang myself with.

'Your meeting with the police this afternoon? They were here to talk about the man in the village and the…beast?'

'Oh that!' she said, almost shrieking with laughter. 'Oh that, yes. Yes, the police did say we needed to take extra precautions.'

'And… Dianna was a good help with the police?'

'Yes, wonderful. Actually, you really have both been a

constant support this year. And without any detriment to your grades. I don't know how you and Dianna do it, I really don't.'

I poured a mental pail of cold water over the flames that had just ignited in my mind. Dianna? A constant support? A constant thorn in my side, rather. A constant interloper on *my* duties, definitely. 'Well, I can't speak for Dianna but I enjoy it, ma'am. I like helping out.'

'Well, you've both been a marvel. How is the play coming along?'

'Oh we're almost there, ma'am. If you'd like to come and watch the dress rehearsal, we'll be starting just after Prayers tomorrow morning.'

'Lovely, yes, I might do that. And talking of Prayers...'

*Here it comes*, I thought. *This is it. This was the moment I've been waiting for.* My heart began to pump like a clubhouse classic.

'Would you be an absolute dear and set out the hymn books first thing tomorrow, please? I meant to ask Clarice Hoon but I never got round to it. Oh and breakfast tomorrow—'

'I can monitor it,' I said quickly, so as to squeeze the information, the golden information out of her just that bit quicker. 'Sorry, ma'am, was there something else you wanted to say about Prayers?'

'Uh, yes, erm, I've forgotten what it was now,' she chuckled. 'I'm sure it'll come to me. I must just tidy up these last few things and show my face at the staff Christmas party. I promised I'd do a little speech and announce Employee of the Year. Any idea where that gold picture frame I got from the mother-in-law last Christmas is?'

'Yes, it's on your tallboy in your apartments, ma'am.'

*C.J. Skuse*

'Oh good, I'll wrap that up quickly and give that as a prize. Was there anything else?'

'Er, no, ma'am.'

She got up from her desk chair as I got up from mine, and went over to her corner armoire and took down a coat hanger from which hung her Christmas end-of-term red trouser suit. 'Be a dear and go up and hang this in my bedroom would you?'

I looked at her. I waited for her to look at me. Any sign, any inkling, any vestige of good news, vanished from her face.

'That'll be all for tonight, thank you, Natasha,' she said finally, with a knotted brow, clicking off her desk lamp and leaving me in darkness.

# 3
## Insidious

I spent a fitful night, worrying about Seb and angsting over Head Girl. Obsessing over why my dad hadn't called me with news. Fixating over why Mrs Saul-Hudson hadn't mentioned some shred of hope that that badge was mine in our meeting. If I got that badge I would be able to cope better with Seb's disappearance, I knew I would. I'd be able to focus myself on my duties and I would stop worrying so much. If I didn't get it, what then? What the hell would I do? Who the hell was I at this school if I wasn't Head Girl? Just some wannabe?

That Tuesday morning, the last day of term, I had a phone call.

I was waiting to be connected to my dad on the public phone outside the school office. There was a shiny prospectus on the shelf and I was absentmindedly peeling through it while I waited. It stated that Bathory School 'prides itself on its record of pastoral care'. I looked through the pages of all the girls, six-year-old Pups, wide-eyed Tenderfoots, spotty Pre-Pubes, proud prefects and perfect Head Girls of years gone by, action shots of athletics and gymnastics, wondrous gazes down microscopes, contented smiles while reading books on beanbags, playing cellos in the Music room, waving through coach windows on the way to Switzerland, Venice or Amsterdam. I'd done all of that. I'd had all these experiences. My parents were paying £9,000 a term for all this and it wasn't as though they were rich, not like a lot of the other girls. My mum and dad ran a bakery, that was all. They weren't loaded by any stretch of the imagination. But they'd sent Seb to a private school, so they sent me too. I knew it was a struggle. I knew I had to do my best.

'Nash, hi, it's your dad.'

I closed the prospectus. 'Hi, Dad.'

'Nashy, it's good to hear your voice, darling.'

I wanted to cry. I'd forgotten how much I'd missed his voice. 'Is everything okay? You don't usually phone this earl—'

'I know, darling.' He'd called me 'darling' twice. This really wasn't good.

'What's wrong?'

'Uh, it's Seb.'

That was all he'd needed to say. The bottom dropped out of my world. I reached behind me and felt for the corridor wall so I could lean against it.

'Nash? Nash, darling, are you there?'

'Yeah.' I didn't dare say anything. I didn't want the silence on the line to be filled with words I'd always dreaded

I'd hear. Words from my nightmares. But I had to ask. 'What's happened?'

'Well, there's still nothing. They think he's gone off the map a bit.'

I sank back in the big leather swivel chair and it turned me towards the wide bay window. He hadn't said dead. He still wasn't past tense. There was still hope.

'Oh,' I said.

I could hear Dad scratching his stubbly chin, another bad sign. He hadn't shaved. By the way he was talking so quietly and slowly, it sounded like he hadn't slept either. He always talked like that when he'd done a night shift. 'They've made contact with three of the lads on his expedition. Apparently, three of them went off to spot a pod of manatee while the others returned to camp. Seb's group didn't come back. I'm sure all will be well. You know Bash. If he fell into a pit of snakes he'd come up wearing snakeskin boots.'

This was Dad trying to make me feel better. It didn't help. All it did was make me think my big brother had fallen into a pit of snakes.

'He's more than likely just gone somewhere remote where there aren't any phones and he can't get in touch.

'We're catching a flight out there this lunchtime. Managed to get a couple of cancellations. So, I'm afraid, you'll have to stay there, baby, at least for now.'

'What?' I said. 'Can't I come?'

'We can't come and get you, darling, we'll have to leave for the airport in a couple of hours.'

'But I could get a train or something.'

'It'll take too long. We've got to get our flight. Look, you stay there, where you're safe. Where we know where you are. We spoke to your Headmistress and she said Matron's going to be staying over Christmas as well so you won't be on your own.'

'So, the Saul-Hudsons aren't staying?' I said. 'First I've heard.' They never went away for Christmas, always New Year skiing, but never Christmas. They always stayed here in case any girls were going home later.

'Yeah, she said they're leaving tonight to go skiing or something in Scotland. There's a few other girls staying as well as you she said. Okay? Nash? They said Matron's very happy to stay instead of them.'

'Okay, Dad,' I said. Cowards, was all I could think. And then my mind went to all the Christmas presents I'd wrapped and put under the loose floorboard in my room. I couldn't wait to give Dad his. It was this board game he used to play as a kid and thought they'd stopped making. I got it on eBay months ago when I was home for the summer. When Seb was there. We'd had a barbecue for his birthday. We were always together for birthdays and Christmases. Always. Always.

'What about Christmas?' A single tear fell into the phone mouthpiece. I rubbed my cheek.

'We'll have our Christmas when we get back. All four of us. Okay? Try not to worry too much, Nashy. They'll find him by then, I know they will.'

I swallowed down a lump of emotion and built a dam for any more tears. There was nothing to cry about yet, I kept telling myself. When I got off the phone, the pain in my throat was worse, but I wouldn't cry.

'There's nothing to cry about, stop it. Stop it,' I said aloud.

Often, at times where I didn't know what to do, I'd hear Seb's voice in my head. He was always full of advice. He always said the right thing.

*Suck it up, Nash. I'm fine. Just fancied being on my own for a bit, that's all. Typical Mum and Dad to panic and get the Embassy involved. I can look after myself.*

I could hear it. But I didn't believe it.

I was in the Chapel, already dressed in my Bob Cratchit outfit for the dress rehearsal straight after morning Prayers. Even though I'd spent a fairly sleepless night, I'd been tasked with setting out the hymn books and assembling the right hymn numbers on the board above the lectern so I focused on the task at hand. I was a mere minutes from the official announcement of Head Girl and I had to put everything else out of my mind.

The Chapel was set apart from the main school, at the start of the wooded valley known as the Landscape Gardens. It was the first building you saw at the bottom of the path. Warm, wooden, bedecked in burgundy and navy curtains, carpets and prayer cushions, it was where we worshipped, where we heard any big announcements and where girls ran if they needed help from a higher source.

'Hi, Nash.'

Clarice Hoon and a couple of her hangers-on, Allie Powell and Lauren Entwistle, sauntered in and took early places right on the back bench. I heard the creaking of their pews, whispering and a few giggles.

I carried on putting up the numbers on the hymn board. Two five six. One one nine. Twenty-three. *Don't get angry unless you have to,* came his voice in my mind. *They're not worth your anger or your tears.* 'Any news about your brother yet?' Clarice called out. I looked over to them. They had their feet up on the pew in front. 'Bet you're worried about him, aren't you?'

I went over to the organ and got the music sheets ready for Mr Rose.

'He's really hot,' said Lauren.

'I saw him at Sports Day last year. He came with your parents, didn't he?' Allie this time—like Clarice was working them both like a ventriloquist's act. More giggles. More whispers. 'Has he got a girlfriend?'

There was a cloth underneath the eagle lectern. I bunched it up and wiped over the top and around the eagle's bald head, trying hard to zone them out. *They're idiots. They couldn't find their own backsides with both hands. Don't even listen. Block it out.*

'Why are you ignoring us, Nash?'

She'd been like this ever since Fourth Form. Last summer I'd reported her for pushing a Pup down the main staircase. There were many things I hadn't reported her for as well.

'Just trying to get this place ready,' I muttered, keeping my head down as I finished polishing the lectern. Now I had done everything I had to do. The hymn books were laid out. The lectern and music were ready. I had to go back down the aisle, past them, to get out of the Chapel and rejoin my class.

I knew one of them would move the moment I was level with them. She blocked my way with her whole body. *Don't vent it. Keep it in check. Stay strong.*

'Let me past, please, Clarice.'

Her face was thick with foundation and blusher. Her breath smelled of sour milk. 'Why won't you talk to us? Are you too good for us or something?'

Acid began filling my chest. 'I have nothing to say to you.' Lava bubbled up in the middle of my chest. *Think of Head Girl. Set the example.*

'Nothing to say? Not like you, is it? You had plenty to

say to Saul-Hudson when you reported me.' She whipped her hair flirtatiously over one shoulder. 'You never report Maggie and she's done a lot worse than I have.'

*Avoid eye contact.* 'You had your revenge,' I said, remembering the start of term. She'd put tacks in my outdoor shoes. She never admitted it, but I knew it was her.

'Why don't you ever report Maggie Zappa? Are you and her lesbi-friends now?'

'I report people who do bad things, Clarice. Maggie doesn't endanger life. Maggie doesn't abuse children.' I still didn't look at her.

She stepped back from me. 'Abuse children?' She looked back at the other two, who were laughing. 'Who have I abused?'

'I'm not going into it now.' I tried barging through her, but she held me in place.

'Whoa there, you can't just say that and then walk off. That's libellous.'

She'd learnt that word in English last week. We all had. 'Actually it's slander, but it happens to be the truth. Now let me past, please.'

'No, you're accusing me of something, so accuse me. Tell me what I've done.'

'Get off me.'

'No. Finish what you were saying. I abuse children or something.'

'You really want me to say it now?' I glanced back at Allie and Lauren. They were transfixed, like they were watching some award-winning movie moment.

'Say it,' she snarled.

I looked just past her, still not focusing on her eyes. 'I didn't tell Saul-Hudson about the five different St Anthony's boys I've seen you sneaking up the back stairs in the past year.'

She went crimson.

'I didn't tell her that you cheated in the Maths test or spat in the school governors' tea. But yes, I did report that you pushed a new Pup down the stairs. And that I've watched you drag a compass across a Tenderfoot's knee in Prep to see how long it would take for her to scream. I report people who do that kind of thing. Not because I'm a lesbian, but because *you're* a psycho. Do you want me to go on?'

I pushed towards the Chapel door. Allie and Lauren looked like two frightened lambs, lined up for the garrotting machine. I was on my way, my foot over the step, almost back out into the crisp, cold morning, when I heard her say it.

'I hope your brother died slowly. In pain.'

*Died*, she said. Past tense. Deceased. No longer with me. *Kill her.*

No more cooling voice of advice. I flew back into that Chapel like a wind and grabbed her by both shoulders, slamming my forehead against hers with an eye-watering *CLUNK*.

The rest I don't remember.

And before I knew it, I was running.

# 4
## Jeepers Creepers

I didn't stop running until I was deep into the Landscape Gardens. I headed straight for the old wooden Wendy House, opened the yellow front door and shut myself in. It was freezing. All I had on was Bob Cratchit's threadbare shirt and torn trousers.

I'd often wondered what the consequences would be if I'd let the reckless part of my brain decide things for me. The part of my brain that wanted to key the cars of people my dad had fallen out with. The part that wanted to touch boiling hot surfaces. The part that wanted to shout back and swear all the time. The part that wondered what it would be like to punch Clarice Hoon in the face every time she laughed when I tripped over or got a question wrong in French. And now I knew. It felt horrible.

I don't know how long I'd sat there on one of the little toadstool seats, my head aching like I'd loaned it out as a wrecking ball, a ready-laid plastic dinner service set out beside me, when Maggie Zappa, still in her Mrs Cratchit dress and bonnet, appeared in the doorway.

She sat down on a toadstool on the other side of the table and pulled a packet of cigarettes from the pocket of her lacy apron. She took one out and offered it to me.

'Go on.'

I didn't think, I just took it with a hand I didn't realise was shaking. She cupped her hand around the end and held the lighter as I inhaled. Seb had taught me how to do it without coughing. I let the smoke out, slowly. 'We're not allowed up here. Mrs Saul-Hudson said it was out of bounds over Christmas.'

'Why are we up here then?' said Maggie, blowing smoke through the little square window. 'You're gonna get a bruise there.' She pushed her finger into my forehead. There was a pulsating ache radiating out from where she touched me and I winced.

'Aargh! God. What the hell did I do?'

'I wondered how long it would take.'

I looked at her as I exhaled the cigarette smoke, shuddering at the taste. I felt warmer somehow. 'What?'

'You and Clarice going at it in the Chapel. I was outside. I watched the whole thing through the window.'

I shook my head. 'I don't know what happened. I can't even remember what I did. My head hurts, I know that.'

'You beat the crap out of her, that's what you did, *ma petite oignon*,' said Maggie, cigarette dangling from her mouth as she laid up one of the plastic plates with bits and pieces from the box of fake food. 'Your head hurts because you headbutted her. I've never seen anything like it. It's all right. She deserved it. She's a total dick.'

'Violence is never the answer.'

'Sometimes it is,' said Maggie. 'Just because her parents own a racehorse and live in Dubai, doesn't mean she owns the world.'

'They own the fifth largest racing stables in the world.'

'So? Some people are born dicks, some achieve dick-ness and some have dick-ness thrust upon them. Isn't that how the saying goes?'

'Something like that.' I sniffed. 'I just saw red. Nothing could have stopped me. I lost it. I completely lost it.'

'She deserved it, don't worry. She's had that coming for a long time, let me tell you. She was born a dick. There's no point going over it, wondering if she has Daddy issues or if Mummy never let her drive the Ferrari. Don't reason with it. You've got to show people like that what's what or they'll stamp all over you. She won't give you any more grief now, just you watch.'

'She said my brother was dead. She said she hoped he died in pain.'

'Ugh, what a cow!' said Maggie.

'I *know* he's dead.'

'You know that for a fact, do you?'

'No.' I dragged on the cigarette.

'Well then. You don't know jack.'

We stared each other out. Maggie wasn't going to be first blinker, so I gave in. I didn't understand what she was doing here. Of all the people to come to my aid, Maggie was the last I'd expected. We'd barely had a conversation since she'd started at Bathory last spring. But here she was, giving me a cigarette and seeing me at my absolute worst, but not judging me. It was just what a friend would do.

'It's been nearly a week since he went missing.'

'Five days I'd heard.'

'I don't know what's happening to me. I haven't slept properly for ages. I'm forgetting chores. There's misspellings all over today's diary. I read over my libretto first thing. I couldn't remember any of my lines for *A Christmas Carol*. I knew them all last week. I knew all *yours* last week too.'

'So? There's more important things in life than chores and a play everyone's seen a million times. And the Muppets did it waaaay better anyway.'

'Yeah, I know, but...'

'Plus them four Pups they've got playing our kids—how come they're all white? At the very least they ought to be mixed race. It's totally miscast.' She dragged on her cigarette until the stem was nearly all ash. 'Or are they not my kids? Did Bob Cratchitt shag around in the book?'

'Not as far as I know.' I came to the end of my cigarette and she offered me another one. 'I'm going to stink.'

She shrugged. 'Just stand next to me. I'll take the blame. I'm like a blame sponge. Ciggy stink. Stolen turkeys. I'm your girl.'

I smiled. 'So you didn't steal them then?'

She looked at me. 'What would I want with three frozen turkeys?'

'I have no idea.' We sat in silence, Bob and Mrs Cratchit smoking their cigarettes in silence. Then I just came out with it. 'I've lost out on Head Girl.'

'What?' Maggie shrieked. 'Who says?'

'No one. But I know I have. I've just punched a fellow

prefect, for God's sake. She's not exactly going to overlook that, is she?'

Maggie shrugged. 'She might. What with all the stress you've been under lately, worrying about your brother and that.'

I shook my head and stared at a woodlouse crawling its way across a plastic apple on top of the cooker. 'Dianna's won. I know she has.'

'Pfaff?' said Maggie. 'Great. That means we're all screwed. Oh well.' She sighed and lit up another.

'Oh well?' I repeated. 'Do you know how hard I've worked to be Head Girl? I've been up every morning to help with Pups or unlock outside doors since…forever. Every single hockey, netball or athletics practice I've been out there, tidying up balls or polishing javelins because no one else volunteers. I monitor Prep, every night.' My voice was getting steadily louder.

'Yeah, yeah, I know.'

'I've got spotless deportment. I miss phone calls home most nights just so I can sit in that study with Saul-Hudson and go through the diary while she sits there on her yogically tightened arse, picking lip hairs and drinking Tesco Finest cocoa while I'm stuck drinking that…value crud she gets for the rest of us!'

'Whoa, it's all coming out now,' Maggie laughed.

'Sorry,' I said, breathing deeply, my head falling into my hands. 'Just can't believe I've fallen at the last sodding fence.'

'You let it out. It's good for you,' said Maggie. ''Bout time you gnashed your teeth a bit. Listen, you don't know Pffaf's been given Head Girl, do you?'

'It's a pretty safe bet. She called for Dianna to talk to the police with her. Not me. She said I've "got enough to deal with". If that isn't a massive hint as to who she trusts the most at this school, I don't know what is.'

'But you practically run this school, Nash. Saul-Hudson would be lost without you. If she'd rather put that chuckle-head in charge of running the place, then let her. She doesn't deserve your respect. What other headmistress would keep me here as long as she has, eh?'

'True,' I said, forcing a small laugh. 'I've failed her big time this week though. She was relying on me.'

'Why do you want to be Head Girl anyway? All that extra responsibility. All it involves is doing the diary and sorting out pissy little tea rotas and wiping Saul-Hudson's arse. Let the Golden Snitch deal with all that if that's what she really wants. I bet your brother doesn't give a crap.'

I laughed. This much was true.

'Seb would want you to enjoy yourself, wouldn't he? You can't enjoy yourself if you're constantly trying to impress other people. All that is for when you're grown up. Now is the time to kick back—at least until you're eighteen. Then you can start thinking about job prospects and contraception and hatchbacks.'

I couldn't help but laugh. 'I'm sorry, Maggie.'

She blew out a thick cloud of smoke. 'For what?'

'For never sticking up for you.'

'You've turned a few blind ones to me, I know you have. So come on, chin up, tits out and let's go get our God on.' She gestured towards the open Wendy House window. A line of students had already begun the trek up the path towards the Chapel on the opposite side of the valley.

'Do you mind if I sit next to you in Prayers?' I asked her as we stepped out of the Wendy House.

'Yeah. If I can share your hymn book.'

'Why where's yours?'

'Kinda flame grilled it yesterday. Don't ask.'

There was a tremendous creak of the pews and everyone stood up to greet Mrs Saul-Hudson, who took her position at her bronze eagle lectern as the organ ceased its hum. I stayed seated throughout.

'Good morning, girls,' she boomed, removing a small hair from the lapel of her red suit jacket.

'Good morning, Mrs Saul-Hudson,' the assembled pupils all droned back at her, apart from Maggie who preferred 'Good morning, Mrs Stool-Softener.' She threw me a look and I smiled, despite myself.

'That woman literally has no neck,' Maggie whispered into my ear, at which I burst out laughing.

Mrs Saul-Hudson threw me a look, full to the brim with disappointment.

I sucked my swollen lip again, spotting Regan Matsumoto staring at me from the choir pews at the front. Why was she always staring at me? I could see no evidence of Clarice Hoon or her vile apostles though and Matron hadn't pitched up either. I figured they were all in Sickbay. Clarice wailing on and on about how I attacked her and pinned her down. The other girls just crying in harmony.

It was as though Maggie had read my mind. She leaned in to me again. 'I see the Hoon Patrol haven't rocked up. Probably in Sickbay getting her face reassembled.'

I looked down at the prayer cushion beneath my feet and tried to decipher which Bible story was knitted into the fabric today. Maggie had Noah and the Ark. On the other side of me, Carrie McKernan had Jonah and the Whale. Mine showed a monster. Maybe it wasn't a monster. Maybe it was the Devil.

'Girls, before I begin our last assembly of term, there are a couple of grave matters which I must discuss this morning,' said Mrs Saul-Hudson. Everyone sat to attention, eager to know the fate that had befallen Bathory in the night.

Maggie leaned into me. 'Bet her husband's been caught dogging again.'

'What?' I said, snapping my head to look at her. 'He was night-fishing,' I whispered back.

'Sure he was.'

Saul-Hudson continued. 'First of all, I'm sure you have all heard by now that a man very sadly died in the village a few nights ago. There have been some rumours flying about the school regarding the cause of his death. I want you all to be assured that he died as the result of a burglary that went wrong and the perpetrators have been caught, so you are quite safe.'

She smiled. Nobody smiled back.

'So he didn't have his guts ripped out by some wild animal and die in agony on his doorstep then?' said Maggie, leaning into me.

'Apparently not.'

Saul-Hudson continued. 'The second matter I must bring to your attention concerns last night's staff Christmas party. A person, or persons, broke into the kitchens and laced the party food with a toxic substance...'

Maggie leaned in again. 'Staff toilets take a bit of punishment, did they?'

'Sssssshhhh!' I said, bubbles of laughter and fear mingling in my belly.

'I do *not* consider this act to be even remotely amusing.'

She scanned us all, daring us with her eyes to laugh or even breathe wrong. 'I suggest the culprit come and see me after Prayers in my office and tell me privately—'

Maggie's hand shot up.

Saul-Hudson honed in on her, thinning her frosty eyes. 'You.'

'Yes, me,' Maggie sighed. 'It was only laxatives though, Mrs Saul-Hudson. Guess you'll be throwing me out of school now, won't you?' She held up her wrists as though a pair of invisible handcuffs were to clamp down on them. But they didn't. All Mrs Saul-Hudson did was clear her throat and say, 'See me after Prayers, please. Now, let us pray.'

There was a shuffling and creaking again as every teacher and all the school's three hundred and four girls arranged their cushions and knelt down to pray for trespassers and daily Hovis.

I clasped my hands and closed my eyes, inhaling the strong atticky smell of the Chapel and the musty old hymn book just beneath my nose. There was a snigger to the right of me.

I opened my eyes and nudged Maggie. 'You still hell-bent on getting chucked out?'

She nodded.

'But why?'

Maggie looked at me. *'Je suis* have *mes raisons.'*

'*...and give us this day our daily bread...* I don't think they'll expel you for putting Ex-Lax in the cocoa. They didn't for spray-painting the pony or putting the custard in the minibus.'

'More's the pity,' she said.

'*...the power and the glory...* She could put you in the Chiller again.'

'...*forever and ever...* Maybe I want to go to the Chiller again.'

*Please, please, let Seb be all right.* 'Amen.'

The Chiller was supposed to be the most feared place in the school, but basically it was just the laundry room where teachers sent girls to 'cool off', tucked away at the back of the school basement. All the younger kids were afraid of it, but it wasn't so scary. It was always warm and smelled gorgeously of clean washing. I'd lost track of the amount of times I'd seen Maggie frogmarched down there to serve a time out. But Maggie was afraid of no one and no place. Whenever I'd gone down there to retrieve her for a teacher, she'd just be sitting on top of one of the washing machines, picking her nails or singing.

'Please be seated,' said our Head when the prayer was over. And we all were. There followed an end of term lecture about not treating our rooms like hotels, news from the past few months (netball victories, a 'positive' visit from the school governors and a new bench donated by one of the trustees—who definitely was not a paedophile) and details about the Christmas Fayre that afternoon; who would be doing what and when. Stallholders would arrive to set up on the Orangery lawns at eleven a.m., the younger ones would be 'making mince pies' (folding impetigo into pastry) and the first year Sixth Formers (our class) would be adding finishing touches to the play, which would start in the Hall at three p.m. The candlelit procession through the Landscape Gardens rounded everything off and then the girls could find their parents and go home for Christmas.

And then it came. The dread in my chest was strangulating.

'And lastly, I have the great pleasure of announcing my

new Head Girl, who will take up her post at the beginning of next year. It's been a very difficult decision, owing to the quality of the candidates I had to choose from, but the girl I'm appointing is kind, considerate, brimming over with focus and dedication. She is accepting and kind to all students and is a keen exponent of fair play. She is also extremely loyal to Bathory and to what we are trying to achieve here.'

She looked directly at me. I, for once, held her gaze.

'This girl will be your representative, your prefect leader, in loco parentis when there isn't a member of staff on whom you can call. I am sure you will agree she is the right person for the role. Your new Head Girl is…Dianna Pfaff.'

There was a lengthy pause between the announcement and the beginning of the applause. The girls were shocked. The news about my 'quite vicious attack on Clarice' had yet to reach the majority of them, but I could feel eyes on me, looking at me for a reaction.

Maggie stared at me, mouthing a string of choice words. I smiled, a rictus grin, and watched Dianna stride along the aisle towards the lectern, where Saul-Hudson pinned the badge to her cardigan. I clapped along with all the others as she made her way back down the aisle to her pew, badge gleaming.

Dianna passed our pew, flashing us a sanctimonious, paint-stripping smile.

'Whatever,' I said, like a bitten apple, feeling itself going bad from the inside. 'Whatever.'

# 5
# Dead and Breakfast

As I made my way to the Refectory that morning after Prayers, I walked slower than everyone else. I was swept along on the tide of other girls who were all just like me, in the same uniform, just trying to get to the same place, The same. Not special. Not the best. I felt like little pieces of the person I was were flying off behind me never to return. I didn't care that there was a little dab of Blu-Tack on my sole, sticking to the highly polished parquet every so often. I didn't care that my tie was slightly askew. And I didn't care if I was late for breakfast. For once in my life, I did not care.

The Refectory was a large, high room, echoing with the sounds of clinking cutlery, loud chatter and the dishwasher whirring in the kitchen through the hatch. It had a parquet

floor and walls decorated with scholarship boards dating
back over a hundred years. Some of the Year Tens on my
table were playing the game where you picked a name from
one of the boards and everyone had to guess which one.
They usually honed in on names like Smellie or Windass—
the favourites were always Ethel Glasscock from 1947 and
Olive Dicks from 1955.

It wasn't long before I spotted Clarice Hoon, three tables
away with all the other prefects. Her left arm was in a sling;
her bottom lip was even more swollen than mine. She'd
brushed her hair so that a curtain of it fell down across the
bashed-up right side of her face, and tried to cover it with
make-up, but she hadn't done a good enough job. I caught
details from the girls along my table. She'd fallen. Down the
main staircase. Probably drunk. It had been known. Someone was covering for me. I felt a pang of guilt. I took a seat
on Table Nine, aka The Rejects Table, and knowing looks
all around me as I sat down told me what a huge statement
I was making by not sitting with the other prefects.

'Could you pass the toast, please?' I called up the table to
anyone who was listening and immediately, the toast rack
was on its way down.

Maggie eventually scuffed in, socks rumpled down, face
like thunder, looking like she'd been heaved through a hedge
by her hair. I guessed by her scowl that she hadn't been expelled. Inwardly, I sighed in relief.

'Don't ask,' she griped, ignoring looks from the other
girls and yanking out the chair opposite me.

'Saul-Hudson still not expelling you then?' I said, pouring
her out some juice. It dripped on the table. I didn't bother
to wipe it up. What a rebel I was becoming. I'd be making
headlines in the school magazine at this rate.

Maggie frowned. 'I'm living in a sea of morons and the only life raft is made from moron trees. Twenty Blue Tickets, an hour in the Chiller and a loooong lecture about why I "mustn't break in to Sickbay and steal laxatives". What's it gonna take to get kicked out of this dump?'

'They'll only send you to another school if you get kicked out of this one. Maybe a worse one.'

'There *isn't* a worse one,' she said, looking like she meant it.

Regan Matsumoto sat down at the end of our table. As quiet as a mouse yet as noticeable as a fart, nobody liked Regan though nobody quite knew why. It was just one of those innate things, like in the wild when mother animals reject the offspring with health defects. We'd all rejected Regan. Picked her last for team sports. Left her to wander the playing fields alone at break to identify insects and talk to people who weren't there. All I really knew about her was that her parents had won money on the EuroMillions and were now so loaded they didn't work, just took holidays. But they never took Regan with them.

A *clickety clack* on the polished parquet tiles signalled the arrival of Dianna Pfaff, our sparkling new Head Girl, a bundle of letters in her hands.

'Hello, Natasha. Margaret.' She beamed, her blonde bob shimmering in the early morning window-shine.

'Hi, Dianna,' I said, biting on both words as though they hurt me to say them. I reached for the milk jug. 'Congratulations.'

She smiled and looked down at her badge. My badge. 'Thanks, Natasha. I really couldn't believe it when she said my name.'

'Yeah, me neither,' I muttered.

'How come you're on post today, princess?' said Maggie, snatching the letter Dianna handed her. 'Thought you'd have a minion running about for you.'

Dianna's bangs quivered with annoyance. 'Drop dead, Margaret.'

Maggie faux gasped. 'I'm shocked. Our new Head Girl using such a callous remark? You get any post from your brother today, Dianna? I've always wondered, do prisoners really stick their envelopes down with spunk or is that a myth?'

Dianna stiffened and leaned over Regan's cereal bowl.

'Very funny, Margaret. You really should be on *Britain's Got Talent*. They're in dire need of comedians.' She seemed really annoyed for some reason and every time she spoke, little flecks of spittle flew directly into Regan's juice glass.

'You're so full of shit, Dianna. That must be why your eyes are brown.'

It went on like this for a while. It always did. I finished my toast and a whole bowl of cornflakes, the war of words still raging around me. Eventually, Dianna was the first to run out of comebacks. 'There's two for you, Natasha.'

She held out two white envelopes. I took them both and saw the handwriting on the top one was Mum's. A Christmas card from her and Dad. I didn't recognise the second one. All around me, the chatter and clinking stopped.

When I looked up, all eyes around the table were on me except Regan's. She was slowly chewing into a slice of toast while watching a money spider crawling over her free hand like it was the most interesting thing she'd ever seen. I ripped into the envelope and opened the letter.

Dianna was still hovering. 'Anything important?'

'Keep your beak out,' said Maggie. 'It's none of your business.'

'Uh, I think it is my business. I am Head Girl.'

'Yeah, and don't we know it?'

'What does that mean?'

Maggie swigged her orange juice then licked her lips, slowly like a cat. 'The only reason you wear that badge is cos you brown-tongued your way up Saul-Hudson's arse. Everyone knows it should have been Nash who got Head Girl, not you.'

Dianna's nostrils flared. 'Well, Natasha fell at the final fence, didn't she?'

'Yeah, and why was that, do you think?' I said. When I looked up, Dianna was staring at me. I opened my second letter.

It was a picture. Hand-drawn and coloured. Trees. Leaves. A large black monster with huge pointed teeth. Between its jaws it held a man's body. The man had blond hair. There was red scribble all around the page. It was supposed to be the Beast. My brother. Blood.

I folded the letter back up and slotted it into the torn envelope. As I returned to my toast, I took a quick scan of the room, fixing my own face into a calm mask.

Clarice.

I picked her out again, three tables away, talking to Lauren Entwistle. She glanced across at me, and quickly glanced away again.

'Who was your other one from?' asked Maggie.

*Choose your battles. Just ignore it.*

'Oh, just my nan. She can't come and get me over Christmas. She's away.'

'Well, my mum's still fighting a big divorce case in LA so

she's not going to be back any time soon either. And Dad's in New York till whenever.'

'Is your dad a lawyer too?' I asked.

'No, architect,' said Maggie. 'Something to do with that new thing they're building on Wall Street or something, I dunno.'

'One World Trade Center?' I said, hardly believing it.

'Summing like that.'

'Wow,' I said.

'Sooo, we can have Christmas here on our own and totally let rip! No parents, no teachers, no Saul-Hudson ramming her big fat honk into our beeswax.'

'Matron'll be here though,' I said.

She grimaced. 'Yeah, but we can outrun her if we have to. Beeyatch.'

'She's been lovely since I heard about Seb,' I said. 'She asks me every morning if I've heard anything and whether I need to use the phone.'

'Bless,' said Maggie, unconvincingly. I knew how much she hated Matron and I didn't wonder why. It was because Matron was usually the one who caught her out. Every single time.

'There's a Pup staying as well,' I said, trying to think of the little girl's name.

'And I am,' said a small voice. We both looked at the stern-looking girl with the plaits.

'Why will *you* be here?' asked Maggie, barely hiding her disdain.

'I'm not allowed to go home for Christmas,' Regan said, matter-of-fact. She pushed her glasses up her nose and dipped her head.

'Why aren't you allowed to go home?'

Regan swallowed down some cornflakes, leaving a milk drop on her chin. 'I'm only allowed home one holiday a year, summer or Christmas. I went home in the summer so...'

'...so you're here for Christmas,' I finished.

She nodded.

'Oh peach parfait,' groaned Maggie, her spoon clattering against her empty bowl.

'Well, I guess we can make the best of it,' I said, trying to find a bright side. 'Plan a midnight raid on the kitchen or something.'

'The devil is at your elbow, my child,' said Maggie with an evil stare and a suggestive eyebrow wiggle.

I laughed.

Regan laughed too, but I don't think she knew what she was laughing at. She still had a milk drip on her chin. 'We can go looking for the Beast that killed the man in the village.'

Maggie and I looked at her.

'It would be better than sitting in the library. I spend a lot of time in the library.'

She didn't say it to court pity. It was just a fact. And it was a fact with a subtext: spending time in the library was code for *I have absolutely no friends*.

'I slept in there on Sunday night.'

'Why?' said Maggie. 'All there is are encyclopedias and crappy books like *Common Sense Beekeeping* and *Fun With Yarn*. Not exactly party central.'

'It's warmer than the dorm. I was reading all the old school scrapbooks that the prefects of the past used to keep. About all the parties and plays. And the Beast.'

'Oh yeah,' Maggie laughed. 'The Beast of Bathory? The

stupidest mythical beast known to man. He only comes out in the winter when there's no food around.'

'He killed Mr Pellett in the village. He was a retired accountant. Lived up at The Old Apothecary.'

'How do you know all this?' said Maggie.

Regan tapped her nose. 'I know a lot of things about the Beast of Bathory.'

I thought about my monster.

'It's just a scary story,' I said. 'The prefects have been telling the Pups ghost stories about the Beast of Bathory for generations.'

'It's more than a story. It's real. A man died last week. It tore him to pieces. Two tourists went missing at the end of last summer and they haven't been found.' She fumbled with her collar and pulled out what looked like a necklace made from green garden twine. Right in the centre of it, there was a tooth. She showed it to us. 'What do you think that is?'

'Uh, looks like a tooth,' said Maggie.

'Looks like a dog's tooth,' I said.

'I found it on the path between the Chapel and the Tree House. It's one of the Beast's incisors. Look at the size of it.' The tooth *was* pretty big, about the length of a Post-it note. And about the same colour yellow too.

'How did you make the hole?' I asked her.

'I did it in the CDT room. Imagine being ripped apart by a mouth full of them.' She looked at the tooth like it was a naked picture of Ryan Gosling.

Maggie threw me a look, grabbing a last piece of burnt toast from the rack. 'It's total and utter rubbish. It's probably plastic.'

'No it's not,' said Regan. 'People have seen it.' She looked directly at me. I poured myself some more apple juice.

'Witnesses swear it's bigger than any beast you would get in a zoo. Twice the size of a tiger.'

Maggie stared at her with wide eyes, almost missing her mouth as her thickly buttered toast rose to greet it.

'Loads of people have been killed in the past two years. And now Mr Pellett. There've been sightings recently. All at night.'

'Convenient,' said Maggie.

'They say it has bright red eyes and growls like a tiger. It's taken sheep from the farms. Everyone knows about it.'

Maggie laughed. 'Bright red eyes. Don't make me laugh. All boarding schools have these stories cos they're so deathly dull. If you go up to the Blue Bathroom and say Adolf Hitler three times in the mirror, he appears and stabs you. And if you stand on the eleventh step of back stairs at eleven minutes past eleven on the eleventh month of the year, some weird leprechaun thing comes up out of the stairs and drags you down to hell.'

'O'Leary's ghost.' I nodded. 'Isn't there one about the ghost girl of Grace's Lake too? The one who sleepwalked there in the night and fell in, all tangled up in her bed sheets?'

Regan was stony-faced. 'The Beast is real. People have died.'

We both looked at her. She really believed it.

'I've seen tree trunks with scratches all up the bark. And I found something behind the Temple. Something awful. Do you want to see it?'

Just then, the bell *dingalingalinggggged* out in the corridor and Maggie and I both jumped out of our skins. Regan didn't. She was just staring at us, waiting for an answer.

# 6
## The Thing

While my form was busily black-bagging up their desk contents and lockers and cleaning the classrooms, I was sent to Mrs Saul-Hudson's office for a ticking off about my attack on Clarice.

And that was all I got. A ticking off. I didn't even receive a billion Blue Tickets for Tudor House or a detention or anything. Just a long monologue about how my parents would 'have to be told', how 'fighting's never the answer' and how it was 'understandable with the amount of stress I was under with my brother's situation'.

And that was it.

The reason for my lack of punishment had little to do with what I'd done to Clarice, and everything to do with what I knew about the Saul-Hudsons. I was the secret keeper, you see. I'd been Mrs Saul-Hudson's right-hand man for a long time. I had intimate knowledge of their private apartments and I knew stuff about them that they definitely wouldn't want spreading around. Punishing me was a risk they couldn't take, despite breaking a golden rule of the school.

Maggie was incensed.

'You break a girl's face and you get nothing? It's so unfair! Not that Clarice didn't deserve it or anything, cos she actually did, but you got nothing? Actual factual nothing?'

'I know. This school is fundamentally flawed, Maggie,' I told her as the break-time bell rang out in Long Corridor. 'It's the reason why you're still here.'

'Must be.'

The three of us hotfooted it across the frosty front lawn, up the flint steps into the valley where the Landscape Gardens began.

On hot summer weekends, being at Bathory School was heaven. I loved being a boarder. We could go outside to do our prep or take the three-mile walk into the tiny village of Bathory for ice cream, and we were sometimes allowed to swim in the pool to cool down. We could sit beneath the hazelnut tree on the Orangery lawn in our vests and shorts or play croquet.

But on winter days like this one, we were rarely let outside, except to walk Brody or go up to the Chapel for prayers and Sunday service. The swimming pool was frozen over and the hazelnut tree bare and stark without its leaves. Our noses glowed red and our breath left cloud trails on the air. I was still glad of something to take my mind off Seb. When I thought about him, I felt myself starting to lose my mind. Bathory just wasn't the place to lose your mind. You might never get it back.

'It's just up here,' said Regan, as she led Maggie and me towards the Temple, right at the top of the bank and up into the woods.

'It's not far now.' She led us deeper in, where the tops of the trees were alive with birdsong.

'Is this really worth it?' said Maggie. 'If we're late, we'll miss the fit work experience boy pruning the Quad hedge.'

The Quad was the square expanse of grass separating the French room from the corridor to the Science lab. 'He's finished,' I said. 'He's not back again till the spring.'

'Aw what?' she groaned. 'He was the one good thing about being here. *Je suis* desolate.'

'He wasn't that fit anyway.'

'He bloody was. Didn't you see him take his top off in the summer? Holy Mary Mother of Abs.'

'There's more to boys than abs and pecs.'

'Not much more,' said Maggie. 'Don't tell me you don't get horny, Nash. You must crave it, we all do. Have the odd fantasy about Keith the bus driver or Mr Saul-Hudson in his golf trousers. Or out of them...'

I couldn't even fake a laugh at that one.

'No, I know who *you've* got the bubbles for,' said Maggie. 'Charlie the Shop Boy.' She wiggled her eyebrows suggestively.

'Shut up.'

Regan looked back at us blankly, and Maggie 'explained': 'Nash fancies the boy who works at Bathory Basics.'

Regan carried on walking in silence.

Maggie gave the back of her head a dirty look. 'God, what a sulk fest.' She stopped to catch her breath. 'Oh come on, let's go back. Bet you any money she's taking us to So-Not-Worth-It-Town.'

'We won't know until we get there, will we?' I said, picking up the pace.

Pretty soon, we were up in the highest part of the valley, where a sloping dirt track, worn by centuries of wooden carts transporting ice from Grace's Lake and Edward's Pond up to the now overgrown icehouse, led to the Temple.

Maggie and I stopped walking. Pigeon-toed, Regan stumbled gingerly through the prickly bushes and crouched down behind the folly.

'Come on,' she whispered, beckoning us with her hand. Maggie looked at me then shrugged, and together we fought our way through. Partially hidden by rotting leaves and damp twigs was something that looked like a long knobbly stick covered in school Bolognese.

'What the frig is that?' said Maggie, batting away an errant branch. 'That's disgusting.'

I pulled my jumper cuffs down over my hands and shoved one across my mouth, trying to push images from my mind: my brother's body, cut into pieces by guerrillas in the Colombian jungle.

Regan poked at the thing with a long twig. 'I found it when I was exploring.'

'You brought us all the way up here in the freezing cold to show us a sheep's leg?'

'It's not a sheep's leg,' said Regan, standing up. 'I don't know what it is. What did you think you were coming to see?'

'That's not a sheep's leg,' I said behind my hand. Neither of them heard me.

'I dunno,' said Maggie. 'A dead body or something? A monster's cave? A tunnel back to civilisation? Not a frigging sheep's leg.'

'I told you it's not a sheep's leg,' said Regan, moving closer and bending down to poke it with a twig. 'I think it's from a cow.'

'I think it's a spine,' I said.

'A SPINE?' They both cried out, in a chorus of disgust.

'Yes. Look at the bottom, there's ribs sticking out of it. And the gunky stuff looks like intestines. It's thick too.'

Regan levered up the end of it with her twig. 'Is it… human?'

I shook my head. 'No, it's way too big. You've seen Bony Bonaparte in the Science lab. A human spine is much thinner than that. This looks to me like it's come from a large animal. A cow or a horse, or something.'

'But why is it here? Where has it come from?' said Regan.

'I don't want to think about that,' snapped Maggie, rubbing her arms. 'I wanna go back inside, not stand here in the freezing cold, debating about some random bone. I told you this would be a big fat slice of nothing.' Without another word, she started back through the bushes.

I waited for Regan. 'I really think the Beast had something to do with this,' she said.

'It's more likely a wildcat or something.' I shrugged, although not even *I* believed *that* theory.

'You haven't seen it closely enough,' said Regan. 'Come here.'

I looked after Maggie, then moved closer and crouched down to look. 'See?' she said, pointing to the top of it.

'Yeah.' I put my jumper-cuffed hand up to my mouth again. 'It stinks.'

'But look at the bite mark on the top. Something bigger than a wildcat did that.'

'A big wildcat?' I said.

'But what if it's not?' She stared hard into my eyes, like she could read the sell-by date under my skull. 'You saw it on the playing field, didn't you? That time in netball. I know you did. Aren't you even curious about it?'

'Regan, the Beast of Bathory is fictional, okay?' I sighed, expelling a huge cloud of white air. 'That's why it's in the myths and legends book in the library. It's a story made up by some weirdo with an Abominable Snowman fetish.'

She wasn't buying it. 'Yes, but you hear about these sorts of things all the time, don't you? Legends made up about beasts and monsters, just to keep people from going to places where they shouldn't. Like Satan. There's a school of thought that says he's just made up to stop Christians from straying from the path of righteousness.'

I snickered nervously, no idea what I was actually snickering about. 'Yeah, well, this conversation is getting a little too deep for me.'

'Satan's not the only one,' said Regan, flicking a plait over her shoulder. 'There are myths and legends in every culture, which came about to stop children being naughty or getting out of bed. The Bogeyman. Baba Jaga. Bloody Bones…'

A branch cracked somewhere in the woods.

'What was that?' I said, a frozen ache spreading all through my limbs.

'Maybe it's the Beast, come back for the spine?'

A distant *ting-a-ling-a-ling* tinkled in the distance. 'Come on, that's first bell.' We were so far from Main House, I wanted to get going.

'There has to be a reason why this spine is here and I want to know what it is,' said Regan stubbornly. 'Either it's here because the Beast is real and it's attacked a cow or a horse—or it's here because someone wants us to *think* the Beast is real.'

I stood up. 'Fine, whatever. I'm going back down now, okay?'

Regan followed me as we picked our way back through the bushes. In front of the Temple, we looked over the valley—I could just see the dot of Maggie walking beside the lake. I started back along the track, but I could tell Regan wasn't following. When I looked back, she was just standing there, outside the Temple; her stare blank and cold, her eyes appearing almost black in the wintry light.

'Regan?'

She didn't move immediately—then, slowly and thoughtfully, she began walking towards me.

'You know it's real. There's fear in your eyes,' she said, as she passed me. Her own eyes were as dead as a shark's.

I shivered as she left me there, wishing Maggie hadn't been so far away.

# 7
## Saw

Dad called me from Heathrow just before lunch, just to say *I love you* and *We'll be back soon*. I could hear everyone back in the Refectory as I put the phone down, pulling their Christmas crackers and cheering as the turkeys were brought out to be carved by staff members at the ends of the tables. It was a joyous time. I just wished I'd felt it.

I rejoined the school midway through the turkey course. Christmas didn't mean the food got any better at Bathory, despite all the little extras—roast potatoes (hard), organic carrots (mashed), peas (frozen), stuffing (God knows), pigs in blankets (raw) and figgy pudding and custard (grim) and though the sight of it all brought bile into my throat, I took a spoonful of each, knowing that if I didn't there was nothing else to eat until dinner. The food at Bathory had always been bad. When I'd first arrived as an eight-year-old Pup, I'd been vegetarian. The first week, when I realised the vegetarian option was either a saucer of grated Smart Price cheese or a grey hard-boiled egg, I quickly switched back to meat to keep myself alive.

On a more positive note, Clarice Hoon hadn't given me any more grief about Seb, aside from the odd snide look as I walked up Long Corridor. This I could handle. *First to lose their cool loses the argument*, Seb told me, and he was right. As always.

Midway through lunch, Mrs Saul-Hudson marched in and dragged Maggie out. It turned out she'd just had a phone call from a pilot at RAF Lyneham who'd done a fly-past the previous day, who'd kindly informed her that the school now had letters crudely daubed on its roof. Instead of assisting with the Christmas Fayre preparations, I gladly spent the afternoon helping Maggie to clean it off.

'Why though? Why not expel me for this? It does NOT make sense!' she shouted, as I scrubbed away at the second S in 'SAVE US'. 'Why keep giving me these stupid mean-ingless detentions? I mean, I've tried EVERYTHING to get out of this place. I've done it all...'

'...even vandalised a listed building now,' I added.

'Yeah. I don't know what more I can do,' she cried. 'Maybe I could get a boy in here. Yeah, that might do it.'

'Why do you want to leave so badly?' I asked. She didn't answer immediately, so I pressed. 'Seriously, you can tell me.'

'I just wanna go home, that's all. I don't need an educa-tion.'

'But they'll only send you somewhere else, won't they?'

'Fine. Then maybe they'll send me back to my old comp

where I was happy and settled and didn't have to wear this cheap scratchy boy-repeller.' She loosened her tie like it was hurting her neck.

'I'd miss you,' I told her.

'Yeah, right.'

'I would. You're the thing that's keeping me going at the moment.'

'Yeah, well, you'll get over me eventually.'

She carried on scrubbing. I felt no padlock on my urge to tell her any more, so I just said it. 'They're paying double the fees.'

'Huh? Who?'

'Your parents.'

'WHAT?' she cried, standing up and slamming her scrubbing brush down on the flat roof where a thousand soap bubbles flew up into my face. 'What do you mean? How? How do you know that? Are you joking me?'

I shook my head, wiping little flecks of foam from my nose and cheeks. 'Your file was out on her desk when I was in there a few weeks ago. I wasn't going through it or anything, I was just putting her cocoa down. And it was there, in your file. I read it.'

Maggie sat back down on the roof. 'Double fees? That's really why I'm still here?'

I nodded. 'There was a letter in the file, open, from your dad. I only read a bit, as I said, it was just there on the desk. He wants you to get your GCSEs here so you can go to a good Sixth Form or get a good apprenticeship when you leave. He doesn't want you sponging off them like your sister does. And because you were kicked out of two other schools, Mrs Saul-Hudson agreed to keep you here, come what may. He thanked her for it. But that was it, that was all I read.'

Maggie shook her head. I sat down next to her. She looked beaten down. Flattened. Lost. 'I can't believe he's done this. He knows how much I hate it here. I'll run away.'

'No you won't.'

'I will.'

'You won't, Maggie. You'd have to walk at least ten miles to the nearest train station.'

'I'll hitch.'

I looked at her. 'Maggie, don't.'

'Why not? My parents clearly don't give a toss. He's leaving me here all Christmas, that's how much he loves me. Git.'

'They're paying £18,000 a term so you can get your education, Maggie. I'd say they love you a hell of a lot. And anyway, I'm here all Christmas too so it won't be so bad.'

'They're sadists. Actual, factual sadists.'

'Why do you hate it here so much?'

'Why?' she repeated. 'Look around you, Nash. We're in the middle of actual NOWHERE.'

I shrugged, looking around us beyond school land towards the moors and the hillsides dusted with icing sugar snow and spindly black trees. Coupled with the cinnamon smells rising up from the Fayre and the tinkling of a carol from somewhere, it felt like we were in a scene from a Christmas card. It was stunning. 'That's not so bad. It's quite beautiful, don't you think? Look at the snow on the hills, on the trees.'

'And I hate nature.'

'That can't be the only reason you want to leave, the isolation.'

'No,' she said quietly. 'The food's crap as well.'

'Yeah it is a bit, isn't it?' I grinned.

'And...'

'What?'

She went to tell me something then stopped herself. 'It's like you said—the place is "fundamentally flawed". Why else would we be allowed up on this very old, probably very unsafe roof, to scrub tiles. No one gives a crap about Health and Safety here, do they? No one gives a crap about us.'

'Look, the parents are starting to arrive.'

Cars were trickling through the top gate at the far end of the driveway. There was the lightest fluttering of snow on the gelid air as a succession of Rolls-Royces, Mercedes, Porsches and Volvos rolled up the drive and parked up, their occupants following the signs through the formal gardens towards the stalls. I stopped scrubbing and walked to the West Turret roof to look down on the Orangery lawn. Stall-holders had been at the school all morning, setting up their Christmas glögg, hickory smoked nuts, handmade crafts, wicker baskets, pomanders and tree ornaments. A ginger girl, Rosanna Keats, was standing at the arched entrance to the formal gardens, with a tray of glögg in little tumblers and a plate of sugared plums. Two girls standing next to her—I think it was the twins Hannah and Heather Bolan-Wood—bore fat chunks of stollen and gingerbread on little red and white napkins.

My mum and dad would have loved to see all this. They'd enjoyed it last year. Dad had gone on about his eggnog for months afterwards and Mum had bought these Hansel and Gretel tree ornaments which she said reminded her of me and Seb. Seb'd taken the piss, as he usually did at my school events, about our indoor and outdoor shoes, our 'no whistling' and 'no TV except on Saturdays' rules. He'd laughed all through the school concert, at the Pups forgetting their words and Regan Matsumoto's tuneless trumpet recital. All the girls in my dorm kept going on about how hot Seb was. I'd just found him annoying. I'd have given anything to be annoyed by him again today.

'Have you seen Regan recently?' I asked, hugging the chimney pot on the Weather Station turret as the eerily distant sounds of the choir singing 'Once in Royal David's City' came floating upwards.

'Huh?'

I sighed and hopped down off the turret roof to rejoin Maggie in the middle. 'Regan Matsumoto. You know. Weird girl? Plaits?'

'Best friend is a spine in the woods? Yeah, what about her?'

'I haven't seen her about this afternoon. Have her parents come to pick her up then? I didn't see her go. She said she was staying here for Christmas.'

Maggie was clearly distracted. 'Ssh,' she said, not taking her eyes from whatever she was looking at on the west side of the school. 'Come and look.'

I moved across to the Observatory turret, where she was hiding behind the chimney, and she pointed towards Edward's Pond. A figure was walking by herself, carrying a white bag, towards the Birdcage. She looked round. It was Dianna.

'What's she doing?' I said.

'Dunno,' said Maggie. 'She keeps looking round, to see if anyone's following her.'

'She looks very furtive,' I whispered.

'What does that mean?'

'Secretive. Like she's doing something she shouldn't. Maybe she is.'

'Oh, she *so* is,' said Maggie, her eyebrows going into suggestiveness overdrive. Dianna looked around again and disappeared into the trees.

'Oh, come on,' I said. 'This is Dianna Pfaff we're talking about.'

'Yeah, I know. The Kate Middleton of Bathory School. Wouldn't swear if her fanny hair caught fire. But what's it about then? And what's in that bag?'

I shrugged. 'Candles for the procession or something? The route goes that way.'

'The route's already marked,' said Maggie. 'I watched Amy Sudbury and Helena Freemantle doing it this morning with white paint and gaffer tape.'

'Okay well—'

'Look, there she is again,' said Maggie as Dianna's blonde head appeared in the gap between the trees and the path from the Birdcage up to the Temple. She still had the bag. Then we lost her. 'Damn.'

'What is she doing up there?' I said aloud.

'I've got to know,' said Maggie. 'I'm gonna go and catch her red-handed.'

'No, wait,' I said, holding her arm. 'Wait until she comes back down and then go and ask her.'

Maggie was just about persuaded. I went back to scrubbing the roof while she watched and waited for signs of movement in the gardens. Pretty soon, the gorgeous sugary smell of roasting chestnuts and the sweet notes of 'O Little Town of Bethlehem' came floating up to greet us from the scene below.

'That bleeding caterwauling,' Maggie muttered. 'Seriously, I've heard better noises coming out of abattoirs.'

'How many abattoirs have you visited then?' I said, swilling off the last white remnants into the guttering.

'Nash, Nash, she's coming back, look!'

I put down the bucket and raced back over to the Observatory turret roof again, hiding behind Maggie as we watched Dianna coming back down the hill. She disappeared into the trees. When she reappeared, we saw that the white bag she had been carrying had gone.

I looked at Maggie. 'Where's the bag?'

'Oh, we have sooooo got something on Princess Di.'

'Like what?' I asked. 'We saw her walking into the valley with a bag. Big deal.'

'Maybe she's the dreaded Beast of Bathory, and in the bag are some more severed limbs! MWAH ahh AH!'

I laughed. 'Come on, seriously.'

'Let's go and ask her about it now,' said Maggie.

'Not yet. We don't want her to know we're on to her. Don't you know anything about espionage?'

'Eh?'

'Espionage. Spying. Look, we're in the driving seat here—we've got something on her. If we go down there and let her know what we know—not that we know much—she'll make up some feeble excuse, and next time she'll be even more careful about covering it up.'

'Covering what up?'

'Whatever it is that she's just done,' I said. 'No, we have to play it really cool, don't let her suspect we know anything. Come on. Let's go and put these back in the yard. I need to get my libretto.'

* * *

Later, as the others squealed off to the dorms to collect luggage and leave with their parents, Maggie helped me put the signs up in the Landscape Gardens saying 'Keep Out' and 'Unsafe: Frozen Water' and then we got two hot chocolates from one of the stalls and played cards in the bay window of the common room. Girl by girl, trunk by trunk, car by car, the school emptied, the Christmas smells disappearing and the chatter evaporating on the polar white air. A Pup called Tabitha Bonham, who was also staying behind until her army parents picked her up some time before Christmas Eve, had latched on to me and was sitting by my feet with a floppy toy rabbit, the ear of which was in her mouth.

'SNAP,' Maggie shouted and banged her hand down on the coffee table between us. I stared out of the window as she shuffled the stack. I longed to see my dad's blue Volvo Estate beetling down the driveway, sweeping round the turning circle at the front of school. To see Mum and Dad get out of the front. To see my brother Seb leap out of the back seat and come running up to hug me. But it was so far away. They were so far away. The night grew darker and emptier.

The door to the common room burst open and Dianna Pfaff stormed in, mumbling and cursing under her breath.

'*Bloody* stupid do this do that. Hateful…'

'Hi, Dianna,' I said. She did a double take.

'Natasha,' she said. 'Margaret. Pup.'

'Princess,' said Maggie, slamming down a jack on top of my jack. 'SNAP!'

'Dammit!'

Maggie smiled, collecting up her cards. I had seven left. It was the third game in a row that I'd lost, but I didn't mind.

I'd seen a bright side—me, Maggie and a fairly sweet Pup on our own with Matron over Christmas. We could make the best of it.

I looked over at Dianna, who was removing a plastic container of Rice Krispie cakes from her locker. 'Everything okay, Dianna?'

She closed her locker. 'No, not really. I just got off the phone to my mother. Looks as though I'll be staying for Christmas as well.'

Then again…

Maggie groaned. 'Oh you are fu—'

'SNAP!' I shouted as Maggie took her eye off the stack. Then the door opened again and the one person I wished had been oven-roasted with our reconstituted turkey strode in and removed her coat.

'Oh, are you staying for Christmas too, Clarice?' asked Dianna.

She looked straight at me. The sling had already gone, not surprisingly—Clarice was all about the effect—though there was still a plaster over her nose. 'Yeah. I am.'

# 8
## Scream

Matron wasted no time in doling out holiday chores to the unhappy band of sisters in the main hall before supper.

'Dianna, yard duty, entrance hall and breakfast washing-up—'

'But I'm—'

'No buts. Natasha, dog walking, common room and litter.'

'Yes, Matron.'

'But, Matron—' Dianna persisted.

Matron wasn't listening. 'Margaret. Margaret?'

I put up my hand. 'She's in the Chill…the basement, Matron, finishing off her detention. Orders from Mrs Saul-Hudson just before she left.'

'Oh yes, of course. Well, Margaret will be on kitchen

laundry, dorms and lunchtime washing-up. I'll inform her when I go down to let her out.'

Dianna looked like she had a bonnet full of bees. 'But Matron, I'm Head—'

'If you say "But I'm Head Girl, I shouldn't have to do chores," Dianna, I shall give you *extra* chores to do. Understood?'

Dianna shut up. My heart gave a little leap of delight. I loved it when she got owned by a member of staff.

Regan appeared behind us on the stairs. A shudder ran through me. I hadn't even noticed her arrive.

'Regan, good of you to join us. You're on bedroom laundry, corridors and Hall.'

'Yes, Matron.' She nodded meekly.

'Tabitha, bathroom, evening washing-up and morning post duty. And sit on your own bottom, please. You are not a baby.'

'Yes, Matron,' Tabitha squeaked. She had been sitting on my lap, but she quickly slid off onto the stairs.

'And Clarice Hoon, dining room, kitchen and Music room.'

Clarice checked the huge pink plastic watch on her wrist. She now had no plasters on her face, but all her Nash-inflicted bruises and thumps had been plastered with concealer. 'Yeah, all right.'

'Yes, Matron.'

'Yes, Matron. Ooh, and Matron?'

Matron snapped her head round like a snake, glaring at Clarice. 'What?'

'Can we have our phones back? Now it's Christmas hols, I want to call my boyfriend.'

'You may not have your phones back until your parents arrive.'

'What?' Clarice cried. 'Why?'

'Because,' said Matron, 'I am under strict instructions from Mrs Saul-Hudson that owing to certain pupils flouting phone privileges, no girl is allowed their phone back until they go home.'

We all knew this meant Maggie and her secret science lesson Snapchats to some boy back in her home town. This knowledge didn't take the sting out of it though. All pupils, both day girls and boarders, had to post their phones in a locked box outside the staffroom every single morning and were allowed them back every night when they went home or after Prep if they were boarders. Woe betide any Bathory girl who smuggled their phone into class and it went off. It was instant detention or, at the very least, five Blue Tickets for their house.

'But my parents don't get back from Australia until Boxing Day at least. What about emails? Twitter? Facebook?'

'This doesn't automatically become a youth hostel once the term ends. You are all still at school. You will continue to use the main public phone at the front of school for phone calls to relatives. You have Margaret Zappa to thank for your absence of phone and internet so take it up with her. The passcode needed to unlock the router is right here,' she said, tapping the side of her own head, 'so don't get any ideas about hacking in to it because that would be impossible.'

'*And internet?* So unfair!'

'This is not a hotel, Clarice. Whilst you are here, you will be expected to attend breakfast, lunch, dinner and Prep and to take part in quiet prayers at the Chapel on a Sunday morning. At all times, you are to wear your uniforms. And

wash that make-up off your face. Unless you're audition-
ing for the circus, I see no reason to wear it. You're not im-
pressing anyone here.'

I swallowed the snigger I desperately wanted to emit. I
could see Dianna straining not to smile too.

'No internet?' said Clarice, flicking her violent red hair
in Regan's face before it fell to her shoulder and sat there
shimmering like a fat red snake. 'What are we supposed
to do instead?'

Matron sighed. 'When we can trust Bathory girls not to
order unsuitable items, download distasteful imagery or
Google how to make incendiary devices, your privileges
may be returned. But until then there remains, as I said,
no internet.'

'But my boyfriend might need to get hold of me. I do have
a boyfriend, and a social life, unlike other people, and they
both need attention.'

'Do you want to mention your boyfriend any more times,
Clarice?' said Dianna.

'Lesbian,' Clarice muttered, before shutting up completely and leaning sullenly against the banisters.

'Do you have a spinal issue, Clarice?' sighed Matron.

'No, Matron,' she grunted.

'Then will you please use the bones God has given you
and stand up straight.'

I wanted to high-five Matron right there. Seb used to have
a girlfriend like Clarice: all lipstick and hair straighteners
and me me me. She hated me too—always commenting on
my lack of boobs, my lack of style and not having a boyfriend. I constantly wanted to slap her around the gills too.

'You may all continue to make your one ten minute phone
call per evening, after Prep, using the payphone outside the

Head's office. Phone cards can be purchased at Bathory Basics in the village. You can go down there tomorrow after lunch. Being here is still a privilege and you may not run amok.'

*Run amok?* I thought. Far be it from me to agree with Clarice, but asking for our phones back was hardly amok-inducing. Unless she thought we were going to arrange bunga bunga parties or heroin drops.

Clarice had a face like a smacked butt cheek. I was the one who really needed a phone. But maybe I didn't really want to hear. No news was good news.

It was as though Matron had read my mind. 'Natasha, you may have ten minutes' phone privilege after breakfast each day as well if you wish.'

'Thank you, Matron.'

'Why her?' scoffed Clarice. 'We're all missing home, you know. Also, shouldn't you be keeping *her* away from me, given what she did to my face? Shouldn't I get some sort of restraining order?'

Matron walked up to Clarice. 'I am under no further instruction from Mrs Saul-Hudson to punish Natasha for what she may or may not have done to you—'

'May or may not have done? She punched—'

'And when your brother's missing, you may also have extra phone privileges. Now I'll hear no more about it.'

Even that didn't stop Clarice. Now she'd pushed past Regan and was right in Matron's face.

'What now?' Matron glared at her.

'Day trips.'

'I'm sorry?'

'When some of us were stuck here for a few days in summer, Mr Saul-Hudson took us to the beach at Gunness-on-Sea. We went shopping and had McDonald's on the way back. What are you going to do about day trips?'

Matron gently but firmly pushed Clarice backwards, as though her smell was offensive. 'And what, pray tell, did you have in mind?'

Clarice shrugged. 'I dunno. Just some days out. Christmas shopping and stuff.'

*'And stuff and stuff,'* Matron mimicked. Tabitha looked at me and smiled. 'And how were you planning on our getting to and from this *stuff*, Clarice?'

'Bus?' she suggested.

We knew there were no bus drivers working over Christmas, and Matron couldn't drive. Clarice stopped talking. I think even she realised it was futile by this stage.

'You should count yourselves lucky you're allowed to stay here for however long your parents have deemed fit. I cook your meals, I lock you in and I report anything suspicious to the Saul-Hudsons. That is that. As for entertainment, you make your own. You will all use the prefects' common room for recreation, to save making the other common areas untidy, and unless you have any relatives willing to spend the day with you, this school will be your whole world until your mother's car rolls up that drive. Do I make myself clear?'

Clarice nodded, sulkily accepting she wasn't going to get the lifeblood that was internet access out of the stone that was Matron, as the woman turned on her polished black heel and left, her key bunch jangling on her hip.

'Such a troll,' Clarice muttered.

Dianna threw her a look, but didn't say anything.

So that was us for the foreseeable—me, Maggie, Dianna, Regan, Clarice and a six-year-old Pup whom Maggie had decided we should call Tabby, her full name being 'way too long to be arsed with'.

As Matron left us on the hallway stairs to go and let Maggie out of the Chiller after her hour's penance, Dianna Pfaff sidled up to me. I was uncertain of the intention but got the distinct impression that a favour was about to be asked.

'Listen, do you want to swap chores with me? She's given me yard duty, entrance hall and breakfast washing-up.'

'That's not so bad. Maggie's got the really bum chores—kitchen laundry, washing-up *and* dorms.'

'I know, but I was only on yard duty a week ago. Could I swap you yard and entrance hall for Brody and outside litter?'

'Why do you want to do those?' I said. 'Brody pulls hard on the lead and does about three craps every time and outside litter is never-ending.'

'I know, but I don't mind. Tell you what, I'll do both and you just do one of mine.'

'Matron'll know we've swapped. I don't think she'll allow it.'

'She wouldn't have to know. I won't say anything. Please?'

I stopped and looked at her. 'You wouldn't be breaking a rule, would you, Head Girl?'

'Please, Nash.'

She seemed desperate. It flashed across my mind that the reason she wanted the outdoor duties was to do with her covert visit to the woods and that big white bag. 'Sorry, Dianna,' I said. 'I don't want to incur Matron's wrath, not since the extra phone allowance.'

Dianna nodded. 'Okay.'

'If there was something you wanted to do outside, I could cover for you…'

'No, I didn't want to do anything in particular,' she said. 'It was just for the fresh air.'

'You'll get fresh air on yard duty.'

'Just forget I mentioned it. You're probably better off with Brody anyway. He likes you.' She did a kind of awkward giggle thing and started up the stairs towards the dorms, her cheeks just beginning to turn a darker shade of pink.

I heard from my dad again that night. He and Mum were holed up in some grotty, boiling hot Colombian motel with no air conditioning, twenty miles from where Seb was last seen. I listened to him in a darkened corridor in a freezing cold school in the middle of nowhere.

'Nashy?'

'Hi, Dad. How are you?'

There was about a three-second delay on the line and lots of crackling. 'Hi, sweetheart, we're fine. There's been a development, honey. We're just trying to…'

'What?'

'…Seb…walking…backpack…he fell.'

'What? Dad, I can't hear you, the line's gone funny.'

'…ash…ash…hear me?'

'DAD? Dad, for God's sake I can't hear you, what's happened?'

I was frantic. The only words I could make out clearly were 'backpack' and 'fell'. He was dead. I knew he was dead.

And then his voice came back to me, clearer than before.

'NASH?'

'Dad?'

'There you are, I think we're back now. Did you hear what I said?'

'No.' I didn't dare breathe out. It hurt too much.

'One of Seb's party, Joe, has been found. He flagged down...bus...to the town. He'd gone to get help for their friend Mike who had fallen down a gorilla trap in the jungle. When Joe came back with some rangers a day later, Seb and Mike...gone. They found Seb's backpack...and there was a rope...trap.'

'So what does that mean?'

'Well, it means that, until two days ago, they were alive, somewhere in the rainforest.'

'Okay.' I breathed out. It was easier to breathe, but it still hurt. They still hadn't found him. Anything could have happened in those two days.

'I think they'll find him, love. I really do now.'

I nodded, not that Dad could hear that.

'Nash? Baby, are you still there?'

'Yeah.'

'Listen, we're going up into the hills tomorrow so we'll be out of range. I won't be able to call in for a few days, okay?'

'Okay, Dad.'

'I've got to go now, honey. We love you. We'll see you really soon, all right?'

'Yeah, okay.'

'Love you, Nashy.'

The line went dead. All I could think right then was how far away my whole family was. Oceans away. A whole continent away. I was nowhere near any of them and had no way of knowing if they were all safe. I felt sick. When I put down the receiver, Dianna was standing behind me and her appearance made me leap out of my skin. 'You made me jump.'

'Sorry. Is there any news on your brother?' she asked.

I pulled my jumper cuffs down over my cold fists. 'Yeah, up until a couple of days ago he was alive. No one's heard anything since. It's just a horrible limbo now.'

She looked like she was searching for the right words. 'Is he a good brother?' she asked.

I looked at her. 'What do you mean? He's just…my brother.'

'Yeah, but there's good brothers and bad brothers. Mine's the worst,' she said. Her voice had a jittery anger to it, like she truly meant it.

'Seb can be annoying,' I said, walking along with her towards the Refectory where we did Prep. 'When I was little he used to tease me and lock me in suitcases and fart on my head.'

'Yeah. I had all that too.'

'But he's good in other ways. He used to build these assault courses in our garden, made out of old fireguards and wardrobes. We used to time each other. And he'd tell me stories at night before we went to bed. Taught me to drive too, on the beach near our house. Once, when he was about eight, he ran away with me.'

'He did?'

'He didn't want my mum to cut my hair so he packed our bags and we ran away.'

'How far did you get?'

'Not far. This busybody neighbour saw us in the High Street and drove us home.'

'He looked after you though?'

I swallowed and rubbed my cold nose with my cuff. 'Yeah. I didn't know you had a brother until Maggie mentioned him at breakfast.'

Her face darkened. 'Don't remind me. Yeah, he's in prison okay, but I don't want to talk about it.'

'Okay. What's his name?'

'Uh…' She took ages to say it. I wondered if she was making it up. 'Leon.'

'That's a nice name.'

'He doesn't deserve it.'

'How come you two don't get on?'

She looked at me. 'Let's just say he's the black sheep.'

Just then footsteps clattered along the corridor and Matron appeared, leading Tabby, Clarice, Regan and Maggie towards the Refectory for Prep. As they passed, I noticed Clarice was walking closely behind Tabby, holding the belt of her tunic. Every time Tabby walked too far ahead, Clarice pulled her sharply back, like a pony, and the front of her shoes scuffed Tabby's heels. Tabby didn't look like she was enjoying herself.

'Are you okay, Tabs?' She looked up at me with the sort of face a puppy might make if its tail were being pulled. I yanked Clarice's hand away.

'Get off me.'

'Get off *her.*'

'Oh come on, we're only playing Horsey. You like it, don't you Tabby?'

'No,' Tabby mumbled.

I looked at Clarice. 'Get. Off. Her. I'm watching you. Remember that.'

Clarice swung her thick red ponytail over her shoulder and laughed.

I thought perhaps I'd got through to her. Perhaps she would get the message now.

I was wrong.

\* \* \*

The next morning, I was tidying the prefects' common room, finding the cases for the three DVDs that were always on the shelf: a science video on photosynthesis, *Mrs Doubtfire* and *Schindler's List*. Prefect boarders could bring their own pre-approved DVDs for common use, but largely these were only ever the ones around to watch. I'd had a terrible night's sleep, dreaming dreams about Seb that didn't have happy endings. There'd been a lot of screaming. Then, out of nowhere, I heard a real scream. Through the bay window, I saw the red blob of Clarice's hair. She was standing on the grass verge, underneath the cobnut tree, and she seemed to be talking to herself. Then she put up her arm. I saw a leg dangling from the branches, kicking it away.

I dropped my duster and ran for the front door.

'Clarice, what are you doing?' I slowed to a jog as I reached her.

She turned to me and sighed. 'She won't come down,' she said to me, hands on her hips and smiling, like they were playing a game. 'She's being very silly indeed. I may have to inform Matron.' Her voice had a threatening edge.

I looked up into the tree and saw Tabby, bundled up on a thick bough just above our heads. She was shaking.

'What's wrong with you? Why do you get your kicks from tormenting the Pups?'

'I beg your pardon?' she said through her thickly pink lips. 'I was trying to apologise to her *actually.*'

'You heard me. Leave. Her. Alone.'

'I think you ought to watch who you're talking to.'

'I know *exactly* who I'm talking to.'

'Why can't you just mind your business, Nash? You

already lost out on Head Girl because you attacked me. Wouldn't want to get expelled as well, would you?'

'Go away, Clarice.'

'Go away, *Natasha*. Don't you have a brother to go and bury?'

Her comment had pierced my nerves like a dentist's sickle. My heart thundered in my chest, but I stayed firm. I stared her out. I heard Seb's voice in my head, or was it Maggie's? *Girls here can be evil. You've got to give as good as you get, or it'll sink you.* I looked her dead in the eye. 'You hurt that little girl again, I will hurt you back tenfold.'

She made a *pffft* noise and laughed like a piglet being tortured. 'Whatever,' she said. 'I'll see you later, Tabby, silly billy.' She smiled and walked past me, whispering 'virgin' in my ear, and headed back towards the school. I waited until she was far away, beneath the portico arch, before I moved closer to the little girl above me.

'It's okay,' I said. 'You can come down now. She's gone.'

Tabby sniffed and climbed down, bough by bough, her knees scraped and her navy blue tights torn. When she reached me, she put her arms out and I lifted her down, intending to put her on the log. But she clung on to me like a wet shower curtain.

'Hey what's wrong? What's the matter?' She settled on my lap as I sat down on the fallen log. 'It's okay, Tabby, it's all right.'

'I want my mummy.'

'I know you do. I know. She'll be here on Christmas Eve, won't she? And Daddy.'

A fresh drip of tears. 'I packed my case ready.'

'That's good,' I said. She began to cry again. 'Tabs, come

on, it's okay.' I pulled some tiny twigs and furry leaf things out of her hair.

'I fell over,' she whimpered.

'I can see by your knees. We'd better go and clean them up, hadn't we?'

'And I saw the monster.'

'Well, you just try to stay away from her—what did you say?'

'The monster. I saw it when I was running, over there.' I followed her arm towards the tennis courts and surrounding fields. There was nothing there.

'Was it Chief Brody? He's not a monster, Tabs, he's just a dog. He's really cuddly.'

'Not Chief Brody. It was the monster.'

I frowned. 'That's just a story.'

'Clarice said it's real. She said it'll come and get me. She said it'll hide under my bed and bite my foot when I'm getting in. She said he'll scratch me and eat me.'

If I'd had fire inside me, I'd have blown smoke out my nostrils. 'No, Tabby, it's not real. Clarice was just being... stupid.'

Tabby put her hand just above my head. 'He was big. As big as you.'

I sighed. 'Was he?'

'And he was black and he had big teeth. I'm not lying, I promise.'

'No, I know you're not lying, Tabs,' I said, hugging her closer. 'I believe you.'

# 9
## The Hunger

The following day was a Thursday. Just after lunch, Matron presented Dianna with a shopping list of odds and ends to pick up from Bathory Basics in the village, permitting her to choose two people to accompany her. As Clarice was in the doghouse over her continued bullying of Tabby, Matron had banned her from leaving the grounds and was now watching over Tabby like a very fierce eagle. So me and Regan were to accompany Dianna on the jaunt and the others gave us their lists.

I still hadn't found Babbitt, Tabby's toy rabbit that had gone missing.

'Give my love to young Charles, won't you?' Maggie winked as I put my coat on.

I smiled. 'Yeah yeah.'

'And see if you can get anything out of Princess Di about the whole white bag thing. She'll tell you, I bet.'

'Yeah right. Listen, will you look after Tabby for me while I'm gone?'

'What d'you mean? I thought Matron was keeping a closer eye now?'

'She is but Matron's busy making dinner and cleaning and doing paperwork and stuff and I just don't want her left by herself. And don't mention beasts or anything. Clarice has taken her cuddly rabbit thing away and put it somewhere too. See if you can find it, will you?'

'God, that girl is one Insane Jane, I tell you.'

'Just make sure she doesn't go near her. I don't know why she's zoned in on Tabby.'

'I told you, she's a dick. That's what dicks do. But yeah, I'll watch the little squirt. She can help me do the washing-up and vacuum the dorms. In fact, she can just do it all. Let's get me out of the equation right and quick.'

'Just don't let her out of your sight, okay? She's on bathroom duty.'

'Got it. Leave her with me. I'll do the business, find the bunny thing and all. I'll be like Cameron Poe at the end of *Con Air*, coming through the flames with the toy bunny for his little kid. Actually, they sell DVDs in the shop, don't they?'

'Yeah—not many though. And they won't be new ones.'

'See if they've got *Con Air* though. I fancy watching that. Plane full of desperate convicts. Nicolas Cage with a mullet. What's not to love?'

I sighed. 'Uh, the plot?'

'So insignificant when you have a plane blowing up in

Vegas *and* the awesomeness of The Cage and his Nickel-back hair.'

I sighed. 'Okay, I'll see if they've got it. Just try not to blow up the school while I'm gone.'

'Killjoy.'


Bathory village was our Hogsmeade, except we didn't have a joke shop or a Shrieking Shack or Butterbeer. What we did have was a small park with swings, a phone box and a surprisingly well-stocked general store called Bathory Basics. Together, they provided the four things any Bathory girl wanted more than anything—freedom, a link to the outside world, decent tampons and chocolate. In Sickbay, Matron only ever stocked the very cheapest sanitary towels that felt like surfboards and made you walk like you'd been riding a horse all your life, so boarders had to make sure they returned from every holiday or exeat with enough period-ware to see them through the term. It was never enough though. There had once been a post office in the village too at some stage, but that had long gone, along with the garage, pub, paper mill and cake shop. There wasn't much in Bathory village, but it was our sanctuary, and we took every opportunity to walk the three miles to reach it. The only downside was that we felt every inch of that walk.

'God, I'm freezing,' said Dianna, burrowing her face further into her scarf.

'So am I,' I lied. I was actually pretty snug in my coat, thick woollen scarf and Mum's cashmere gloves, and the anticipation of seeing Charlie again was keeping me warm. 'I think it's going to snow soon.'

'And my shoe's rubbing.'

'So's mine, right on my heel,' Regan added.

The road was an endless grey stretch, sided by fenced-off fields. In the distance were the moors, already iced with a light fall of snow. The temperature and distance were very unforgiving on our thin regulation navy pea coats and Mary Janes. I walked beside Dianna and Regan stayed behind us. Every so often, a car would thunder past and we would bunch up together and smoosh ourselves into a hedge.

'Gross!' Regan shrieked, as we all dived into the hedge for the fourth time in as many minutes. She had unwittingly discovered a fresh roadkill badger by treading in it.

'Oh my God, that's disgusting. What did you do that for?' said Dianna helpfully.

'I didn't see it,' cried Regan, standing stock-still and looking like she was going to be sick, modelling the dead badger like a grotesque new shoe. I wrapped my hand in Matron's Bag-for-Life and plucked it off her foot by its ear, swinging it bodily through a gap in the hedge. The dead weight made it very heavy.

'There, gone,' I said, peeling the Bag-for-Life from my hand and balling it up. Regan smiled at me in thanks, and examined her gunk-covered heel. 'Wipe it on the grass, maybe?'

'That was vile,' said Dianna, carrying on walking.

'She couldn't help it. How come you chose us two to come anyway?'

'Why?' she said, as we stopped yet again to allow a Land Rover to pass. 'Because Maggie can't stand me, Clarice is weird and Tabitha's a liability.'

'You'd like Maggie if you got to know her.'

'She hates me.'

'She doesn't. She just doesn't like being bossed around, that's all. If you tried…'

'What?'

'I don't know, being a bit less bossy with her maybe…'

'I'm supposed to be bossy. I am her boss, technically.'

'You're not, Dianna,' I laughed.

'I kind of am. I'm Head Girl after all.'

'Don't remind me,' I muttered, waiting for Regan to catch up.

'Do you hate me?'

'What?' I said, readjusting my scarf.

'For getting made Head Girl. I know you were first choice.'

'I don't care, Dianna. No, seriously, I don't.'

Dianna stood still too. 'You did mind though, at the time. I saw your reaction when it was announced in Prayers.'

'I smashed Clarice's face in, Dianna. No way was Saul-Hudson going to make me Head Girl after that, was she?'

'I'm not doing a good job, though. I've just got so much on my plate at the moment, I'm not thinking straight. And the other girls hate me.'

'They don't. Do they, Regan?'

'Yes,' said Regan. 'Everyone hates her.'

Dianna exhaled. 'I knew that. They all like you, Nash. I don't know why they made me Head Girl. You'd have been a much safer choice.'

The phrase *because bullshit always beats brains* was dancing around my head, but I mentally flicked it away. 'No, listen: they don't hate you. They don't like your tone sometimes, maybe. How you go running to Saul-Hudson about every single little thing.'

'But that's what being Head Girl means, isn't it? I'm supposed to be the eyes and ears of the Headmistress among the student body.'

'Yes, but sometimes you could just turn a blind eye. Like when Maggie wore her indoor shoes outside the other week. I always just looked past stuff like that.'

Dianna seemed fragile. Broken. Was now a good time?

'Dianna, is something going on with you?'

She looked back at me briefly, but didn't slow her pace. 'What do you mean?'

'You seem a bit guarded. And when you asked me to swap chores…'

'I told you, I wanted some more fresh air.'

'Yeah, I know, but you get plenty of fresh air, we all do. Is there something else? If you want to talk about anything…'

'No, I don't,' she snapped, as a beer lorry thundered past, scaring us all half to the grave and cutting my line of questioning dead in the process. She deliberately increased her pace, pulling away from us.

We arrived at the sign for the village. Another two hundred metres and we'd be at the shop.

As we rounded the bend and saw the swinging ice cream sign outside Bathory Basics, Regan asked, 'Nash, do you think the Beast killed that badger?'

'No, I don't,' I replied. 'It was roadkill. The End.'

'All right, I only asked.'

'Well, I'm sick of hearing about this Beast of Bathory. It doesn't exist, Regan. I was mistaken. You were mistaken. You have to stop thinking about it.'

'Tabitha said she saw it yesterday. She told me at breakfast.'

I stopped and faced her. 'Have you been talking to her about it?'

'Yeah. She believes me.'

'So that's why she thought it was the Beast. Look, stop

filling her head with stuff. It'll give her nightmares. It was Chief Brody that she saw. Remember him? Big black dog?'

'No, it wasn't.'

'It was. Just stop with the Beast stuff. It's getting really boring, okay?'

School was a scary enough place to be stranded during the Christmas holidays without some starey-eyed imp like Regan banging on about man-eaters and things that go *rawr* in the woods.

She said nothing more, but she gave me that look again. That lingering look, like she was peeling back the layers of my lies, silently telling me she knew I'd seen it.

At last the warm glow of the Bathory Basics window, with its tantalising display of home-made jams and chutneys and sign promising 'Freshly baked bread and cakes', filled our vision. It was the only shop within five miles and there were lots more than just the basics inside. It was like a Tardis—a lot bigger inside than it looked and there were different little nooks and rooms depending on what you wanted. There was a cooked meat counter, a cheese counter, magazines, cold drinks, milk and yoghurt, a pharmacy area for medicines and dressings, an ice-cream freezer in the back of the shop, sweets and a small room to the side which offered toys, books and jigsaws. There was the odd Beast of Bathory souvenir in there too, for the tourists. It was a trove of precious jewels; a little chunk of paradise to us all.

And Charlie Gossard was the paradise pin-up. Him and Maggie had a long-running spat going. She started it last June by pulling down his shorts and running out of the shop screaming. In return, he posted her a dead mouse. She posted *him* a live cockroach. The next time she went to the shop, he glued her hand to a Lion bar. She spread a rumour there was dog crap in their doughnuts. If memory served, it was Charlie's turn.

He was crouched on the floor, rearranging the display of charity Christmas cards when we walked in. His shoulder blades looked amazing.

'Oh hi, Nash.' He smiled, looking up at me.

'Hi,' I said, taking the briefest look at him before looking everywhere else *but*. I consulted the lists Tabby and Maggie had given me and began putting items in my basket.

'Do you need any help? Anything from the counters on either of those?' He jumped to his feet and craned his neck over my shoulder so he could see them more closely.

'Uh yeah, actually,' I said, feeling hot. 'I think Matron wanted cheese and some slices of ham, didn't she, Dianna?'

Dianna was reading a paper. She snapped her head up. 'Pardon?'

'Cheese and ham? Matron? You've got her list, haven't you?'

'Yes,' said Dianna. 'Uh, somewhere.' The list was dangling from two fingers beneath the crease so I grabbed it and handed it to Charlie. Dianna seemed jittery. I hoped she didn't fancy Charlie too. She did have a smaller waist than me.

He took Matron's list. 'No probs. I'll sort that all out for you. We're out of mince pies though. They didn't come in with the delivery this morning for some reason. I can drop those down to you when we get the next one, if that's all right?'

'Yeah fine,' I said, secretly watching every movement he made as he strode towards the counter. He looked almost as gorgeous from the back as he did at the front. He'd had a haircut recently too. There was a slightly-too-long tuft of blond hair on his neck that had been missed. I had a barely controllable urge to kiss it.

'Does that say two pounds or ten pounds of Cheddar?' he said, squinting at the piece of paper he'd placed on the top.

I joined him to look, moving my face closer to his. I wasn't taking the blindest bit of notice of the list but I knew the answer anyway. 'Uh, two, I think.'

He started slicing Cheddar behind the counter as I put the rest of the stuff on Maggie's list (big bar of milk chocolate, tampons, chewing gum and *Con Air* on DVD) and Tabitha's (Smarties, iced gems, pink hair bands and a pony comic) in my basket. His dad came in from the back of the shop with a stack of bread crates and set them down before him.

'Put that lot away when you've finished,' he said, not looking at Charlie. Charlie didn't look at him either.

'Maggie not come today then?' Charlie asked as Regan passed by, her basket already full of items from Clarice's list (hair serum, hair dye, shampoo, condoms and painkillers).

'No, not today,' I laughed, even though it wasn't funny. 'You're quite safe.'

'That thing with the doughnuts really hurt us, you know. We chucked out over a hundred quid's worth of stock.'

'Did you? I'm sorry.'

'You didn't have anything to do with it.' He cling-filmed the cheese and labelled it, then started on slicing the ham. His eyes were Pacific in their blueness. The word 'gooey' was created for these exact moments.

His dad sidled past him, straightening up the wall clock as he went. 'Three o'clock we have to be there, isn't it, Charlie?' he said.

'Yeah,' said Charlie, continuing to slice the ham. I loved

watching the movements of his forearms as he sliced things. I could spend more time looking at his forearms than I could at a priceless statue. Looking at how tanned they were. At the tiny blond hairs. At his cluster of friendship bands.

'You sure you're all right down here then, son?' said Charlie's dad

'Yes, fine.'

'I'll get on with some paperwork then, all right?'

'Yes, again,' said Charlie, and his dad patted his shoulder and left through the curtain at the back of the shop.

'Have you got to go somewhere?' I asked him, as he bagged up the ham and weighed it out.

'Yeah, the doctors,' he said, rolling his eyes. 'I've got to have this check-up thing about my asthma.' He removed a small pill bottle from his jeans and rattled it to show me.

'Oh,' I said, my heart skipping the smallest beat. I did like vulnerably lovable boys. 'You've got asthma?'

'Yeah. They changed my tablets, which made it worse, so they're gonna put me on some different ones.'

'Oh,' I said. 'My brother has that, but he has inhalers.'

'I used to have inhalers, but I'm allergic to steroids,' he said. 'These are preventers. No steroids. They really work too, I've had way fewer attacks this year.'

'Oh right.'

He must have it really bad, I thought. I remembered when Seb had a bad attack at his school sports day and had to be taken to hospital. I'd never been so scared in my life, waiting for news. Until now, of course. Charlie put the ham next to the cheese by the till. I smiled at him, hoping somehow he'd translate what it meant into words.

'Anything on your list?'

'Um,' I said, playing for time as I looked down at my

piece of paper—Frosties and Post-its. 'I'll have some Cola
Cubes please. And toffees. About two pounds worth of
each.'

'Coming up.' He smiled, walking round to the other counter where the sweet jars were. I continued to watch his forearms as he took down the Cola Cube jar and began weighing
them out.

'You don't have *Con Air* on DVD by any chance, do you?'

He frowned as he crouched down to get the toffees from
the bottom shelf behind the counter. 'Not sure. Have a look
on the rack.'

I picked my way through the DVDs, desperately trying to
think of something else to say, something to ask him, but everything I could think of was a platitude. The weather. The
shop. School. I wanted to ask him something about himself,
something that would segue us into a conversation about
going out or something, but I couldn't think how to do it.

Amazingly, I found *Con Air* with a £3 sticker on the front.
I put it in my basket.

'So when do you go home for Christmas then?' Charlie
asked me.

'Some of us are here till Boxing Day, others for the dura-
tion. My parents are in South America. I'm not sure when
they're coming.'

'That sucks,' he said, looking genuinely sad for me.

'It's okay.' I shrugged.

'How many of you are left?'

'Six, not including Matron. Maggie's there till the New
Year I think.'

He nodded. 'Cool.'

'How come?'

He smiled, winding round my sweetie bag. 'Just good to

know, that's all.' My hopes sank like a plank. I knew why he had asked about our Christmas plans. He was going to play a prank on Maggie, that was all. Nothing to do with my availability for a date or anything.

He looked around, seemingly checking for his dad who might be lurking to pounce on him if he wasn't working hard enough, then he leaned forwards over the counter. 'So, do you get any time out?'

'Huh?' I said, picking up a two pence piece that had dropped out of my purse.

'Do you get allowed out anywhere?'

'Um…'

'I thought you and me could, I dunno, maybe go into town or something?' His dad popped his head through the curtain. 'Yeah?' said Charlie.

'I'm going upstairs to change, all right? There's a delivery coming in a bit. Keep an ear out?'

'Yeah.' When his dad had gone, he seemed to relax a bit more. 'So anyway, there's a Christmas fair on over at Dyerston. Or we could go up the Gorge or something?'

Jackpot. My mouth was out-of-control smiley all of a sudden. 'Really?'

'Yeah.'

'What, all of us?'

'No.' He smiled, 'I thought just you, maybe.'

'Um,' I said, still smiling. 'Well, yeah, I'm sure I could ask Matron. Though I don't know about going into town. And I'd have to be back for Prep at six o'clock.'

'That's all right. We could hang out here, but there's not much to do in the village really. There's crazy golf up at the Gorge and some caves and shops and stuff. I think there's a petting zoo or something as well. It'll be dead quiet now it's winter.'

'Will your dad let you off work though? You seem to be quite in demand here.'

'Yeah, no worries. I'm due some time off. And anyway, it's Christmas, right? Spirit of goodwill and all that. I'll handle him, don't worry.'

The *Gorge*, I thought, scrolling in my head through the number of times of Bathory girls had said they'd been taken 'up the Gorge' by some boy or another. It was *the* hot spot in Bathory for first dates, first kisses, first anythings with a boy. I felt so proud Charlie had asked me, I could have sprouted wings from both shoulders.

Before my mind could list all the other obstacles, problems and worries I just said, 'Yes, I'd love to.'

He smiled back at me, brilliantly, and it was like the sun came out in my chest.

# 10
## Village of the Damned

The shop bell tinkled and an old woman came in, wearing thick brown snow boots and dragging a shopping trolley behind her, its two wheels caked with mud. She had a waxed hat pulled down over her face, and her woollen coat was covered in white dog hairs.

'Afternoon, Mrs Renfield,' Charlie called out. Mrs Renfield grunted a greeting and went about her business. I was on tiptoes reaching for the Frosties when Charlie beckoned me back to the counter. 'Got to keep an eye on her. Likes the odd five-finger discount.' I could feel his breath on my ear.

I smiled at him and watched as Mrs Renfield made her way over to the bookshelves where Regan had picked up a thin pamphlet on Bathory folklore. No doubt she was looking for information about the dreaded Beast. 'For God's sake,' I muttered.

'What's up?' said Charlie at the till, as he rang through some sweets for three local kids.

'Regan and this Beast thing. She doesn't shut up about it. It's really annoying.'

'The Beast of Bathory?'

'Yeah. She's obsessed with it.'

'You seen it yet?'

I frowned. The kids had moved over to the magazines and were laughing at some pictures in one of the papers.

'No, no one's seen it, that's the point. It doesn't exist.'

'It does, Nash,' said Charlie. 'There's too many people round here who've seen it in action.'

Regan's ears had pricked up. Now she scuttled over. 'How do you mean, seen it in action?'

'I mean, seen it tear apart their dogs, or had people they've known go missing.' Dianna came over too, and passed him her full basket of Matron's shopping. He totalled it up. 'Thirty-five pounds seventy-two pence, please.'

She gave him Matron's forty pounds and took the change. 'Can I cancel the newspaper delivery for the school as well, please, while I'm here?'

I frowned. 'Did Matron ask you to cancel it?'

She looked at me. 'Yes. Is there a problem?'

'No, not at all,' I said.

Then it was back to the land of make-believe.

'People have actually *seen* it kill things?' said Regan, eyes wild.

'Yeah. Old Mr Renfield has for a start, hasn't he, Mrs R?'

'Caw, has he?' said the woman. 'Bloody thing took enough sheep to put us out of the farm years back.' The old woman came waddling over to us. 'Did all we could, but there was no stopping it. Came in the night it did. Always came in the night and always at this time of year.' She parked her backside on a small wooden stool on the customers' side of the counter.

'It ate your sheep?' said Dianna.

'Some of 'em,' she replied. 'Others it killed and left. Some had broken necks, some of 'em ripped right down the front and hollowed out. You heard about that nice Mr Pellett from the Apothecary, didn't you?'

We nodded.

'I heard the screams. Farmers round here been moanin' about the bloody thing for generations, but nothing gets done. Cos it's not very often, you see. Only every now and again it'll turn up. Took them two on the moors in the summer, and that walker last winter. Loads more gone missing. Visitors. Tourists. But you can set your watch by it coming at Christmas. He goes for the turkeys, cos there's so many of 'em about.'

'Could it be a fox?' Charlie suggested, putting the last of Dianna's own goods, including shaving foam, in a carrier bag and asking her for the £26.48 she owed him.

'A fox can't bite a turkey in half, my love.'

'It bit a turkey in half?' said Dianna.

Mrs Renfield shook her head. 'Not just one. Dozens. Don't you get talkin' to my old Henry about no foxes. My Henry saw that evil thing with his own two eyes not five winters past. Hasn't slept a full night ever since.'

'What did it look like?' Regan persisted. 'Was it black? Is it as big as they say? Did it have evil red eyes?'

'Bigger. And blacker,' said Mrs Renfield. 'They say the eyes are as red as cherries.'

I had a bad taste in my mouth. She was wrong. I wanted to argue. Its eyes weren't red; they were yellow. Golden yellow. Quite beautiful. But I said nothing.

'It starts when you don't hear the birds any more,' Mrs Renfield continued. 'Then there'll be the footprints in the snow. Then they'll go missing, one by one.'

I felt sick. 'Oh my God.' I held on to the counter and put my basket on top so Charlie could start ringing my and Maggie's stuff through.

'Who will go missing?' asked Regan, in a state of near desperation by this point.

Charlie totted up Regan's shopping, bagged it up and held it out for her, but she didn't take it from him—too busy salivating over every detail. 'Here you go.'

'I've found things,' she told the old woman. 'Up at the school, in the woods. I think they're signs the Beast is around.'

'What sort of things you found then?' the old woman croaked.

'Severed limbs and animal entrails. I've found three now—a spine, a sheep's carcass and some innards.'

Dianna frowned, changing her heavy-looking carrier bag between her hands. 'What were you doing up in the Landscape Gardens, Regan? They're out of bounds at the moment. You were there in Prayers when Mrs Saul-Hudson said.'

'It is weird though,' said Charlie. 'We've had a couple of carcasses go missing from the bins out the back. Not just taken either, ripped from bin bags. Normally we'd blame badgers or something but...'

'...but you think it could be the Beast?' said Dianna.

Charlie shrugged. 'It's possible.'

'Why would it take carcasses all the way from here up to Bathory Woods? It's miles away,' said Dianna. 'Why not just eat them here? That doesn't make any sense.'

'Because his lair's up there!' Regan shouted. 'I know it is!'

'Oh calm down, Regan,' said Dianna. 'You're acting like a baby. The Beast of Bathory is a myth. Even the Pups and the Tenderfoots don't believe in all that guff.'

Regan got right up in Dianna's face. She said, very slowly, 'There is something in those woods. Something living. I've heard it. I've found things.'

'For goodness' sake…'

'I'm going to find it, Dianna.'

'Oh yes, Regan, I'm sure you are.'

I could have told everyone I'd seen it too, backed her up. Regan knew it and I knew it.

She was standing her ground pretty well though. 'I will find it and I'll show all of you. Even if I have to camp out in those woods I'll find it. I'll show you.'

Dianna glared at her. 'You're not camping in those woods. Mrs Saul-Hudson said that whole area is out of bounds over Christmas. Nash has put the signs up.'

'I will if I have to.' Regan shrugged.

'You're not, Regan. I'm warning you. I forbid you to.'

'Tough.'

'I'll tell Matron.'

'Only a fool would go looking for that thing,' warned Mrs Renfield, placing a jar of marmalade and two tins of tapioca and peach halves on the counter and removing her purse from her trolley with her knobbly hands.

'I don't care,' said Regan, sounding more like Maggie than her usual meek self. 'Call me a fool if you like. It's no worse than what people call me already.' She looked dangerously close to crying.

'Weather forecast is saying snow's coming, mind,' said Charlie, doling out Mrs Renfield's change.

'Good,' said Regan, definitely sulking now.

'The temperature is plummeting every day. You are *not* going camping in those woods. It's suicidal,' said Dianna.

Did she really care or was she more worried about what Regan was going to find in those woods? Something she didn't want anyone to know about?

'If you do go looking for it, don't do what my Henry did,' said Mrs Renfield. We all turned to look at her. 'Whatever you do, don't run. Make yourself as big as you can, make as much noise as you can and with any luck he'll leave you alone. It's the quiet ones he goes for. If he starts running after you, there's no getting away. Not from the size of them claws.'

Nobody said a word in reply.

'We'd better get back,' I interjected, killing the silence. 'It'll be dark soon.' I looked at Charlie. 'We have dinner at five. If we miss it, we don't get anything else until breakfast.'

'Jeez, they run that place like a Gulag, not a school,' he laughed.

I tried to laugh but I still felt sick at all the talk about the Beast. Dianna waited outside as Regan carried on talking to Mrs Renfield and I said my goodbyes to Charlie, hoping he would bring up the subject of the Gorge again before I left. And he did.

'Here,' he said, scribbling something down on a white paper sweet bag and handing it to me. 'My number. Text me when you've got a free afternoon, yeah?'

'Might be a problem with that,' I said. 'We aren't allowed our phones.'

'What?' he said, clearly outraged.

I shrugged. 'Yeah, not until we go home. Maggie…well she did something so now we're not allowed them. It's just like you said. Gulag.'

He took the bag back and started scribbling something else.

'And don't give me an email address. We're not allowed internet either. Our Matron's blocked the WiFi.'

He looked shell-shocked, like I'd just said we're not allowed oxygen. 'Was that Maggie as well?'

I nodded.

'Well, all right then, I'll call you on the school phone,' he said, handing me the paper again so I could write down the number, which I then did. 'We could go out and do something, somewhere. You're allowed one phone call a day on a landline, surely?'

I took the paper, tearing off a strip and writing down the school number. 'I'm allowed two,' I assured him and smiled. He smiled back. We were getting good at this smiling thing.

'Bye, Charlie.'

'Bye, Nash.'

I dipped my head, about to blush, and, as I walked out of the shop, I noticed the newspaper display was all back to front and sports pages up. I told Charlie.

'I'll sort it out, don't worry. Kids,' he huffed, coming around the counter again.

I felt a little pang of sadness as we left the warmth of the shop to venture out into the dim, cold outside world.

'You won't be allowed,' said Dianna. 'Matron won't let

us watch soap operas, let alone allow us out on day trips with random boys.'

'I'll tell her he's a relative,' I said. 'We're allowed day trips with relatives.' I waited for her to respond with some threat that she'd tell Matron herself, but she didn't. She just carried on walking. 'Hey, where's Regan?'

And with that, Regan came running up behind us, waving something in her hand and shouting. 'Guys, guys! Seriously, you're not going to believe what Mrs Renfield gave me.'

Dianna stopped. Twenty metres behind her, I stopped. We both looked at Regan and waited for her to catch up. The closer she got to us, the clearer we could see it.

Clutched tightly in her grasp, about half the length of a long ruler, was a thick, black, sharp, bloodied claw.

# 11
## Near Dark

'"But it was not the sight of her body, nor yet was it that of the body of Hugo Baskerville lying near her, which raised the hair upon the heads of these three daredevil roisterers, but it was that, standing over Hugo, and plucking at his throat, there stood a foul thing, a great, black beast, shaped like a hound, yet larger than any hound that ever mortal eye has rested upon. And even as they looked, the thing tore the throat out of Hugo Baskerville, on which, as it turned its blazing eyes and dripping jaws upon them, the three shrieked with fear and rode for dear life, still screaming, across the moor. One, it is said, died that very night of what he had seen, and the other twain were but broken men for the rest of their days".'

'Oh good. Glad you're not filling her head with scary

Beast stuff,' I said, upon finding Maggie in the Fiction Library. Tabitha was on her lap, sucking her thumb and holding the copy of Arthur Conan Doyle's *The Hound of the Baskervilles* for her to read.

'She chose it,' said Maggie, as Tabitha climbed off her lap and came over to greet me.

'I got your stuff, Tabby,' I said. 'Take it up to your bedside chest and don't let Matron catch you with it.' I handed her the bag and her change and she went to the Roald Dahl shelf, pressed it hard and it popped out, as though on a spring, revealing the Hidey Hole behind it. She stepped inside and the shelves moved back in place as though she'd never been there.

'Handy that, innit?' said Maggie, gesturing to the shelves.

'Yeah, but we're only supposed to use them in an emergency.'

'Well, not being arsed go to all the way to the front hall to get up to the dorms *is* an emergency.'

Maggie got up off her beanbag and came to the table. 'Clarice hasn't bothered her. 'I gave her a "stay away" stare earlier and I haven't seen her since.'

'Good. So Tabby's been okay?'

'Yeah she's been fine, stuck to me like frickin' superglue. Why are you so concerned about the little squirt anyway? You her real mum or something?'

'I just worry about her. I remember what it's like being that small at boarding school. Prefects like Clarice can be horrendous. And what with both her parents being in a war zone and all that.'

'Oh yeah. That's pretty cruddy.'

'Any sign of Babbitt?'

She shook her head. 'Nope. *Rien du tout.*'

'This Beast thing's annoying the hell out of me too.' I slumped down into a chair at the reading table beside a shelf full of Enid Blytons, so old they still had the racist bits in. 'Regan refuses to let it die. This old woman at the shop gave her some claw she's been carrying about in her handbag for decades.'

'Never mind that, did you get any goss out of Princess Di? Did you see Charlie Cheesepuff? Did he ask you out? Did you do Upstairs-Outsideys?'

'Don't be silly.'

'Downstairs-Outsideys?'

I just looked at her.

'Did you get my chocolate? What about *Con Air*?'

'Which would you like me to answer first?'

She thought for a second. 'The most important one, did you get my chocolate?'

I slid the large slab of Dairy Milk across the table towards her and she tore the packet open, breaking the corner with her teeth, immediately dying of ecstasy, closing her huge brown eyes to savour the moment. 'Oh my God that's worth waiting for.' I started counting out her change. She pushed it away. 'Keep it. Honestly. I've got more goddamn coins up there than Scrooge McDuck.'

'Oh, thanks,' I said, scraping them all off the table into my pocket. 'There isn't much change anyway. I got your *Con Air* as well,' I said. 'I put it on your bed.'

'Wicked!' she said. 'We'll watch that one night. Get some corn popping and stuff.' She went back to her chocolate. I wondered if they should be left alone, so adoringly was she gazing at the slab. 'So, did you see Chucky Cheese then?' she asked through another mouthful of brown sludge formerly known as Dairy Milk.

I nodded. 'Charlie? Yep. And he saw me.'

'And?'

'And, nothing really.' I started picking at an old boiled sweet stuck to the side of my chair. 'He cut the cheese.'

Maggie frowned. 'He farted? In front of you? Well, that's not gonna get you dropping your knickers, is it?'

I fell into hysterics. 'No, I mean literally. That's what he was doing. He cut some cheese for Matron. And some ham. And he bagged up some sweets. And he has asthma. I learned that today too.'

'*Très intéressant.* Not.'

'And he asked me to go to the Gorge with him.'

'Oh my God!' Maggie almost choked on her chocolate. 'That's it, tick virginity off the list then! Consider it passé!' She held up her hand for a high five but I didn't take the bait.

'It's just to see the caves or go for afternoon tea, that's all. He said there's crazy golf too. I think he just felt sorry for me being stuck here all Christmas.'

'You're going to play crazy golf? That's basically code for "don't bother wearing knickers".'

'No, it's not!' I couldn't help smiling. 'I am excited though. It'll be nice. If he meant it.'

'Stop pouring cold water on it.' Maggie sighed. 'He likes you. I could sense it that time we went in there last month. He couldn't take his eyes off you. Wake up and smell the erection. You and he are going to have hot sex up against the cave wall in Bathory Caverns or my name's not Margaret Lynette Zappa.'

'Is your name Margaret Lynette Zappa?'

'Yep.'

I sighed. 'I gave him the school number as I couldn't give

him mine and he said he'd call but I don't know. I don't think he will. I think you're more his type actually.'

'*Moi?*' Maggie squawked, breaking off another chunk of chocolate. 'He can't stand *moi*, remember? He's gonna prank the living daylights out of me next time I see him. Serving it well cold, obviously. I'm surprised he didn't send you back with a pie for me filled with chicken and razor blades.'

'Yeah, but the pranking is just flirting, isn't it?'

'Oh no. We mean business. He's not my type anyway.'

'What, loyal? Hard-working? Nice?'

'Always got blood under his fingernails,' she finished.

'No, he hasn't. They were very clean today as a matter of fact.'

'Ooh, get a good long look, did you? What else did you get a good long look at I wonder? Pecs out, were they?'

'Like bullets.' I grinned and we both fell about in hysterics. As soon as I caught sight of the wall map above the bookcase, I felt bad for laughing, for forgetting about Seb for one moment. I honed in on Colombia and all the blue space between here and there. It immediately sucked all the joy out of my thoughts.

'Charlie will call you, I know he will,' said Maggie. 'He likes you and I can tell you really like him.' She finally folded down the packet of her half-eaten chocolate bar and shoved it in down her jumper. 'Mm, major noms. So what deets did you get out of Princess Di about her woodland shenanigans?'

I leant back against the Point Horror books. 'Not much really. Actually, not anything. I think she might have told me something if I'd kept on but...'

'But what?'

'There's definitely something about her and those woods.'

'Seriously?'

'Yeah. I just can't add it all up. She's hiding something in there, I know she is.'

'Come on then, Sherlock,' said Maggie, leaning back on the creaky wooden chair. 'Hit me with it. What could it be?'

I stood up and paced the floor, jingling the coins in my pocket. I paced back, past the Judy Blumes, towards the Point Horrors and back again. I stopped and looked at Maggie. 'No, that's not helping.' I sat down again.

'Okay, what are the facts then? Sherlock always collates his facts first.'

'We saw Dianna going up to the woods with a full white bag. About half an hour later, we saw Dianna returning from the woods *sans* bag.'

*'Oui,'* said Maggie.

'She refuses to talk about what's on her mind, which isn't unusual, but might be noteworthy.'

*'Vrai...'*

'She wanted to swap chores with me so that she could do the two outdoor chores, litter and walking the dog. And she got quite agitated when I said she couldn't.'

'Which means?'

'Which means she wants to be outside more. Which *could* mean she wants free rein to go into the woods whenever she wants.'

'Right.'

'Oh, and another thing. You know I said Regan got given this claw? The old lady who gave it to her was saying she had first-hand experience of the Beast. Or rather, her husband had. They used to own a farm and he saw it attacking his sheep once. It took some turkeys at Christmas. Regan

said she was going to camp out in the woods so she could
see it.'

'Yeah...'

'Yeah, and Dianna got annoyed and forbade her from
camping in the woods.'

*'Forbade?'* cried Maggie.

'Yep. And since when has Dianna *forbidden* anyone from
doing anything ever?'

'She does it all the time!'

'Does she?' I said.

'Yeah. She forbids the Pups from touching her muesli
and forbids the cooks from using her wholemeal pasta in
the big pot with everyone else's spaghetti.'

'Yeah, but it was the way she forbade her,' I said, pacing
again. 'Like, in anyone else's mind it would be like "Okay,
Regan, you wanna go and camp in the woods overnight to
look for some abominable thing, you go right ahead", but
Dianna said it like she was afraid of what Regan might find
if she went up there.'

'But *what* might Regan find if she went up there?' Maggie urged. 'Come on, Nash, think. What could it be?'

I slumped. I'd peaked too early and I had absolutely nowhere to go but down. 'I have no idea. Something to do
with the Beast maybe? She seemed to get pretty het up
when Regan was banging on about it. We need evidence.
Why don't we sneak up there tonight and have a good look
round?'

'It's dark already,' said Maggie.

'So?'

'So, we won't be able to see anything.'

'We'll take our torches.'

Maggie seemed like she was looking for an excuse. I called her on it.

'You're not afraid of this Beast thing too, are you?'

'No, of course not,' she scoffed.

I didn't know how long Regan had been at the door, but when I turned my head she was just standing there. The door was wide open. Neither of us had heard her come in.

'Yes?' I said, rather too abruptly.

'There's a phone call for you.'

I instantly feared the worst. If it was about Seb, it would be all my fault. I'd barely given him a second thought all afternoon. 'Oh God. Who is it?'

'It's that boy from the village shop, Charlie.'

I breathed out. Maggie was wolf-whistling and catcalling and generally just acting like a complete and total winder-upper.

'Ooh, see, I told you. I told you he'd ring!'

Still recovering from the shock, I smiled embarrassedly at her, as Regan stood aside to let me through the door.

When I reached the school phone, on the shelf outside the staffroom, the receiver was resting on the telephone directory. I picked it up.

'Hi, Charlie,' I said, unable to keep the smile out of my voice.

'Nash, hi. Yeah, uh, how are you?'

'I'm still okay, thanks. I only saw you about an hour ago.'

'Yeah, I know. I thought, well, no time like the present. I wondered if you'd be free on Wednesday to go to the Gorge. You know, like, with me, kind of thing?'

My ears were ringing with bells. 'Oh, that sounds lovely, Charlie. So your dad let you have the day off?'

'I haven't asked him yet, but Wednesdays are always quiet so it'll be fine. What do you say?'

'I'd have to ask permission.'

The line was silent at his end.

'I'm sure it's okay though. The school knows your dad and everything so there shouldn't be any problem there.'

'Great, that's great. Well, what's say I pick you up about ten o'clock in the morning or something and we'll just go up the Gorge?'

'Okay,' I said, smiling down the receiver.

I could feel him smiling too. 'I'm looking forward to it,' he said.

'Me too. I'll see you at ten then, all being well.'

'Yeah. Text me…sorry, let me know if you're not allowed and I'll come up to the school and we can just chat or something.'

'Okay. I'll send a carrier pigeon maybe. I think they still allow us to send one of those out from time to time.'

He laughed like I'd said the funniest thing he'd ever heard. Then he stopped. 'Bye.'

'Bye, Charlie.' The line went dead for a few moments. I hadn't heard a click.

Neither of us had hung up.

'Charlie?'

'Yeah.'

We laughed. We did this a couple more times, said bye and then stayed on the line. I have no idea why it was funny but it was. I hadn't been relaxed enough to laugh like that in a long time. Eventually, when we did both hang up, I knew this was what I needed. Time away from the school, time with someone who wasn't really connected with the school or my family. Time just to play and be happy and worry about nothing.

The staffroom door opened and Matron appeared, locking it behind her with one of the many keys on her bunch.

'Hello, Matron.'

'Natasha.'

'May I be excused on Wednesday twenty-first to go out with a friend?'

'Where with a friend?'

'To the Gorge. Just for the day.'

'Who is this friend?'

'Charlie Gossard.'

'From Bathory Stores? I don't know, Natasha, that doesn't sound very—' She stopped talking all of a sudden and looked at me. I must have visibly deflated without realising it. 'His father will need to sign a permission slip.'

A smile cracked my face in half.

'But be back in good time for dinner and Prep.'

'Yes, Matron.'

I stopped just short of hugging her or curtseying, and bounced back along the corridor in the direction of the dorms. Matron had a bad rap at Bathory for her harsh features and there were some unkind rumours that had always persisted about her once being a man. But I liked her, always had. So what if she *had* once been a guy? Matron was kind and fair to me so I had no reason to dislike her at all. At that precise moment in time, I loved her to death for letting me go out with Charlie.

Barely containing the ear-piercing squeak of joy caught in my chest, I two-stepped it up the back staircase, passing Regan Matsumoto in the middle. She stared at me, her eyes not leaving mine until I had made it to the top and rounded the corner.

# 12
## Bride of Chucky

Knowing I was going out with Charlie on Wednesday made the days in between seem slightly sweeter than they had done. We all passed the time in relative harmony; Maggie, Tabby and I played games and got Matron's permission to use the Art room to create huge murals and make sculptures with clay. Regan was still watching every move I made, and coming back from the woods with tiny animal skulls and soil tinged with red stuff, which she swore was blood. Dianna was still doing her disappearing act every so often and coming back pretending she'd been out jogging or taking the air or, the best one yet, 'I thought I saw a rare bird in the foliage and went to investigate.' I didn't really care what Clarice was up to, but she was out of mine and Tabby's hair and that was all that mattered.

I had another phone call from Dad on Sunday morning, just to say there was still no news but that he and Mum were fine. On Monday, Matron got us all sorting and dusting the library books *all day*, and on Tuesday she had us washing floors, repairing hymn books and redoing the House noticeboards *all day* in preparation for the new term.

By Monday, the weather was starting to worsen and Matron banged on about our battening down for a big heavy snowstorm. I was worried our date would be called off, but on Wednesday, Charlie was as good as his word. I watched the clock on the common room wall tick over to 09.58 a.m. and, at the far end of the drive, I saw a small silver car rolling in. I watched it come all the way down the drive, go round the turning circle and stop by the front entrance. The clock struck ten just as he was ringing the door chime.

'He's here,' I said.

Maggie and Tabby were in there with me, getting just as excited as I was. Well, maybe not quite as excited as I was.

'Have an amazing time and I want *every* single detail when you get back.'

'Okay,' I said, taking one last look in the mirror. I smoothed Tabby's hair. 'You will keep an eye on her, won't you, Maggie?'

''Course I will, now go on. Go forth and enjoy oneself for once.'

Matron came to the door in her aproned uniform, smudges of flour on her cheeks and stains of pasta sauce on her hands, and escorted me to my visitor in the main hall.

'Now you have your spending money?' she checked.

'Yes, Matron.'

'And he knows to have you back here in time for dinner at five o'clock sharp, yes?'

'Yes, Matron. What are we having?'

'Well, it was going to be stew but…have we had stew recently? I could have sworn there were five pounds of stewing steak in the bottom of the utility fridge. Anyway, we're now having lasagne followed by jam sponge and custard.'

'Lovely,' I said. 'I'll see you later, Matron. Thank you again.' I think she could tell I really meant it.

I didn't think Charlie could look more beautiful than he usually did in his white t-shirt, jeans and apron, but he'd made a real effort today and worn a white shirt with a soft blue jumper over the top of it and navy trousers with creases in. I'd never seen him out of trainers either. Today it was polished shoes. He looked older than his seventeen years and I felt as weak as a kitten. My heart was racing as I greeted him at the front door.

It was freezing outside and the clouds were heavy with snow.

Charlie handed the signed permission slip from his dad to Matron and we got in the car. He didn't say anything until we'd both put on our seat belts then he turned to me and said, 'You look really nice.'

I could smell the aftershave on him. He usually smelled of biscuits and meat.

'You *smell* really nice,' I said.

'Do I?'

'Yeah.'

He started the engine. Before putting the car into gear, he opened the glovebox and pulled out a leaflet. 'Things to do at Bathory Gorge,' he said. 'Have a look through and see what you think.'

His tablets fell out into my footwell.

'Oh, sorry.'

I bent over, picked them up and put them back in the box. 'Did the doctor change them for you?' I asked.

'Yeah,' he said. 'I'm much better, he said. I've got to keep an eye on it though.'

'Do you get it bad?'

'Yeah, every now and again. It's worse in summer, you know, with the pollen.'

'Yeah, it must be,' I said, looking over the tourist leaflet. 'Erm, well we could do the fudge factory?'

'It's a bit crap,' he said. 'You can't actually go in, you just sort of watch through a window. Might be free fudge though.'

'Hmm. Crazy golf?' I suggested. 'Oh. Looks like it shut on December seventh.' The car sped out of the drive and onto the road. 'There's rock climbing at the far end of the Gorge?'

'Not this close to Christmas,' he said.

'There's a cliff-top walk?' We looked at each other. 'Bit cold?' we said simultaneously.

'How about the caves?' he suggested.

I looked for a mention of them. There was also mention of the entrance price. 'Twenty-five quid?' I cried.

Charlie laughed. 'Jeez, it used to be about a tenner when I was younger. They must have bumped up the prices when the overseas tourists started coming. I can pay for you though if you want to see them?'

I was still recovering from the shock of it. 'No way. I wouldn't go in on principle, not just to see a bunch of rocks.'

He laughed again, the car swerving a little on the road. I wasn't surprised; he was going so fast. 'Whoa. Icy. There's an underground cavern and a witch's grotto and a stalagmite shaped like Vernon Kay.'

I giggled. 'Yeah, right.'

'I swear!' he said. 'Look, it says on the leaflet. There's Vernon, Harry Styles and Shrek riding on Donkey's back.'

'Still not worth twenty-five pounds each.'

'No, maybe not.' The car swerved again on a patch of ice. 'Sorry. My alignment needs looking at.'

'Yeah, maybe you should…slow down a bit. Or something. Maybe.' I clutched the armrest on the door.

'Nah, it'll be fine. You're better off going at top speed on ice. It's safer.'

'Safer?' I laughed. 'Who taught you that?'

'It's a well-known fact. There's tea rooms open all year-round. And a cinema, but it's pretty tiny and it's all Disney films over Christmas, I think.'

'There's a cheese shop. It's got the area's only haunted cheese.'

'Oh yeah,' said Charlie. 'The owner's got it in a glass case. Says it moves every now and then. I've got my doubts.'

'How about the museum?' I suggested, scanning the Tours page of the leaflet. 'Oh and it says there's a guided double decker bus tour through the Gorge and surrounding villages. That'd be nice.'

'I think that's a summer-only thing, isn't it?' he said, an embarrassed look on his face.

'It's okay, I don't mind where we go. It's just nice to be out of school. I haven't left the village since September. Well, we played a netball tournament at Toppan Academy.'

We'd reached the end of a road and Charlie indicated left. 'How come you have to stay there anyway? Where are your folks?'

I sighed deeply. I guess spending the day together in a tourist town where pretty much every single tourist attraction was shut would mean we would have a lot of time for talking. So we talked. I told him about Seb. I told him about my parents having to fly over to Colombia to meet the ambassador.

'Blimey. So how long's he been missing?' he asked.

'Uh, nearly two weeks now.'

'And there's no news at all?'

'There's bits of news,' I said, as the car slowed down for a tractor to pass us along a narrow stretch of country lane then roared off again at top speed, even though there were multiple warning signs for ice around. 'Nothing for certain. It's the not knowing more than anything. Every time they say I've got a phone call, I freeze. It's like the world just stops for a split second, and I know I'm on the precipice of unbelievable joy or unbelievable pain. And it's never one thing or the other.'

'Must be horrible.'

'Sorry. I'm putting a dark cloud over the day already, aren't I?'

'No, no, not at all,' he said, gripping the steering wheel like his life depended on it. His knuckles were white. I glanced across at the speedometer. He was doing nearly sixty miles an hour on a country road. On an icy country road.

'God, I'm really sorry, Nash. What's his name?'

'Seb.'

He nodded. He seemed like he was groping for more words but none would come. Nobody could ever think of the right thing to say. I was tired of all the *Don't worry*s and *They'll find him*s. Then he just said, 'I think you've just got to have faith that he'll turn up. Until then, there's nothing else you can do, is there?'

I looked at him. He snatched his eyes away from the road for a second to look at me.

'That's what you'd do?' I asked, noticing the car freshener stuck to one of the vents was in the shape of a football boot. Seb had one just like it in his car.

'Until you know for sure, then just have faith. I think that's what I'd do.'

'Then that's what I'll do,' I said, feeling slightly better already.

I made up my mind: I'd think about it when I got back. If there had been a phone call while I'd been out, I'd handle it. Now was about me. And Charlie.

After a short discussion about the freezing weather, another couple of skids on black ice, and a tiff about the music on the radio, which he wanted to turn up but I didn't, we arrived safely at the main public car park in Bathory and Charlie went to get a ticket from the pay and display machine. I breathed a sigh of relief when I got out and when I held out my hand, it was slightly trembling. I had to admit though, he was a good driver. He'd probably seen a few too many *Fast and the Furious* movies, but he knew how to handle a car, that was for sure. When he came back, we started walking into the street that we would follow right up through the Gorge.

'I wanted to ask you out for ages,' he said, taking my freezing, gloved hand in his own bare, warm one as we passed a jewellery shop.

'Did you?' I said.

'Yeah. Ages and ages. I couldn't stop thinking about you. But I didn't know whether I should ask you out or what you'd say. Bathory girls tend to be a bit...well, stuck-up.'

'You thought I was stuck-up?' I said.

'No, no, not at all, I didn't mean that.' He blanched. 'No, I…'

'And how many Bathory girls have you asked out in the past, may I ask?'

'Uh, well, not many, I mean, it…you're definitely the first. I just meant…'

I laughed. 'It's okay. I know what you meant. Bathory girls aren't supposed to fraternise with boys. It affects our studies. Apparently.'

'Will it affect your studies?' he asked.

I shrugged. 'Probably. I might not be able to stop thinking about you.'

He grinned and squeezed my hand tighter. 'I might not be able to stop thinking about that,' he said.

We just sort of looked at each other, for the longest time, as we walked. Then he inadvertently careered straight into a wooden chef's sign for fresh vanilla fudge. I couldn't stop laughing. He didn't laugh, though; he just looked angry with himself for his slapstickery.

The setting was undeniably beautiful. It was a proper Christmas card scene. At the top of the picture was this colossal rock, split in half by the road snaking down through the village and dotted with tiny shops and tea rooms that twinkled and shone with decorations and fairy lights. Most of the shops sold local crafts like ciders, jams and home-made sweets, while others were devoted to items like mountaineering gear, wax jackets and guidebooks or pure sheepskin leather jackets and slippers. Some shops seemed particularly enamoured of the Beast myth; their neon signs yelled out 'Come inside for your Beast of Bathory Souvenirs!' which comprised everything you could think of with a black wolf logo on it: cuddly toys, tea cosies, tea towels, belt buckles, even cutlery.

It was starting to snow and we were heading dangerously towards a perfect movie moment, one where we would be making snow angels and walking in a winter wonderland. But there's one problem with winter wonderlands.

They melt.

# 13
## Black Christmas

I wanted to walk up to the top of the Gorge, let the clean winter air launder my lungs and throat, but Charlie spotted an arcade centre called The Sunspot and wanted to go in there, so we did that for an hour. I didn't mind; it was warm and there was tinsel draped across most of the fruit machines. It still felt like Christmas.

'Which one do you want to play? Gears of War? Call of Duty? Guitar Hero?'

'Death on Castle Mars,' he said, without hesitation. As the name suggested, it was about a castle. On Mars. And there was a lot of death. The player was this extremely muscly soldier with a neck as thick as a tree stump and covered in tattoos, gun straps and strings of bullets and he had to run in and out of all these spooky corridors, machine-gunning aliens until they burst into flames.

'I'm brilliant at this,' he said gleefully, pumping the slot full of pound coins. 'I'm up to level seven at home. I played it for seventeen hours straight last week. I haven't got this version though. Dad's getting me it for Christmas.'

'Cool,' I said, and hung around the machine for what seemed like an age listening to him yell things at the screen like: 'Stop running. You know you can't outrun me. I'm too quick. I'm just too damn quick for you'; 'Oh I've got you now, Busta Rhymes'; 'Yes! Yes! YEAAAAS!'; 'Eat lead!'; and, 'You are deader than dead now, Martian Mike'. All of which would be followed by him gritting his teeth and punching the air when the scores flashed up. He only stopped, begrudgingly, when a man came over and started queuing for a turn. I think he'd have happily stayed there all day.

Halfway up Gorge Road, there was a sign for 'The Beast of Bathory Museum'.

'Can we go in there?' I said to Charlie, who was looking in the window of the fancy dress shop next door.

He looked at the sign. 'It's pretty crap,' he said. 'It's only, like, one room. I haven't been in there since I was a kid. Probably hasn't changed.'

'I'd like to,' I said.

He shrugged and followed me up the steps to the museum. He was right too; it was just one room. A room with a large, glass-topped table in the centre. The walls all around detailed the history of Beast sightings, sites of corpses ascribed to the Beast and alleged victims. A little old man was seated on a chair by the entrance with a small tin marked

'Donations', and Charlie and I both put in some coins. He nodded thanks.

The first sign on the wall was entitled 'The Strange and Colossal Predator'.

*Since just before the First World War, there have been over forty-six reported sightings of a strange and colossal predator, roaming the fields and villages. Despite official inquiries purporting to disprove local lore as nothing more than superstition and scaremongering, many people in Bathory maintain that one or more large black animals stalk this area.*

The second sign was entitled 'Sightings and Eyewitness Reports'. I caught the words 'large wolf' and 'as big as a horse'. There was a mocked-up drawing of what an eyewitness claimed to have seen. It looked like a picture Tabby drew in Prep a few nights ago.

*It is feasible,* said a quote from someone from the Government who checked the area out in the late eighties, *that a turn-of-the-century entrepreneur who lived in the area and privately owned a small group of big cats may have let them go when he was thought to be contravening the laws of the Dangerous Wild Animals Act, and that, since the early part of the twentieth century, these animals have been living hidden in the Bathory countryside.*

'That actually makes sense,' I heard myself saying, thinking back to Regan and her refusal to believe that the myth was just that: a myth. This was in front of me, in black and white, and seemed perfectly believable. I felt a bit ashamed of the way I'd spoken to her.

The third sign on the wall was entitled 'Victims of the Beast' and it talked about all the bodies of animals that had been found on farmland. I recognised a couple of the farm names—Daisy Brook and Willow Mead—they were the farms either side of the school.

Across the room, Charlie was laughing at a papier-mâché model a local primary school had made of the Beast. Its eyes were crossed and its teeth were wonky, with several chipped off. It did look pretty ropey, but behind it were black-and-white pictures of sheep lying dead in the fields, the black on their wool denoting blood, though it was hard to tell as the photos were so grainy.

*Over the last century, a total of 128 sheep and lambs have been killed by the Beast of Bathory,* the sign read. *Fifty-seven cows have been reported killed or with mysterious long scratch marks on their hides. But perhaps most chillingly of all, seven people, mostly hikers and travellers, have been reported missing, having been last seen in the Bathory area.*

'Blimey,' I said aloud.

'What?' said Charlie, who was now looking into the glass tabletop. Inside it was a scale model of Bathory village and the surrounding areas of Gunness-on-Sea, Toppan and Barfield. All around were little red dot stickers.

'What do those mean?' I asked him.

He read the little sign: '"The dots denote where traces of victims, both man and creature, have been found".'

'Traces?'

'Yeah. Body parts and stuff, I guess.'

'I thought it was just a couple of tourists last summer and a walker last winter. That's what Mrs Renfield said in the shop.'

'Yeah, but they found evidence of them,' said Charlie. 'They never found the others.'

'They're all near the school,' I said on a long exhale. 'The fields. The woods. The farmland.' The dots encircled Bathory School. I was starting to feel just the slightest bit ill.

'Took that one too,' said a voice not coming from either of us. We looked across at the little man by the door with the collection tin. 'Last week. Fella in the village. The Beast what did for him 'n' all.'

Charlie leaned in and whispered, 'Don't worry, he has to say that for the tourists.'

'It's true,' he said. 'I saw him carried out his cottage. Covered in blood.'

I felt a sense of dread, as though a heavy cloak had been thrown upon my back.

The old man continued, scratching his pepper-stubbled chin. 'You don't go walkin' at night. You keep your doors locked. You don't go lookin' for it in the winter. Winter's when he takes 'em. Takes 'em back to his lair. Stores 'em up. Feeds on 'em till spring.'

I didn't understand. 'Why would it hunt in the winter? Surely it would spend the summer hunting, and then in winter—'

'Not this un, lassie. Winter's when he comes out. He don't hunt when the tourists are about, do he? Always in the wintertime. Always this time of year.'

Another of the signs read, 'Theories about the Beast of Bathory'. The page was split into four different headings: 'Prehistoric Legend', 'Escaped Zoo Animal', 'Alien Cross-Dimensional Traveller' and 'Native Wildcat'.

'So what do you think the Beast is?' Charlie asked the man.

He shrugged. 'Could be any of 'em.'

'Even an alien cross-dimensional traveller?' I laughed, even though it wasn't funny.

The old man gripped his chin and stared straight ahead. 'I don't know, lassie. You just heed my words. Don't go lookin' for it. Don't go bein' a hero. You hear anything or see any sign of it, you call the police proper quick. That's what the others didn't do. That rambler and those tourists. Don't believe the other stories. That thing's real all right. It's evil, straight from the jaws of Hell.'

'Yeah, can we go now?' I muttered to Charlie.

'Thanks for your…time,' said Charlie, as he guided me back through the door before him and down the steps.

'Whoa, that was intense,' I said, as soon we were safely back outside in the freezing cold air. 'Better not tell Regan about this place. She'll want to move in.'

'He's been in there years, that old bloke. "That thing's evil straight from the jaws of Hell, I tell thee!"' he mocked.

'Stop it,' I said, pushing him so he stumbled on the pavement.

'You got a bit scared then, didn't you?' He smiled.

'I did not.'

'Oh, you so did,' he laughed. 'You couldn't wait to get out of there.'

'That's so not true!'

'So you don't want me to hold your hand then?' he said.

I looked at him. 'I didn't say that.' I reached for his hand and held it in my own.

He was shaking. 'Sorry,' he said.

'Are you cold?'

'Yeah. And nervous.'

'Nervous about what?'

'About, I dunno, you. I dunno. I like you.'

I smiled at him and held his hand tighter. 'I like you too. So you can stop shaking.'

We walked a little further down the street, holding hands all the while, though he didn't stop shaking. He was obviously frozen to the bone. I spied a shop that sold Bathory souvenirs and fossils and gemstones so we went in to get out of the cold. I had always been a bit of a magpie when it came to shiny objects and rocks, even when they were no more than bits of overpriced tat. For that day only, they would be precious jewels.

'I'll be over here,' said Charlie, heading towards a vast wall of local ciders and local chutneys as I made a bee-line for a home-made jewellery display. There were some beautiful pieces—amethyst rings, quartz bracelets, tourmaline earrings and brooches, and all sorts of different unpronounceable rocks strung together as necklaces with tags claiming they 'helped aid fertility' and brought the wearer 'peace and harmony' or 'a long-lasting marriage'.

There was the most stunning bluey-green necklace of little smooth rocks strung together on a wire. The tag said the rock was called 'Howlite—a calming stone used to relieve stress and restore order to the wearer's life. Wear the Howlite to absorb worries and your peace shall be restored.'

'Ha, fat chance,' I said, seeing the back of the tag also read twenty-three pounds and I only had ten pounds in the world. I put it back and decided to buy something for Charlie as a gift for bringing me out for the day. I spied some novelty car air fresheners in the shape of the Beast of Bathory and I remembered the football-shaped one in his car, which had run out of smell. I decided to buy one, plus a small button badge that said 'I've Seen the Bathory Beast' for my collection. I never could resist a badge. I caught up with Charlie by the tills.

'Pick a hand,' I said, holding out both fists out before him.

He looked at me. 'Okay.' He touched the top of my left hand. I opened it, empty. I opened the right and handed him the air freshener. 'Aw, sweet,' he said. 'Mine's just run out. You didn't have to get me that.'

I shrugged. 'Just a tiny thank you, you know, for today.'

'You're welcome.' He smiled.

We walked up the entire length of the road running up through the Gorge and looked into all of the shops. Charlie went in the phone shop to see about a new SIM card for his Samsung, and I helped him choose some Christmas presents for his mum and sister in a lovely high-end gift shop called *Seymour's*, then we went and got something to eat.

The tiny tea room we both liked the look of was halfway down the Gorge on the other side of the street. It was up a short flight of stone steps and from the window it had a great view of the village and the little bridge crossing the river. The place was called The Wishing Well and there was a wishing well by the entrance. Legend had it that wishes came true if you made them there. I knew exactly what my wish would be.

'It's just another money-making scheme,' said Charlie, as a lady in full maid's regalia greeted us and showed us to a table for two in the corner, right next to a little inglenook fireplace and the window with the perfect view. 'The bloke who owns this place owns most of the tea rooms and shops in the Gorge. He's loaded.'

'That's very cynical,' I said, pinning my Beast badge to my jumper in the empty spot where the Head Girl badge would have gone.

He handed me one of the little leather-bound menus. I noticed his hand was still shaking. The barometer on the wall said two degrees centigrade. 'I've made about a dozen wishes in there over the years and none of them have ever come true.'

'What were your wishes?' I asked.

He frowned. 'I can't tell you.' His leg was jiggling under the table.

'Why not? If it's just a cynical money-making scheme, then it doesn't matter if you tell me, does it?'

His eyebrows rose. 'I guess you're right. It was usually material things, like I wanted a scooter a couple of years ago. And I wished my dad got over his cancer.'

'Did he?'

'Yeah, but…'

'There you go then.'

'I never got a scooter for my birthday though.'

'Did you get money?'

'Yeah.'

'And what did you buy with your money?'

'Well, I bought a scooter but it wasn't bought *for* me, so the wish doesn't count.'

'I think you're underestimating the power of the wishing well,' I said, looking at a picture on the wall conveying the history of the restaurant. 'There, see?' I said, pointing up at the picture. '"People who've visited the wishing well over the last seventy years have reported wishes coming true when they've thrown coins in the water, from finding lost objects to relatives recovering from illness and even miraculous conceptions!" See, told you.'

'That doesn't prove anything,' he said, both legs jiggling now.

'Weren't you the one telling me to have faith?' I smiled.

'I used to wish…my mum came back. She left us. I thought at first that the Beast had taken her in the night.'

'Oh, Charlie,' I said, speechless of anything useful. 'She didn't…'

'No, no,' he said. 'We found a note. She'd just left. Couldn't stand it any more at home. There was a lot of arguing and stuff. She went to the city. She wanted me to come too, but I stayed with Dad and ran the shop. He needed me.'

'Of course. I'm sorry, Charlie.'

'Yeah, well.'

'Do you still see her?'

He shrugged. 'Hey, do you want to know a secret?'

'What?'

'Dad didn't give me the afternoon off. I snuck out.'

If I'd been a cartoon, my eyes would have popped out on stalks. 'You lied to him?'

'No, I just didn't tell him. He thinks I'm out delivering turkeys.'

'So who signed the consent form?'

'Me.' He grinned and his eyes twinkled in the café's dim lighting. 'I knew he wouldn't let me take you out and I really wanted to see you.'

Something broke in my chest. 'Aww. I wanted to see you too.'

'Don't laugh but…' His head dipped and when I saw his eyes again they were sparkling. 'I think we're quite similar. I feel a connection with you, Nash. I've never felt it with anyone else.'

'Me either,' I said, cheeks flushing with heat. Just then, the Maidy Lady came over to take our order. Charlie ordered a flat white, which I'd never heard of, but he made it sound nice so I had the same. We also ordered two cheese toasties and a couple of the enormous iced Danish pastries we'd seen behind the chilled cabinet glass when we'd come in.

'Got us through the Blitz,' he said.

'What, hardened arteries?' I said.

'Here,' he said suddenly, reaching into his trouser pocket and presenting me with two clenched fists. 'Pick a hand.'

I touched the top of the right one. He opened it and it was empty. I sighed and he opened the left one, revealing the little Howlite necklace from the shop.

'Oh my God! I was looking at that!' I cried.

'I know. I got it while you were picking out that sheep thing for your little friend.'

'Wow. It's so pretty, isn't it?'

'Take it,' he said. I did. I looked at it. Then I went to hand it back to him, but he frowned. 'No, it's for you.'

'What? I can't accept this, Charlie.'

'Why not?'

'Because it was twenty-three pounds.'

'So? Call it a Christmas present, if you like. I just wanted to buy it for you.'

'Charlie…'

'Look—' he leaned in closer to me across the table and lowered his voice '—I really like you. And I know that it's gonna be tough because you're at the school and when you're not at the school you live nowhere near here but…well, I'd really like us to…I'd like to be with you. Like, go out with you. If you want to, like.'

He looked so nervous. His eyes were wide and his hands were shaking and his leg was still jiggling under the table for all it was worth.

I couldn't stop my mouth stretching into a smile. 'I'd like that too,' I said, clasping his frozen hand in mine. 'But you don't have to buy me stuff.'

'Well, it'd look stupid on me, wouldn't it?' He smiled. 'It doesn't match my eyes.'

We were still grinning when the Maidy Lady brought over our coffees and food.

As we were leaving, it was snowing heavily and, on our way down the steps, I handed Charlie one of the two pound coins I had left from my change.

'Here you go,' I said, standing beside the wishing well.

'Oh come on,' he said, 'you're not serious?'

I closed my eyes, turned on the spot and threw my coin into the well, looking over the railing and peering in until I heard a faint but definite *plop!* when it hit water.

'Done. Now you.'

Charlie trudged back up the steps and closed his eyes before chucking the pound into the air. Fortuitously, it headed over the lip of the well. We both waited for the *plop!* that time.

'What did you wish for?' I asked him.

'To kiss you,' he said, holding me gently around my waist. I couldn't help noticing the burger van in the lay-by opposite. There were some wild goats eating the stale buns by the trailer's wheels. I put my finger against Charlie's mouth, just as he was approaching mine.

'Not here,' I said, and took his hand, leading him down the steps and along the pavement towards the little cobblestone bridge. I stood right in the centre and took his hand.

'Here,' I said and he leaned into me and we kissed away everything for at least five minutes. He kissed hard, but it was good. It was perfect and powerful and I felt it in every sinew, fibre and vein and didn't ever want to let go.

I heard myself kind of yelp as he pulled away. He kept his forehead against mine.

'You like me, don't you?' He grinned.

I nodded. 'You like me too, don't you?'

He nodded. 'We've still got some time before I have to get you back. Anywhere else you want to go?'

'Um, yeah,' I said, still panting slightly. 'There isn't an internet café round here anywhere, is there? I just want to see if there's anything from Seb—emails or anything.'

'Yeah. At the bottom of the Gorge.'

'I haven't had a sniff of internet since—I can't even remember.'

'Your wish is my command, my lady,' he said with a sweeping gesture.

I dealt with all my usual admin when I had internet access—checked both email accounts for anything from Seb or Mum or Dad, checked Facebook for friend requests (four), checked Twitter for @mentions (lots, though mostly bots), checked Tumblr for any good posts to reblog (one of a cat falling into a swing bin and another of Alice in Wonderland smoking a joint which I knew Seb would like). I also had a quick look on the main BBC News site, just to see what else was going on in the world—an uprising in the East, a market downturn in the West and the finding of a dead mouse in a malt loaf. I had just clicked away from the main screen in order to log off, when my eyes caught a headline. My chest constricted.

'Oh my God,' I whispered, clicking back onto the internet and typing 'BBC' back into the search bar. It took me back to the news page. I scrolled down and searched all over for the headline again. I scrolled up. And there it was, right at the top, on the scrolling ticker tape. It felt like being in a dark tunnel when a juggernaut's coming right at you, all honking loudly and screeching brakes.

Invisible hands clutched at my throat. I forgot how to breathe.

'Charlie,' I said.

'Yeah, you all done?'

'Yeah.' I looked in my pocket for my last few coins. 'I just need to print this off. Then, could you take me back to the school, please?'

'Yeah, sure. Is everything all right?'

I nodded. At least, I think I nodded. I was no longer in control of my own mind. It was only on one thing—that headline. I needed to get back to school as soon as possible.

# 14
## The Vanishing

'Has something happened?' he said, as his car turned the corner into the driveway. It was snowing ever so lightly now. 'Is it your brother?'

A huge invisible fist clenched around my ribcage. 'I just need to get back, that's all. I told you. Matron gets really funny if we're late for dinner.'

He wasn't buying it. He swung the car round and pulled up with the handbrake on, the engine still running. 'Have you changed your mind about us, or something? Is that it?'

'No, not at all, don't be silly,' I said, opening the door.

'Is it something I've said? Did I do something?'

'No, no.' I felt the first droplets of snow hit my ears and cheeks. 'I had a lovely day. And thank you for lunch and my necklace and everything.'

The passenger window buzzed down. 'Did I do something?' he asked, a desperate fire in his eyes.

'I'm sorry, Charlie. Thank you again.' I sounded like I was thanking my driving instructor. I cringed. His face as he yanked down the handbrake and roared off back down the driveway told me everything I needed to know.

But when I got into the hall, I didn't have time to give my news. I had a welcoming committee waiting for me. They all stood there: Maggie, Clarice, Regan, Dianna and a stricken-looking Matron.

'Natasha, thank goodness you're back. Have you got Tabby with you?'

'What? No, I haven't. Why?'

Matron took a huge breath and carried on buttoning up her coat. 'She's gone missing. We have to search the whole school.'

'What? How long has she been gone for?'

They all looked at each other. Matron answered. 'About an hour.'

'She'll be hiding,' I said. 'She does this. She's the smallest Pup, so she can get into the tiniest holes. She'll be playing a game, that's all.'

'She's not playing this time,' said Matron.

I turned on Maggie. 'You said you'd look after her.'

'I *did* look after her! I had to go and put the stupid laundry on, didn't I? I left her with Matron for five minutes—'

'And I had to take a phone call from Mrs Saul-Hudson,' Matron interrupted. 'She was checking in, making sure everything was all right. I was only out of the room for moments.'

I looked straight at Clarice. Her face was a Mona Lisa smile of non-committal, the only one of us who didn't look worried at all. I walked across the paisley carpet and got right up in her face.

'Where is she, Clarice?'

'Nash, for heaven's sake!' cried Dianna.

'What have I got to do with it?' Clarice laughed. She backed into the sideboard, making the tennis trophies rattle and clang. 'God, this is…this is victimisation. She's really got it in for me.'

'Just the sort of thing you'd do, isn't it?' said Maggie.

'Where is she?' I repeated, staring her down.

'I don't know, do I? I've been cleaning the kitchen for the last hour. God's sake.'

Matron, unbelievably, gave her the benefit of the doubt.

'Natasha, come along, this isn't helping.'

'It's helping me,' I raged.

'I don't think Clarice has anything to do with it,' said Matron. 'She's just wandered off somewhere, I'm sure.'

'Yeah,' said Regan. 'Maybe she's in the common room, watching a DVD?'

It was no good. I couldn't prove Clarice knew where Tabby was.

Main House was turned practically upside down. Dorms. Classrooms. Music room. Science lab. Art room. CDT room. Old dormitories in the fourth-floor attic space, which were only used to store old costumes now. The Hidey Holes we knew about, which ran between the two libraries and up to the first floor dorms, the Laundry room to the Sickbay and the Science lab all the way to the trap door at the back of the stage in the gym. We found absolutely nothing.

With every minute that passed, my chest grew a little

more tight. We called for her. Bargained with her. Berated her. Anything to get her to poke her head out, admit she was hiding, but of course she didn't. She just wasn't anywhere.

One thing we *did* find in our classroom excavations was Babbitt, Tabby's toy. Maggie brought it to me as I was just turning out the light in the changing rooms.

'One down,' she said.

'Oh, good,' I said, slightly cheered by the sight of it. 'Where was it?'

'Stuffed into the corner by the lockers.'

'Bloody Clarice,' I seethed. 'Psycho.'

'All right, all right. Here.' She handed Babbitt to me and I held him close to my chest. He smelled of biscuits and marker pens, just like Tabby. 'I feel sick,' I said.

'You're really worried about the little tyke, aren't you?' said Maggie as we walked back along the corridor. 'She can't have gone far, Nash.'

'How the hell would you know?' I cried. 'You were supposed to be looking after her, Maggie! Why can't you take responsibility for anything?'

'Excuse me, I said I'd keep an *eye*, not become her foster mum like you are.'

'What if she's gone outside, into the woods or something? It's dark.'

'She wouldn't have gone out there,' Maggie said. 'Not with Regan's friend about.'

'Not by choice, no,' I said.

We came to the PE cupboard, and I unlocked it, using the key Matron had given me. The door opened and a pong of new rubber and old socks wafted out to us. But except for large nets of basketballs and netballs, a bundle of javelins, a cluster of rounders posts, knots of skipping ropes and tubes of tennis balls, the cupboard was bare. I locked it back up again.

'I'm sorry. You're right, she's not your responsibility.'

'Yeah. Well, I do feel guilty about leaving her. Let's just find her, eh?'

Footsteps down the corridor heralded the arrival of Regan.

'Matron thinks we ought to form a search party and try the grounds. Doesn't look like she's in the school.'

'Cool,' said Maggie.

'She wants everyone in the Hall in cold-weather gear in five minutes with torches.'

'Fine,' I sighed. The three of us began walking back towards the stairs, down to Main Hall and the cloakrooms where our coats and wellies were.

'I hope we're not too late,' said Regan.

'What?'

She looked at me. 'What if the Beast is out tonight? It's a full moon, you know.'

I could feel myself losing control. 'Oh, so it's a werewolf now, is it?'

'I don't know what it is—no one does. I just hope it's not got her scent.'

'And what if it has, Regan? What then?'

Regan shrugged.

'No bright ideas, huh? What exactly are *you* going to do if there *is* some kind of monster out there and it's ripped Tabby to pieces? What will you do *then* about your precious Beast?'

'Take it easy, Nash,' said Maggie, stepping in between me and Regan on the stairs.

'No. I'm sick to death of all this talk about the Beast of Bathory. There are other things out there, *real* things that we need to worry about. Freezing cold weather for one. Strange men for another. And the fact that a senior Bathory girl is sadistically picking on Tabby for no apparent reason. *There* are your Beasts. *There* are your monsters.'

I was boiling like a geyser, ready to blow at any moment. I marched to the back of the cloakrooms and sat down in the dark on the bench, between two pegs laden with navy coats. My hands were shaking—I could just about see them in the moonlight beaming in through a top window. Then I heard voices outside, low and urgent.

Maggie appeared in the doorway a few moments later. 'Nash?'

'Yeah, I'm here,' I said, swallowing a lump.

'Why did you mention strange men?'

I shrugged. 'She's a kid, isn't she? A kid—on her own. We've got to find her, we've just got to. I won't rest until we do.'

She plucked my coat from its peg and pulled my folded-up wellies from the pigeonhole under the bench, then handed them both to me. 'Then neither will I. Come on.'


It was nearly seven o'clock by the time we'd congregated on the swirly red carpet in the main hall. Tabby, the expert hider, had been missing for over three hours.

'Right then, all of you,' said Matron, as Maggie and I walked in. 'Dianna, you and Regan search the formal gardens, tennis courts and Orangery. Clarice, you and Margaret, the Pups' classrooms, Portakabins, barns and sheds. It's snowing, so we don't have much time.'

'I'm not searching with her,' said Maggie, clutching a white banister. 'There's only two people I trust here. One of them's me. The other's not her.'

'Go with Clarice I said, Margaret,' said Matron, her voice shaking by this point. She handed each pair a fire whistle and a torch. We all saw her swallow the sob. 'Natasha, you and I will search the upper landscape and the woods with Brody. If she's out there we have to find her ASAP. There's more snow forecast for the early hours. Temperature's dropping by the hour.'

It was Dianna's turn to protest, as I knew she would.

'Matron, I could come with you to search the Landscape Gardens. Regan can handle the formal gardens by herself, I'm sure.'

Matron turned on her heel, grabbed Brody's lead from the coat hooks and attached it to his collar. 'Don't argue. And stay together at all times. We need to find her, girls. Please.'

We followed our breaths along the pathway, up the flint steps to the right of the drive and into the Landscape Gardens, all the while calling out Tabby's name. We could barely see the trees for the lines of snow falling silently upon us. The air had grown considerably colder since I'd gone out with Charlie, and I tucked my scarf right up around my mouth to breathe some warm into the wool. The winter moon was full and blurry with black clouds gliding past it. Moving, always moving. Time was moving on. We walked along the path by Edward's Pond and Matron shone our torch over the still surface of the water. It was frozen solid.

'Tab-beeeeee!' she called out. I called out too. Our

voices echoed in the valley, then disappeared on the night breeze. I think we were both holding our breaths.

'What do I say?' asked Matron to nobody. 'What do I say to her parents? They're in the Middle East, for God's sake. She's supposed to be the one who's safe and looked after.'

Did she expect me to answer her? It felt rude not to.

'Matron, we'll find her.'

'I shouldn't have let this happen.'

'You didn't let it happen, it's just one of those things. We'll find her.' I didn't sound sure, because I wasn't sure. If she wasn't in the grounds then there was no telling where she was. Someone *must* have taken her. I didn't dare think about who that might be any more.

'There's still hope, Matron. You've got to have faith that we'll find her.'

'I don't know what to do, Natasha,' she said. She was crying by this point. 'I really don't know what to do.' We made our way up the snaking path towards the Wendy House. I had to take charge—Matron was losing the plot, fast. I took the torch from her and opened the door, shining it inside.

'Tabby?' I called. Nothing.

I came back out and shook my head. Matron's face disappeared through a white cloud of exhaled breath.

'Let's go along to the Temple.'

As we were walking along the uneven path, I looked out and down into the valley. A shape caught my eye in the trees ahead—I shone the torch over it, but there was nothing out of the ordinary. The path sloped down and we went with it. Matron's sobs had become more woeful.

'It's so cold,' she said, trying to rub some warmth into the fingers of her torch hand.

'We'd better pick up the pace,' I replied.

The Temple was as still and quiet as the Wendy House. There was nothing there, and no sign that anyone had been. The same for the path down to Grace's Lake and the Bird-cage at the far end. The wire door creaked open and I shone the torch around. Just a carpet of brown leaves and the golden bars shone back at us.

'This is hopeless,' Matron complained, as we crossed the wooden bridge over the lake to the opposite side of the valley where the tree house was. Chief Brody sniffed the ground eagerly. I wondered what he could smell. He had the scent of something.

Then I saw something in the trees again.

'What was that?' I said, my torch hand shaking as I shone the light behind us.

'What? What did you see?'

I couldn't call out. I was too afraid to disturb whatever it had been. 'I don't know,' I whispered. 'I thought I saw something moving in the trees.'

I didn't think. I knew. Brody barked. He knew too.

'Tabbeee?' Matron called. 'Tabbeee, if that's you, then come out here this instant!'

But, again, nothing but silence.

Matron slapped her hands by her sides. 'Well, that's it, isn't it? I'm going to have to call the police. We've looked everywhere.'

'No, we haven't, Matron. We haven't got as far as the Chapel yet.'

'She won't be in there, I know she won't,' Matron shouted. 'I've lost her, haven't I?' She was nearly hysterical by this point, sobbing and panicking, completely uncontrollable.

'Matron, please stop—this isn't helping Tabby,' I said, holding her forearms like it was going to help. 'Please stop.'

'We can't help her. What if it's taken her? What if we find something?'

'What? What if what's taken her?'

'The Beast,' she said.

'Oh, for God's sake,' I muttered, exhaling. 'There is no such thing as the Beast of Bathory.'

Matron sniffed up a line of clear snot from her top lip. 'I've seen it, Natasha.'

'What? When?'

'A few years ago.' We walked along the path towards the waterfall. 'It was this time of year. I'd come back from chaperoning Year Eights on a trip to London. I was on the drive, clearing out the minibus. Night was as quiet as a church. I heard a noise, coming from the flint steps. I can only describe it as a…grunt.'

I felt alarm in every bone. Should I tell her I'd seen it too? No. She was already in a state of panic. *Stress makes you stupid*, I thought, another favourite saying of Seb's. *Think calm and you'll be calm. Panicking helps no one.*

'Once my eyes had adjusted to the darkness, I saw its eyes, shining in the moonlight. Then I made out its head, and then its body. It just stood there, at the top of the steps, looking at me. It was enormous.'

The wind whipped up around us, filtering through all my layers to my skin. Brody strained at the leash. 'Okay, well, let's keep looking.'

'I just froze. Couldn't even bring myself to call out.' She stared into the distance. 'In seconds, it had gone, but I never forgot it. I knew I wasn't dreaming or seeing things.'

'I believe you,' I said. 'Come on, let's try the Chapel.'

Matron stopped at the end of the path, leaving me to walk up to the building and try the door handle. It was locked. I turned to her and shone the torch down the path.

'She won't be in there,' said Matron, completely without hope.

'We should try it, at least,' I said, gesturing for her to give me the key.

Inside the building, the usual smell of must and sweet wood hit me and I shone the torch over the pews and altar. It felt colder than it was outside. Everything was still. I walked down the aisle, shining it down both wings and calling for her again.

Nothing. As with every other folly, the place was empty and silent. I looked back at Matron. 'I think we should call the police now, Matron.'

She looked at me and nodded.

'Let's go back to Main House. It's even chillier in here.'

Suddenly a bell rang inside my head. I grasped Matron's arm. 'I know where she is,' I said.

'Where?'

'The Chiller. I mean, the laundry room. We didn't look in the basement at all. It's the only place we haven't tried. Oh God, why didn't we think?'

'But why would she go down there?'

'I don't know. What if Clarice locked her down there? Come on.'

'No,' said Matron, fumbling with her key bunch for the basement key, 'you run on, you're faster.'

'Okay,' I said. 'Should I take the torch with me or leave it for you?'

'Just take it and run. I'll be behind you. I've got the dog—I'll be okay,' said Matron.

I bolted down the valley path and back along the pond until I got to the side of the school and the steps down to the basement where the window with the broken catch was—the quickest way in and down to the laundry room. It opened easily and I shone the torch inside. Back up in the woods, I could hear the dog barking constantly.

'Tabby?' I called out. The torchlight was fading. I shook it to get the beam back and shone it along the unpainted stone corridors of the basement. Jumping down onto the concrete, I ran along the corridor to the main room where the junk was stored.

'Tabb-eee?' I called out, the scents of clean laundry and mouldy stone in my nostrils.

Nothing.

I climbed over broken chairs and old gym equipment stuffed down there after inspections, pianos with flat keys, towards the archway beyond which was a narrow passageway and the Chiller itself.

There was a light coming beyond the archway. The light bulb outside the Chiller door was on. Someone had been down here.

'Tabb-eeee?' I called again.

And, this time, a little voice answered. 'Nash?'

I barged through the rest of the chairs and sprinted down the passageway towards the room. The door was locked, but I could see her through the little round window, bundled in a ball, tears streaking her dusty little face.

'Oh thank God, thank you God, thank you God.' I exhaled, almost crying myself by the time I'd pushed hard enough on the door to get it unwedged where it had become stuck on a little rock. 'You're okay now, it's okay.' I didn't know if I was saying it to Tabby or myself.

The door released and Tabby flew into my arms like a ball into a baseball mitt. I cuddled her into me. 'Oh, thank goodness you're safe. We were so worried about you. What happened? Did Clarice lock you in?'

'I was looking for Babbitt,' she huffed. 'And the door shut and I got locked in.'

'Tabby, are you sure Clarice didn't lock you down here?' She shook her head. 'You're sure?' She nodded. 'It's all right, you're safe now, okay?' I hugged her again, a sob stuck in my throat, and tried not to think about the apology I would now have to make to Clarice.

I switched the light off outside the Chiller and carried Tabby down the passageway and across the junk to ground level, wrapping her inside my warm coat when we got outside.

'Found her!' I called out into the night air and, within moments, quick footsteps came running up the path. 'I've found her!' I blew my fire whistle and we waited on the path by Edward's Pond until we heard more footsteps coming from behind us.

It was Regan. She'd run all the way from the tennis courts. And she was by herself.

'Oh, thank goodness!' she cried, wheezing for air but smiling with relief. She looked quite pretty when she smiled.

'Where's Dianna?' I asked her.

Regan guppied her mouth open and shut. 'I don't know… She went to the toilet. That was about twenty minutes ago now though.'

Maggie came running up from the direction of the barns,

followed by Clarice, who wasn't running but walking, her arms folded and looking smug about something.

'Thank God for that!' heaved Maggie. 'Where was the little squirt?'

'The Chiller,' I said. 'The door got wedged and she couldn't get out. It wasn't anybody's fault.' I couldn't look at Clarice. 'I'm sorry I accused you.' Tabby cuddled into Babbitt on my chest. 'I was wrong.'

'I should think so too,' she huffed. 'I'm not as bad as you seem to think.'

I wanted to say, *Oh but you so are,* but I held it in.

'Where's Matron?' asked Maggie.

'She was up at the Chapel,' I said. 'She said she was right behind me.'

We all looked up into the dark, featureless valley. Maggie called out for Matron.

'We've fooooooooounnd herrrrrrrrrr,' she yelled again. But nothing came back. We could see the Chapel. I put Tabby down and shone my torch beam up towards it, sweeping it over the scene. There was a shape in the darkness. A shape and a tinkling sound. It was coming along the path, towards the pond. A big, black, loping shape.

Maggie stepped back, right into me, then stepped aside. Clarice got behind me too. Tabby cuddled into my leg. Regan stayed where she was.

I shone the torch directly on the thing.

It was the dog, Brody. He was on his own, his lead dragging on the path, paws leaving dirty paw prints as he walked.

'Oh my God, Brody!' Regan cried.

I shone my torchlight onto the Newfie as he came to a stop in front of us.

'Brody! What's happened? Where's Matron, eh, boy?' cried Regan as she skittered over and crouched down beside him.

'Is he all right?' said Maggie, going over to inspect him too.

I shone my torch over the paw prints he'd left all along the path. They were red.

# 15
## Psycho

'I think Brody's injured,' said Clarice.

'Dianna hasn't come back yet,' said Regan. 'And Matron's still out here.'

'We need to go inside. Now.' I picked up the dog's lead and lifted Tabby up again, taking the path back towards Main House. They followed me with no protest.

Maggie caught up with me as we came down the flint steps near the front entrance.

'What's happened, Nash?'

'I'll explain when we get inside, okay? Just move.'

'What about Dianna?'

'She's got some serious explaining to do,' I said. 'Come on.'

We ran down the rest of the steps and across the turning

circle to the front door. Once we were all safely inside, I put Tabby down and deadbolted the front door, top and bottom.

Regan stared at me. 'What are you doing? We can't lock Matron out.'

'I don't think Matron's coming back.'

'What do you mean? Where's she gone?'

I walked over to Brody, who was panting, but otherwise fine. I gently lifted up one front paw, then the other, inspecting all over his face and ears and down his legs and back. His black fur was slick and glistening on his back, but there were no other signs of injury. When my hands came away from him, they were red.

Clarice screamed a scream that could have broken crystal.

'Jesus Mothering Christ,' breathed Maggie, as Tabby jumped up into her arms and hid her face in her neck.

Regan put her hand to her mouth like she was going to vomit.

At that moment, the door to the Refectory corridor opened, and in breezed Dianna like she'd just come through the airport arrivals gate. Her sudden appearance caused Clarice to scream again.

'What are you all doing?' Then she saw Tabby. 'You've found her! Where was she?' She took in my red hands. 'What on earth…'

'Where the hell have you been?' Maggie yelled.

'I was looking for Tabby. I'm so pleased you're safe!'

'You were supposed to be in the formal gardens with Regan!'

'Yes, I was. I'll thank you to lower your voice, Margaret. It might be the end of term but I am still Head Girl, you know.'

'Oh, like anyone cares,' Maggie spat. 'Where were you?'

'I just told you!' Dianna shouted.

'You said you were going to the toilet,' Regan interrupted.

'I did. Then I thought I heard something in the woods, so I went up to investigate. What's that on your hands, Natasha?'

'You weren't anywhere near the woods.' Clarice scowled. 'How could you hear something from the toilet?'

Dianna had no answer. 'Why are you all looking at me like that? What's happened?'

Nobody else had anything constructive to say, so I stuck my oar in. 'Matron is missing. And Brody has come back from the woods covered in…this. It's all over the paths out there too.'

'My God,' said Dianna.

'Dianna, if you're hiding something in those woods, you'd better start talking.'

'What?'

'Is it the Beast?' said Regan. 'Have you seen it too? Do you know where his lair is?'

'Oh, Regan, have a day off, will you?' sighed Maggie. 'You're starting to get right on my greatest hits.'

I tried to breathe out the poison air in my lungs. 'I don't think this has anything to do with the Beast at all. Regan, I need you to go and give Brody a wash in the dog shower.'

She seemed disappointed. 'Where's the dog shower?'

'In the first utility room next to the kitchens. It's just a shower tray and a hose. There's dog shampoo in the second cupboard along and towels on top of the tumble dryer. And, Tabby, go with Regan and find the Chief some food and some water, okay? He needs his dinner. Can you do that job for me?'

Tabby reluctantly slid down Maggie's hip and took Regan's hand. They led Brody out of the hall and down the corridor towards the kitchen.

I waited for the door to close behind them before I turned to Dianna. She laughed, a nervous giggle that didn't ring true, and looked from Maggie, to Clarice, and back to me.

I took a breath. 'I know what your secret in the woods is, Dianna. I know why you've been going up there.'

'Natasha, I don't—'

'Stop lying,' I said. 'Someone is dead tonight because of your lying.'

'Don't say that!'

'Tell her the truth then!' yelled Maggie.

'What's Dianna got to do with this?' said Clarice. 'D'you think…*she* killed Matron?'

I reached into my coat pocket and took out the colour-printed page I'd taken from the internet café in Bathory. I unfolded it and read it aloud:

'"Hunt for killer Leon Pfaff sparks airport alert",' I read. '"Ports and airports have been put on alert by police hunting an escaped murderer".'

'Oh my God,' Maggie mumbled.

'Oh my God,' said Clarice.

'"Convicted killer, Pfaff, twenty-two, had been serving a life sentence for the robbery and murder of a man during a raid on an apartment block. He was in the hospital wing at maximum security HMP Pickton when he overpowered two officers and made his escape".' I held up the page with the picture of Leon Pfaff's mug shot. He had the same brown eyes as Dianna, but jet-black hair and a razor-sharp jaw. I noticed he was the same age as Seb, but I tried hard not to think about it.

'No way,' said Maggie. 'He's up there? You've hidden a murderer in the woods?'

I nodded. 'She's been keeping him up there, in the Tree House, I'm betting, since he escaped. Haven't you?'

Dianna said nothing, but a single tear began its path down her right cheek.

'Nice and warm in the Tree House, isn't it?' I said. 'Warm and safe and hidden out of the way of anyone in the winter months. How long did you intend on keeping him there?'

She didn't answer me. I looked at the piece of paper again. '"Anyone with information on his whereabouts has been urged to contact police or Crimestoppers. This man is believed to be armed and extremely dangerous. Do not approach under any circumstances". And you've let him into a girls' boarding school! I think you've got a phone call to make.'

'No, please—I can't…'

'How are you even going to justify this, Princess?' said Maggie. 'Look at Nash's hands! That dog was covered in blood.'

Dianna was breathless. She kept clinging to my forearm, but I pulled away. 'It can't have been him. Why would he do something like that?'

'Because he's done it before,' I said, coldly.

'Yes, but it was in self-defence.'

'He killed a man, Dianna.'

'No, it wasn't like that. It was two years ago. He was defending himself. He got into some drug stuff and he was trying to get away from it. The man was a known drug-dealer. A pimp. A bad man.'

'Oh, he did the world a favour then, is that what you're saying?'

'I'm saying he didn't go there to kill him. But he didn't have a choice. You have to believe me.'

'Why did they put him away for a life sentence, then, Dianna?' Maggie asked.

'Well…he used a knife. But he hasn't done anything while he's been here, I promise. I've been watching him like a hawk. Why would he kill Matron?'

I shrugged. 'What if she came across him in the woods tonight? What if she recognised him from the newspapers? Oh, hang on a minute, you cancelled the daily papers, didn't you? While we were at the shop the other day.'

Dianna said nothing.

'I wondered about that at the time, but I didn't pay much attention—you said Matron told you to do it. That's why all the papers were face down on the shelf as well, isn't it? So we wouldn't see his face all over them. His name. I thought some kids had been messing about with them or something.'

'I knew what you'd say,' said Dianna. 'I knew you'd put two and two together.'

'Well, I can't,' said Clarice. 'What are you saying here, Nash? What's Dianna done?'

'Oh for God's sake, draw her a picture, Nash,' huffed Maggie. 'Dianna's been hiding her brother, her *sadistic, murderer* brother, in the Tree House. *Comprendre*?'

Clarice was silent, shell-shocked. Her face turned robotically back towards Dianna, eyes brimming over with tears.

Dianna gripped my forearm again, and again, I shook her away. 'Nash, listen to me, I know Leon didn't do anything bad tonight. I know it for a fact, because I was with him. I went up to see him the moment we all split up. I told Regan I was going to the loo—'

'Yeah, we knew you were lying about that,' said Maggie.

'I was with him the whole time,' Dianna continued. 'We even saw you running back down towards the school. He hasn't left the Tree House all night. He's too scared to. I've been telling him about the Beast of Bathory and...'

'What, he's too scared of the big pussycat, is he?' said Maggie. 'A convicted killer and he's afraid of an urban legend? Do me a favour.'

'How can you be sure he didn't go anywhere after you left him?' I asked.

'He wouldn't have. I told him to stay in there. He doesn't want to cause any trouble, really he doesn't. He just wants to get out of the country. He won't come near the school.'

'What do you mean, "near"?' I said. 'He's on the premises already.'

'Has he got black hair?' said a small voice. We all looked around. It was Clarice's voice. 'I think I've seen him. Well, I think I've met him. In fact I think... I've kind of been... seeing him.'

Another dark penny dropped. 'What?'

'He said he was homeless,' she said, sitting down on the bottom stair. 'He said his name was Eddie. Eddie Dantès. I wouldn't have gone up there if I'd known he was really... oh my God, he tricked me!'

'You've been seeing him?' cried Dianna.

Maggie guffawed with laughter, folding her arms. 'Oh, this just gets better.'

'Eddie Dantès?' I said. 'Didn't his name ring any bells?'

'Well, no, it's a fake name,' she blubbed, hiding her eyes with her hands.

'Edmond Dantès is the escaped convict in *The Count of Monte Cristo*,' I cried. 'You'd have known that if you'd ever paid attention in an English lesson.'

'I didn't know who he really was, did I?' she sobbed. 'I brought him food and…we talked and I got to know him. He said he loved me!'

'Uh, I think he was lying?' Maggie suggested. 'Is this the amazing boyfriend you wanted your phone for?'

'No. That's a different one. Back home.'

Maggie threw Clarice a look, but said no more.

'I thought I was the only one who knew he was there,' said Dianna softly. 'I can't believe he kept this from me.'

'What, your sweet, innocent pimp-murderer brother?'

'I could have been killed too,' cried Clarice.

'More's the pity you weren't,' said Maggie, folding her arms. 'How stupid can you get?' She looked at Dianna and Clarice in turn. 'You hide a killer in the woodshed and bake him cakes and bring him magazines while *you* clean his pipes out for him on a daily basis. He's living the life of Riley up there. You're *un*believable.'

'Oh, don't give me that,' said Clarice, wiping her nose. 'I just found him up there.'

'Up where?' said Maggie with a smirk.

'In the Tree House. I saw him and I, just, like, befriended him. We were friends first. We talked. He's lovely once you get to know him. If you'd known there was a boy hiding in the Tree House you'd have been up there like a shot.'

Maggie tilted her head in thought. 'Probably. But I *didn't* know he was up there, did I?'

Clarice hid her face in her hands. 'What if I've got some prison disease?'

'You could be up the duff. Murderer babies!'

'Shut up! You can't talk. You're always getting into trouble.'

Maggie laughed. 'I put custard in the minibus and super-

*C.J. Skuse*

glued our French teacher to her chair. You've banged a convicted killer. That's, like, number one on the list of school rules thou shalt not break, Clarice.'

'Shut up! Shut up! Shut up!'

'But why bring him here, Dianna?' I asked, through Clarice's squealing.

Dianna wrung her hands. 'The first place the police would look for him is home. It was all a bit last minute. He had to go into hospital for an appendix operation. He saw a chance and he took it. Mum told me to hide him in the school somewhere and look after him until she got back from Spain. We knew the Saul-Hudsons were going away for Christmas, so it seemed ideal. She's getting him some fake documents, visas and passports and things. She said she'll be here on the twenty-third—she'll have all he needs, and he can go abroad and—'

'Kill people there?' I finished. 'You're an accessory now, you know that?'

'I wouldn't be doing it if I didn't love him.'

'I thought you hated him.'

'I hate him for making me do this, of course I do. I haven't been sleeping, I've been physically sick every day since he got here.'

'Bless,' spat Maggie.

'That's why the police came here last week, isn't it?' I said, a piece of jigsaw knitting into my brain at last. 'That's why Saul-Hudson asked for you to be in the office when she talked to them. It wasn't about the dead man in the village, it was about Leon, wasn't it?'

'Yes,' Dianna admitted. 'But I managed to throw them off the scent. I told them he'd been thinking about going to stay with a friend in Scotland. I have to help him, Nash.

You must understand. Someone needs to have faith in him, give him a second chance. If they lock him up again, it'll finish him.'

Maggie growled. 'If he was an animal, you'd have him put down.'

'Don't say that.' Dianna looked genuinely hurt.

But Maggie was just getting started. 'He's a dangerous creature, Princess. He shouldn't be on the streets, let alone in the grounds of a boarding school. Don't you know killing gets easier after the first one? Some people get a real taste for it.'

'Do they?' said Clarice, chewing the strap on her thick pink watch.

'Uh, yeah? He's got seven people stuck here for the winter, all to himself. He could spree it if he wanted to, take us all out in one go.'

Dianna turned to me. 'He wouldn't, he's my *brother*. Nash, you of all people should understand that.'

There was a hot violent mist in my peripheral vision. 'Don't you dare bring my brother into this!' I snarled. 'Seb's worth twenty of him.'

But she didn't stop. 'What if Seb was Leon? What if he came to you, begging for help? Would you turn him away?'

'Seb wouldn't kill anyone, even to save himself!'

'I know what you'd do, Nash. You'd help him. You'd do what you could.' She was holding my arm again. Finger by finger, I peeled her away.

'Shudder to think what's going on in those woods,' Maggie chipped in. 'He could be out there right now. Doing unspeakable things to Matron's corpse.'

'Oh stop it, Maggie, just shut up,' Dianna raged. 'He's

not some freak. He's a burglar, yes, he's killed someone to defend himself, but he's not insane. He's just—'

'Drawn that way?' Maggie suggested. 'Misunderstood? Deprived of parental love?'

'Scared,' Dianna corrected, wiping the tears from her face.

I shone my torch through the window. It was snowing heavier than ever outside. When everyone stopped talking, I could hear the *pat pat pat* of the larger snowflakes against the pane. The night was growing ever stormier. I thought about what the old man at the museum said.

*You don't go walkin' at night. You don't go lookin' for it in the winter. Winter's when he takes 'em.*

'It's not safe outside,' I muttered into the cold glass.

'What, Nash?'

I turned to Maggie. 'We can't do anything tonight. We can't search. It's snowing too hard and it's pitch dark. We need to make this place secure and get some food inside us and some sleep. We'll all have to sleep in the same dorm tonight, to keep safe.'

'What about Matron?'

'We'll go out and search for Matron first thing.' I looked at their frightened faces. 'We can't risk ourselves.' I looked down at my hands.

Maggie nodded. 'Yeah, all right—I guess.'

Clarice began to cry, even louder than before. As I looked at her, I caught sight of the Head Girl badge glinting on Dianna's lapel. She'd moved it to her coat from her jumper so that it would always be visible.

She caught me looking at it. 'I know,' she said. She bowed her head and unpinned it from her coat, handing it to me. 'Take it.'

'No.'

'We need a leader, Nash. You're in charge now.'

'I don't want it,' I repeated. 'In fact…' I pulled open my coat. There were my netball, hockey, swimming, tennis and athletics badges, all equidistant down one side of my cardigan V, my prefect's badge in perfect alignment with the base of my half-Windsor knotted tie. I ripped them all off, including the one I'd bought at the Gorge saying 'I've Seen the Bathory Beast'. 'None of us are any better than the others, all right? Not any more.'

A single tear rolled down Dianna's cheek, dripping onto her empty lapel. She put the Head Girl badge in her coat pocket. 'But we don't know what to do.'

The grandfather clock struck nine p.m. Its chimes echoed in the silence around us.

Dianna, Maggie and Clarice were looking at me.

I breathed in deeply.

'Okay. Dianna, go and help Maggie lock up.'

'How?' she cried. 'The main key bunch was on Matron's belt loop.'

'Okay, but all the doors have bolts and the ones that don't have chairs in the rooms that you can wedge them with. Do that. Bolt both the internal doors on the long corridor too. Clarice, check the windows. If we have any lights on, the curtains should be closed so we don't draw any extra attention to ourselves.'

Clarice nodded. 'Okay. What are you going to do?'

I looked down. 'I'm going to wash my hands.'

I turned to leave the room, the blood dry enough now on my palms that I didn't leave a print on anything I touched. I walked down the corridor into the kitchen, where Regan and

Tabby were drying Brody off with a large, scruffy-looking beach towel. 'Is everything all right, Nash?' asked Regan.

'No,' I told her, making my way over to the sinks. 'Dianna's been hiding her brother in one of the follies. He's…' I looked at Tabby's innocent little face. 'He's a bad man. Escaped from prison. And Matron hasn't come back.'

'Oh my God,' said Regan. 'And he's out there? Loose?'

'Well, in the Tree House. We hope,' I replied.

'Let's hope he stays up there then,' said Regan. You know—just in case.'

She was still convinced the Beast was out there, even after this.

'Well, I don't know anything for sure,' I said, rubbing my hands into a foamy pink lather then swilling them off in the rinser. 'Apart from the fact that I'm tired and hungry.'

She stood up and came over, lowering her voice. 'Tabby was asking questions. About the blood. I told her it was paint, and that Brody must have knocked over a pot of it somewhere. Was that all right?'

I smiled at her. 'Yeah, I think that's good.'

Regan took a deep breath. 'Look, I know what you think of me, well, what everyone thinks of me really, and I know you think all this…' she hesitated '…all this b.e.a.s.t. stuff is just me being stupid, but I really think…'

'I know,' I told her. 'I'm sorry I doubted you, Regan. Who am I to say the you-know-what doesn't exist?' I felt very tired all of a sudden. 'But we've got another kind of monster to worry about now, so we should probably concentrate on that for the time being.'

Regan twitched a brief smile back at me. 'Okay.'

'I'm hungry,' said Tabby softly, rubbing Brody's ears.

'Yeah,' I said, 'let's lay the table and have some dinner, shall we?'

It was well past nine o'clock. Matron's lasagne and a jam sponge and jug of custard sat on one of the worktops under a clean tea towel, all ready to be heated up. That morning seemed like such a long time ago. My day out with Charlie. My excitement. Walking around the museum. Our kiss.

I walked over to the oven and flicked the dial over to 'on' as Dianna, Clarice and Maggie appeared at the kitchen door.

'I'm going to warm up the lasagne,' I said. 'Go and lay the table.'

# 16
## Dead of Night

We barely said a word at dinner. Even Maggie was quiet—
I think she'd run her batteries down. But for the howling
wind outside, the huge Refectory was still of our noises.
Everyone seemed to be waiting for someone else to call the
police about Leon Pfaff, our resident weirdo. I was thinking
about Seb and how I'd barely thought of him all day. Now
he merely appeared in my thoughts.

Maggie scarfed down her lasagne, as did I. Regan ate like
she usually did—slow and considered, like she was counting the bites. Clarice pushed her pasta round her plate. I
knew things must have shifted between us because the sight
of her wasn't making me baulk as much as usual. She was
even taking orders from me without so much as a whine.
Tabby had three mouthfuls before her head lolled and she

fell asleep on the table. And Dianna watched me like a hawk throughout, probably afraid that at any moment I was going to call the police.

'Thought you were still working on your thigh gap?' Clarice said to Dianna, watching as she suddenly filled her mouth with a giant forkful.

Dianna stopped chewing, then started again, slowly. 'I am.'

Clarice raised her eyebrows and nibbled a tiny mouthful of mince. She'd pushed all her pasta to one side of her plate.

'Eat,' I said. 'All of you. There isn't much food left in the larder and we don't know how long we're going to be here.'

'But I don't want it,' said Clarice. 'I don't like pasta.'

'It's fuel,' said Regan. 'You'll need it to keep warm and keep…'

'I don't care,' said Clarice.

'Can we watch *Con Air* after dinner?' said Maggie. Nobody answered. She actually hurt. She mumbled something about girls having no taste in movies and then a sound out in the main corridor made each one of us jump in our seats.

The main phone was ringing. We all stopped eating, or sleeping, or pushing food around, and just looked at each other.

'I'll go,' said Dianna.

She left to answer it and we all went back to eating and being silent again.

Mum had called me courageous in her last letter. How did you know when you had courage? I just felt scared, about everything. Scared of the phone ringing. Scared about what we'd find when we went looking for Matron tomorrow. Scared about calling the police and what might happen to us if they found Matron's body in the snow. Scared about meeting Leon Pfaff. Scared Charlie Gossard hated me.

Tabby was snoring on the table and the rest of us were halfway through our jam sponge and custard when Regan spoke.

'Jam sponge is nice.'

We were all suddenly visibly sad. Matron had made that sponge. It was the last thing she'd done for us, and now we were completely on our own.

'Do you think she will come back, Nash?' said Clarice. I think it was the first time she'd ever directly addressed me without sarcasm.

'No, I don't think so.'

When Dianna came back in, she'd been crying. She sat back down in her chair, snuffling, but didn't offer an explanation.

Begrudgingly, Maggie eventually asked, 'All right?'

'No,' she said. 'My mother was due to fly back from Spain tomorrow. All flights have been cancelled or diverted because of the snow. She said it's chaos. She doesn't expect to leave Malaga for at least another three days.'

'I wonder if my mum and dad will be delayed too,' said Maggie.

'And mine,' said Clarice.

'And mine,' I said.

'They all will. Anyone trying to board a plane to or get away from England right now is snookered.' Dianna sniffed.

'We need to get the latest news,' said Clarice. 'Or internet, where can we get internet?'

'Here if we can unlock the damn system,' said Maggie. 'Nash, where's the router for the WiFi?'

'By the main phone but there's no way we can get into it without the code. And that's in Matron's head.'

Clarice batted her eyes at Maggie. 'Nash, you said there's an internet café at the Gorge, didn't you?'

'Yes, but it'll be shut now,' I said. 'Besides, look at the weather.'

The snow and wind outside howled and clawed at the windowpanes like hungry white wolves.

'Okay, Plan B,' said Maggie. 'We *must* be able to get internet access in the IT room or the Reference Library.'

'It's blocked,' said Dianna. 'Didn't you hear what she just said? We can't do anything without the router passcode. Thanks to you sexting in class and Googling Molotov cocktails.'

'I wasn't actually going to *make* them,' said Maggie, rolling her eyes. 'If we could just bypass the code. Can we do that, Nash?'

I looked at her. 'How?'

'I don't know.' She shrugged. 'You're good with computers.'

Dianna looked at Maggie as though she'd just sneezed her out. 'Do I need to get crayons out or something? As we've established, *Matron* is the only one who can give us internet access, and she's. Not. Here. Is. She?'

'No. I. Wonder. Why,' Maggie threw back at her. 'Perhaps because she tripped and fell on a certain someone's meat cleaver, fifty or sixty times.'

'I told you, Leon wouldn't have—'

The phone rang again, its shrill chimes tinkling along Long Corridor, foreboding as a wagon full of clowns. This time, Maggie shoved her chair back.

'How about the TV in the common room?' Clarice suggested. 'We must be able to pick up Sky News or BBC or something on there.'

'There's no aerial going to that TV,' I told her. 'It's just for DVDs.'

'What about in the Headmistress's quarters?' said Regan. 'She'll have a TV in her apartment.'

'We're not allowed up there, are we?' said Dianna.

'I think she'd overlook it just this once,' I said.

'Well, *I'm* not going up there. I don't want to get into trouble when she comes back and finds we've been rooting through all her things.'

'We won't be rooting through her things, will we?'

Dianna huffed. 'Maggie will. You can bet the house on that.'

'She won't,' I said. 'But we need to find out what's happening, Dianna. Find out when the planes are expected to run again. It would be good if you could lead us up there.'

Dianna weakened. 'Yes, all right. It would be for the common good. And we do need to know what's happening at the airports. But they'll be locked, won't they? And the apartment keys are on the main key bunch—on Matron's belt loop.' She put her spoon back in her bowl with her half-finished pudding.

Maggie came back from the phone and confirmed all our fears.

'My mum's getting a flight out on Christmas Eve. She thinks it'll be all right by then. Dad's plane from New York had to land in Dublin. No one can get into any of the English airports in the south cos of the snow. Couldn't be more screwed.'

'So your dad's in Dublin?' I said.

'Yeah, in a hotel by the airport. I don't know how long for. How long's a piece of string, Mum said. Guy at the airport said he'd never seen snow like it in forty years.'

'Typical, isn't it?' said Clarice. 'It was the same when that bloody volcano erupted. That mucked up my chances of going to Euro Disney.'

'The weather doesn't do it to spite you, Clarice,' Maggie snipped.

I shuddered. 'We just have to make the best of things—keep safe and not panic.'

'Keep safe?' said Maggie. 'How are we supposed to keep safe, Nash? We've got a frigging murderer running loose about the hills, there's so much snow out there I keep expecting a Yeti to come hiking through it at any minute, and we've got no internet connection. How do you expect us not to panic?'

'Leon's not running about the hills,' snapped Dianna. 'He's in the Tree House. It's too cold to go out in this. He's probably just as frightened as we are.'

'Poor baby,' said Maggie. 'Are his lil' stabby hands getting all frozy-wozy?'

'Shut up, Maggie!'

'Maggie, leave it,' I said.

She picked up her spoon and shoved it in her mouth.

The phone rang, yet again, out in the long corridor.

'I bet that's my mum and dad,' said Clarice. 'Bet they're stuck at Sydney Airport right now, ringing to say the same thing.'

Maggie licked her spoon on both sides. 'Go and answer it then. You should get them to ring the clap clinic and book an appointment while they're there. Find out what you've picked up from Jailbird Jim.'

'Oh will you just *shut* your pie hole for one minute, Maggie!'

The phone was still ringing, but nobody else was volunteering. 'I'll go.' I pushed my chair back and ran out, hesitating before I picked up the receiver.

'Bathory Girls School, Natasha Staley speaking, how can I help you?'

'Nash?'

A man's voice.

'Hello?'

'Nash, is that you?'

The line was so scratchy I could barely hear him.

'Dad?'

'No, it's me. Nash?'

A younger man's voice. A boy's voice.

Seb's voice.

'Seb? *Seb*. Oh my God, is that you? Seb?'

'I'm not going to make it… I just wanted you to know. I love you…'

The line went silent. And then, the line went dead.

And then, all the lights went out.

A small cacophony of screams floated up the corridor from the Refectory, the loudest of them coming from Dianna. How had he got a phone? Maybe he had reached a village. Maybe he had reached a town. What was wrong with him? Was he injured? Why would he say that? My heart was banging as I ran back to the others.

'It's okay, it's okay,' I said. 'I'll get the torches. Stay in here, all right?'

Sobbing—Dianna's sobbing.

'Nash, what happened?' Maggie's breathless voice.

'Power cut, I think. Just stay there, everyone. Don't move out of this room.'

I felt my way back into Main Hall, where the wind was whistling through the cracks under and over the front door, and grabbed all our torches from the table in the middle. I was in automatic pilot mode now, trying not to think about the phone call. I found my torch and flicked it on to guide me back to the Refectory.

'What's happened, Nash?' said Clarice, waveringly.

'What do you think's happened?' I said, handing Dianna the torch I thought was hers. 'There's a storm outside. The power's been tripped. I need to find the fuse box.'

'I'll come with you,' said Maggie.

'We'll all come with you,' said Clarice.

They needed me. I needed them.

'Okay, stay together, then, and don't run. Maggie, grab Tabs. Follow me.'

Maggie picked up Tabby, who, to her credit, wasn't crying, and we trailed our slow and silent conga into the passageway between the kitchens and utility areas.

The brooms, brushes and mops were kept inside the third utility room, along with a chest freezer and the bins by the back door. On the door were hooks where the cooks hung their coats and bags. To the left, high on the wall, was a large grey box. I saw a small stepladder in the corner of the room, which I opened up so I could reach the box. I flicked down the cover to reveal a long row of small black levers, most of which were in the ON position.

'What can you see, Nash?' said Regan, as though I was getting a bird's-eye view of Narnia from a rocky outcrop.

'Nothing much, just a bunch of little levers.' I spotted one lever at the end of the row that was in the OFF position, and flicked it up.

Immediately, a light came on in the kitchen passageway. Regan broke away from the group and ran back towards the Refectory. 'They're back! They're all back!' she called out.

'Great,' I said, replacing the cover and climbing back down. 'Check the phone too.'

'Yay, Nash!' said Maggie, jiggling Tabby about on her hip.

Tabby rubbed her eyes and smiled wearily, laying her head back on Maggie's shoulder.

'Well done, Nash,' said Dianna.

We piled up the plates and ferried them all back into the kitchen where Clarice offered to wash up. While we were all standing in a state of shock, Regan came in with unwelcome news.

'Um, everything's come back on...except the phone. It's dead.'

'What do you mean, the phone's dead?' said Clarice.

'She meant what she said. The phone is dead,' said Maggie.

'It can't be. We've all used it tonight,' I said. 'The pylon must be down at the end of the drive, or something.'

'Is it?' asked Clarice.

'I don't know, do I? I'm not a telephone engineer. It's happened before, a couple of years ago when we had that big storm. When the tree went over on the lawn.'

'But you fixed the lights,' said Clarice. 'So you can fix the phone.'

'I didn't fix them. The trip had flipped, that's all.'

'What are we going to do?' said Regan.

I rubbed Tabby's back as she snored contentedly against Maggie's neck. 'Look, she's knackered, we all are. We need some sleep. We'll deal with it in the morning.'

'Can't we at least go and look for our own phones?' said Clarice.

'They'll be in the staffroom,' I said, my voice as flat as

a dead man's heart monitor as I tried to push the phone call from my mind. 'It'll be locked. I don't have the key.'

*I'm not going make it. I just want you to know. I love you.* The words pushed their way back to the forefront of my thoughts. Around and around and around. Seb… Abruptly, I left the Refectory.

Annoyingly, everybody followed me up the stairs to the dorms and began making up their beds. Maggie and I undressed Tabby and settled her in her bed next to mine, then Maggie took the bed next to hers. No one said a word until lights out.

Then the thoughts came back, fast and strangulating. The tiny sound of my tears hitting my pillow on both sides of my face was interrupted by Maggie's voice.

'I forgot to ask, Nash, how did your date with Charlie go?'

'It was nice,' I managed to say, without sounding like I was crying. 'But I blew it.'

'Blimey, you're a fast mover,' she said.

I couldn't laugh. My brain was throwing up all these memories I didn't want. Me and Seb at home on the hearthrug one Christmas, watching *Karate Kid*. Him teaching me some of the moves: the Crane Kick, Wax On, Wax Off. Other than kicking him in his crown jewels (and the *oooooffff* noise he made every time), I couldn't see the fun in it and kept sneaking off to steal chocolates from the Christmas tree. But he said I needed to know how to defend myself. He showed me moves that weren't in the film.

*You go for the eyes. The throat. Weak points, see?*

*Can I kick you in the crotch again?*

*If you must. Use any means necessary. Just don't give up.*

Eventually I allowed the sound of the roaring wind and

the dumb pummelling of the snow against the windows to lull me into a twitchy, troubled sleep.

The next thing I knew, I was being awoken by someone vigorously shaking my shoulder.

'Nash.'

'What?' I croaked. I opened my eyes to see Maggie, her tiny clip-on book light clutched in her grasp, illuminating one side of her face. She was looking at nothing and everything all at once, like her eyes were searching for sounds. 'What is it?'

'I heard something,' she whispered. 'Something outside.'

'Like what? What sort of noise?'

'I dunno. I was in the bathroom and I heard it through the toilet window. Sort of scuffling. A scrabbling noise. Should we go and check it out?'

I nodded, grabbed my own book light from my bedside drawer and clicked it on, settling it on my tissue box while I found my pea coat and slippers. I swept my tiny light around the room. There were four lumps in the other beds: Clarice, Regan, Dianna and Tabby. All seemed to be sleeping soundly.

I joined Maggie at the window. We drew back the curtains and stared out into the dark night. It was still snowing, though there didn't seem to be any wind. The only things we could see through the cold panes of glass were the pitched snow on the ground outside and the reflections of our book lights.

'I can't see anything,' I said. Then I heard a noise. It sounded halfway between a roar and a cough. And not too far away either. Maggie's gaze locked onto mine.

'What. Was. That?' she whispered.

'I don't know,' I said, craning my neck to try to see further through the window than the freezing single pane would allow. 'It definitely came from out there, though.'

We heard it again. Further away now. And another noise accompanying it. A rumbling noise. Like a…

'Purr,' we both said at the same time. 'Definitely a purr.'

'Okay, what do we do, what do we do?' Maggie whispered.

'What do you mean, what do we do?' I whispered back. 'What *can* we do?'

'That thing's out there right now. That stupid little gimp Regan was right!'

'We don't know that,' I said. 'We don't know what that was.'

'We both heard a purr, Nash. The kind of purr a mahoosive cat with great big teeth makes.'

'I know. But even if it is, we're helpless, aren't we? We've just got to stay put, in here, where it's safe.'

There came another noise, even further away now. An echoey, throaty growl from the direction of the Landscape Gardens.

'You heard that too, right?' said Maggie, her breath fogging up the glass.

'Yeah. I heard that.' I caught my breath. 'It's gone away now, over there.'

'It was stalking the school, wasn't it? Looking for a way to get inside. That's why I heard it in the girls' bathrooms and why we just heard it then. It knows we're in here, Nash.'

We waited at the window for what seemed like an hour. There were no more noises. I looked across at the digital clock on Clarice's nightstand. It had just gone one a.m.

188 *C.J. Skuse*

'All the doors downstairs are either bolted or wedged. Nothing's getting in. I checked it all when we came up.'

'You're sure?' said Maggie.

'Yes,' I said firmly. 'We're safe.'

She looked at me and gulped. 'I need a drink. My mouth's gone all dry.' She went back to her bed and opened the door of her nightstand, retrieving a mostly empty bottle of Evian. After swigging down the remaining dregs, she screwed the lid back on and flung the bottle onto the rainbow rug beside the wardrobe. It landed with a dull *bonk*.

'Probably was a fox or something. They make some weird-assed noises, don't they?'

'Yeah,' I said, drawing the curtains again and removing my slippers and coat.

'Morons,' she muttered, clutching her book light.

I smiled. 'Yeah. Foxes are morons.'

'And badgers. I hate badgers. And stoats. And them things that build dams.'

'Beavers?'

'Yeah. Bloody stupid noises.'

I laughed.

'Nash?'

'Yeah?'

'What if it's…the Beast?'

'It won't be, Maggie.'

'Are you sure?'

'Yeah. Go back to sleep.'

'I can't. Nash…I'm scared. I wanted to leave this bloody place *before* I knew there was a real-assed tiger or something in the woods but now it's like… Oh God, there it is again.'

I sat up in bed, my heart pumping for all it was worth.

There was no point denying it any more. We both had ears.
And that had been a definite growl. 'Even if it was…that,
it can't get in. All the doors downstairs are bolted. We're
safe. I promise.'

'Sure?'

'Yeah, I'm sure.'

'You don't think we should go down and get some javelins out of the sports cupboard, just in case?'

'Do you want to go down two flights of stairs, all the
way down Long Corridor, past the gym, down towards the
cloakrooms and break in to the sports cupboard and get a
javelin? In the dark?'

'No.'

'Well then.'

'Okay. Night.'

'Night.'

I found it oddly refreshing that Maggie was more scared
than me. That Maggie was scared of anything at all. She
was always so fearless. Even when we played netball against
some really rough schools, who ripped us mercilessly for
our long pink socks and tidy hair and straight partings. We
were all petrified, but they never messed with Maggie. But
all the while she'd been carrying this fear about the Beast
and I hadn't seen it. I mean, I was fearful of whatever the
Beast was too, and the fact we had a murderer in the vicin-
ity wasn't filling my mind with Christmas mirth, but these
weren't the biggest monsters in my mind. The phone call
was the thing keeping me awake. That had chilled me to
the marrow.

'Nash?' Maggie was back under her duvet now, pulled
up tightly to her chin.

'Yeah?' I said, getting back into my bed.

'It couldn't have been the madman, could it? You know, Dianna's brother.'

'He hasn't come up to the house before, has he?' I replied. 'Why would he start tonight? He wouldn't risk anyone calling the police to report an intruder.'

'Yeah, but we can't call the police, can we? The phone's out.'

'He doesn't know that,' I said. 'Try to get some sleep, okay?' I reached out for the switch on my book light.

'Nash?'

'What?' I said.

'Leave the light on for a bit, yeah?'

# 17

## The Cabin in the Woods

We were all up before first light. Maggie hadn't said another word about what we'd heard in the night, either because she didn't want to look scared in front of the others or because she couldn't be sure she'd heard anything out of the ordinary. Nights in the countryside *were* full of odd noises and creatures crawling around that didn't do so in the daytime.

I'd slept for about two hours in the end. Everything was now coloured a sick grey by my new certainty that my brother was either dying or dead. Getting the news was a mere formality. I had to stop hoping.

When I was showered and dressed, I put on the greeny-blue Howlite necklace Charlie had bought for me up the Gorge, tucking it beneath my collar so it couldn't be seen and feeling the cold stones against my neck. I padded downstairs to the payphone and checked to see if a dialling tone had magically returned to us in the night. It hadn't. The world outside the windows was white and silent in every single direction. None of us knew how deep the snow was, but we all knew roughly where the ponds and lakes were so we could steer clear of them. I cleaned the massive kitchen oven while I waited for the others to come downstairs. It had congealed red and yellow drips of lasagne sauce on the metal shelves inside, and I needed to keep my hands busy. It kept the thoughts at arm's length.

Leaving the two long oven shelves in the big sink to soak, I joined the others in the main hall to formulate a search plan. Bundled up in tights, jumpers, coats, boots and anything else to keep the cold air out, we gathered at the foot of the main stairs.

'Dianna, why don't you take this one?' I suggested, sitting on the bottom stair and leaning against the warmth of Brody's deep soft fur.

Her eyes swivelled from me to Maggie to Clarice, and then back to me. 'Take what?'

'The lead. Decide who's going to do what, where we're going to search first.' I felt sleep tug at my heavy eyelids.

'No, I can't, Nash. I don't know where to start.'

I looked at Clarice. She had so much make-up on I was surprised she could hold her head up. No help there.

'Okay,' I said sleepily, getting off the stairs. 'Someone needs to stay with Tabby.'

Dianna and Clarice both shot their hands up.

'Dianna, you stay. Keep Brody with you. See if you can find Mrs Saul-Hudson's spare set of keys in case we can't find Matron's.'

'Aye aye, Cap'n,' said Dianna, doing a weird salute thing, and seemingly delighted with her new role as Tabby's nanny. Removing her coat and boots, she took Tabby's hand and led her and the dog off in search of DVDs and colouring books.

'What do you need me to do, Nash?' said Maggie, and a little burst of warmth flooded into my chest. I knew I could rely on her. 'How about weapons?'

'Weapons?' cried Clarice. 'Why weapons? We're a search party, aren't we?'

'Will you keep your voice down!' whispered Maggie. 'I think we need weapons because there's an escaped murderer out there.' She looked at Regan who was rubbing the tooth on her yarn necklace. 'And who knows what else. We should be prepared.'

'Yeah, you're right,' I said. 'We probably won't need them, but it would be good to have them on us all the same.'

'What did you have in mind?' said Clarice, more quietly this time.

I shrugged. I didn't really know what I meant. My mind was too fogged up with flashing images of us finding a body in the snow. Frozen blood on the ground. Gnashing teeth. 'Knives?' I suggested.

'I couldn't stab anyone,' said Regan. 'I just couldn't. I'm not strong enough.'

'Ooh, I don't think I could either,' said Clarice.

I looked at Maggie. 'I probably could,' she said. 'If I had to.'

'What if your life was at risk? Or someone else's life was at risk?' I said, turning to the two naysayers. Neither of them said anything.

'All right, fair enough then,' said Maggie. 'How about if one of them goes with each one of us? We'll take a kitchen knife each and one of these two pussies and we'll go off in two directions, yeah? Bagsy not going with Clarice.'

Maggie and I found two small, sheathed fruit knives in the kitchen. She tied one loosely to the belt loop of her coat while I shoved mine in the top of my drawstring tote bag and carried it on my back. I didn't think I'd be able to use mine. I'd been attacked by a little dog once when I was younger, and I'd just stood there, frozen to the spot, without the courage to bat it away. We also grabbed three javelins from the PE cupboard for poking the snow.

'It's too heavy. I can't lift it,' Clarice moaned, so she had to make to with a rounders post, sans base. Outside, the air was bitterly cold and the snow was still flurrying down in light drifts. The place was white and crisp as a new duvet and the landscape was completely snuggled up for winter. White had enveloped the trees, the flint steps—even the school minibus was just a large rectangular white lump. It hid everything that had been green, brown or grey. And anything that could have been covered in blood. I didn't know if that was good or bad.

'There's no footprints anywhere,' I said. 'No one's been wandering around in the night, which is good. Maybe Leon hasn't left from the Tree House, just like Dianna said.'

A red blush quickly developed over Clarice's face, even on her eyelids.

'It might not mean that,' said Maggie, pulling her scarf away from her mouth and nose for a second to sniff the air. 'He might have gone the back way round, past the stable block. He could be… What's that smell?'

'Smells like burnt toast,' said Clarice.

'Yeah, it does,' said Regan, snapping her head round to look for a source. 'It stinks.'

'Never mind that,' I said. We'd reached the large white expanse that used to be Edward's Pond, the gateway to the Landscape Gardens. 'We need to start looking for Matron. Clarice and I will check the top path by the Chapel, cos that's where I last saw her.'

'The Tree House—' Regan muttered.

'Yes. Maggie, you and Regan take the bottom path that runs parallel to ours and check the bank in case she's fallen somewhere. And we'll meet up by the Tree House.'

'The Tree House—' said Regan again.

'Yes, we'll go there once we've checked the paths, in case she's still alive.'

'No, the Tree House!' said Regan, for a third time.

'What?' I looked behind me, fearing the worst, but see-ing something I didn't expect. It was the burning shack from my dream.

'Yeezus wept,' said Maggie.

'Oh my God,' said Clarice.

Except I wasn't dreaming. There was a fire burning, up in the trees. A ferocious orange bonfire, vomiting huge grey plumes of smoke up into the sky on the far left side of the valley. It was where the Tree House used to be.

# 18
## Don't Look Now

I ran along the valley path, stumbling and slipping and kicking up powdery snow the whole way until I was parallel with the burning Tree House. Then I scrambled up the snowy bank. Someone—Maggie—was yelling my name.

'Nash, what are you doing? Come back!'

I scrabbled desperately to get a foothold on the bank of slippery snow, the stench of burning wood strong in my nostrils. Inch by inch by inch, I climbed, finally grabbing some knotweed to pull myself up to the upper path.

'Seb!' I called out.

'What the hell are you doing?' I heard Maggie call out behind me.

Ducking underneath the tree canopies, I found the

wooden ladder to the Tree House and began to climb, feeling the heat blasting down at me from above.

'Nash!' That was Regan's voice, now. 'You'll fall. It's not safe!'

Her voice got closer as I kept climbing, getting my head just above the floor of the Tree House. I had to keep closing my eyes in the heat, but I saw it. A long sausage-shaped lump, in the corner underneath the window hole. A sleeping bag.

'Hello? Is anyone in there? Can you hear me?' I shouted. As I took another step up the ladder, the rung snapped and broke away and *down down down* I fell until I *thump*ed hard onto the snowy ground below.

'Nash!' Maggie's voice again. My body ached all over. When I opened my eyes, I saw only a blinding white sky above me. Then Maggie's panic-stricken face came into view, leaning over me. 'Jesus Christ, what the hell were you trying to do?'

'He's in there, Maggie. We've got to get him out.' I struggled to my feet, everything aching, my vision swimming. Regan came running along the path from the Chapel, Clarice bringing up the rear.

'Nash, are you okay?' she puffed.

'Leon's in the Tree House. Nash saw him,' said Maggie. 'Nash, we can't get him out. The whole thing's on fire and the ladder's broken.'

'Oh my God!' Clarice started to cry. 'Oh God, we've got to do something.'

'Nash, listen to me,' said Maggie, holding both my wrists. 'You can't get him out, you'll both be barbecued. It's not Seb, okay? It's not Seb!'

I yanked back from her. 'I know that, Maggie. Whatever he's done, we can't leave him to burn to death.'

'But there's nothing we can do!' she shouted.

'We've got to try something,' Clarice wailed. 'Water, we need water…'

'The lakes are frozen,' said Maggie. 'Even if we had buckets, we couldn't get any water out. Are you sure it was him? Not just…a pile of clothes, or something?'

'I only saw it for a second before the ladder broke. I saw a sleeping bag.'

'So he might not have been there?'

'I don't know.'

'He would have got out,' Clarice cried. 'He would have seen it and got out in time.'

'I can't smell pork,' said Regan.

'What?'

'They say burning human flesh smells like pork, don't they? I don't smell it. It's just that woody smell, isn't it?' I looked at her. 'I'm saying it's a good thing.'

'Just…don't put that image in our heads, okay?'

Just then, Clarice screamed. 'Guys, there's blood! There's blood, here—on the ladder and on the ground.'

'Check yourself, you might have done it when you fell,' said Maggie, looking at me.

I rubbed my legs and hands. 'It's not me.'

The broken ladder lay in pieces on the ground. There were bloody fingerprints on two of the broken rungs, and a couple of tiny red puddles on the ground.

Regan picked up a twig and poked at the puddles. 'It's coagulated. This has been here a while.'

All of a sudden, there was a tremendous creaking above us and, as we all ran as fast as our panic would afford us, the whole structure, wood panels and roof and everything it had been resting on, came crashing down through the tree canopy and scattered all over the ground.

'Blimey,' I said, fogging my own face with my rapid white breaths.

We looked down the path. The sleeping bag was lying open on top of a pile of broken, charred wood. It was just a sleeping bag. 'Oh thank God,' said Clarice.

'We need to get back and call the police,' I said. 'This is just getting more and more weird. We can't handle this by ourselves.'

'Nash is right. This is a game changer,' said Maggie. 'We need to get people here. Ambulances. Firemen. Police.'

'How are we going to do that?' said Regan. 'The phone's still out.'

'We'll look for our mobiles again. There's got to be some way of getting a message to someone. Let's just get back inside for now.'

The three of them followed me towards the Chapel and down the winding path towards the flint steps near the entrance to Main House. None of us said a word, although the silence was deafening. We were all looking round, looking for signs of Leon the Murderer, of life, of death, of the Beast.

We were halfway down the flint steps, carefully dodging the patches of compressed ice our footprints had made earlier, when Clarice sidled up to me. I didn't like that her arm was grazing mine as we walked. I moved away.

'What are you going to say to Dianna?'

'About what?'

'About Ed—about Leon?'

'I don't know,' I said. 'I'll have to tell her about the fire. That's all I really know.'

'What if he's run away?'

'Well then, he's not our problem, is he?'

Dianna must have heard the front door opening and closing. In seconds, she and Tabby were there in the main hall.

'Oh, thank God you're back. Did you find anything?' she asked, clutching Tabby's hand. 'Any sign of Matron?'

We all looked at each other. Regan shook her head.

'What, nothing?'

'It snowed too heavily in the night,' I said, turning to make sure the front door was bolted. Tabby left Dianna and came to stand between me and Maggie, holding both of our hands. Dianna was standing alone now, opposite us.

'Nash?'

'Did you find any spare keys?' I asked her, delaying.

'Yes,' she replied, delving into her tunic pocket and pulling out a bunch of assorted silver and gold keys. 'I found these hung up in a kitchen cupboard. Well, Tabby found them.'

I looked down at Tabby and smiled. 'Good. That's great. That's really great.'

'What's happened? What did you find?'

I could see myself in her face. I could see myself when that phone eventually *did* ring and it was Dad, telling me they'd found Seb. 'Why don't we go into the library?' I said.

'Tell me, Nash,' she said, through clenched teeth.

As I reluctantly opened my mouth, there was a loud *thud* on the glass behind us.

Our heads whipped round, but there was nothing at the window—just blinding white as far as the eye could see. On the glass, there was one tiny patch of snow.

'What the hell was that?' said Clarice.

'I think it was a snowball,' said Maggie, going to the window to inspect it. There followed a sharp intake of breath.

We ran over to the windows. On the snowy patch of grass in front of the house, a man was lying on his back, another small ball of snow in his hand. There was a thick red streak on the ground, leading from where he lay right across the lawn and disappearing around the side of the building. He had dragged himself here.

'Oh my God!' cried Dianna, rushing to unbolt the door.

'Dianna, what are you doing?' said Maggie.

'It's Leon!' she screamed, fumbling with the locks. 'It's my brother!'

# 19
## Hellraiser

'My leg—don't touch it, don't touch my leg! Arghhh!'

There was blood on one leg of his jeans and he was shivering like a newborn foal. 'Need to g-g-g-g-get inside,' he mumbled. 'Get m-m-m-me inside.'

'Oh my God, what happened?' wailed Dianna.

'I went out for f-f-firewood,' Leon stammered, as me and Dianna helped him to his feet and put both of his arms around us for stability. 'It chased me up the ladder. I kicked it down, but it…arghh…it got in. Don't leave me out here, please. Help me.'

'Oh my God,' said Regan, inspecting the leg. 'Have you been bitten?'

'Never mind that, we have to get him inside,' I said.

'Are you mad?' said Maggie. 'We can't take him inside!' Brody growled at our visitor in apparent agreement.

'We can't leave him out here, can we?' said Clarice. 'Poor baby.'

Maggie frowned. *'Pourquoi?'*

'What do you mean, *pourquoi*? Look at him!'

Maggie shrugged. 'Yeah, I'm looking at him. He's just burned down the Tree House to get a free ticket indoors.'

'I didn't… I kn-n-n-nocked over a lamp.' He shuddered painfully.

Brody was barking his head off.

Maggie folded her arms and stood watching us. 'We can't just take him inside.'

I knew Maggie had a point, but I couldn't leave him in the snow. 'If he stays out here much longer he'll freeze to death. He's halfway there already.'

'I say we leave him out here. We don't know what he's capable of. He's a murderer, remember? Even the dog knows he's a wrong 'un.'

'Tabs, take Brody inside!' I told her angrily, his bark beginning to gnaw on my patience. Tabby obediently led the dog into Main House, coaxing him with some iced gems from her pocket. 'We're not leaving him out here. He could be hypothermic. We need to warm him up. Come on!'

Maggie stared at me. Regan and Clarice fluttered and flapped around us and me and Dianna helped Leon across the driveway and towards the front door where, reluctantly, Maggie held it open for us.

'He's shaking,' she said, as we struggled past her, settling Leon down on Main Hall's bearskin rug.

'He's freezing,' I said. 'We need to dry him off and remove his clothes.'

'Things are looking up, eh, Clarice?' said Maggie.

'Oh, shut your face,' said Clarice, looking helplessly at Leon like he was her brave soldier who we had carried back from the Somme.

'He'll need a warm drink or soup or something too,' I said. 'Dianna, the keys you found, was there a bunch on there for the Saul-Hudsons' apartment?'

'Yes, I think so.' She patted her tunic pocket and there was a *chink*. She pulled out the bunch and began rifling through them to find the right one.

'Okay, we'll get him upstairs and lie him down on their bed. It'll be more comfortable for him.'

'I'll go and grab some warm blankets from the airing cupboard, shall I?' Clarice offered. I almost didn't recognise her voice.

'Yeah,' I said. 'That would be good.'

'Shall I make him some soup, Nash?' said Tabby's little voice.

'Yeah. Go into the kitchens and see if you can find where Cook keeps the tins. Don't open any though. Regan, go and help her. And take Brody with you, okay?'

'It's a bite, isn't it?' said Regan, looking at Leon's blood-soaked jean leg.

'Just *go*, Regan,' I barked and she quickly took Tabby's hand and Brody's lead and left the Hall.

Dianna and I started to take Leon upstairs, still with no help from Maggie who sat right in the middle of the stairs. 'He's covered in blood, for God's sake. He could have diseases. And we don't know what caused that injury. Who's to say that Matron didn't do it in self-defence? What if he found her in the woods, she fought him off, maybe injured him?'

'If you're not going to help us, move out of the way,' said Dianna.

'I'm just saying, there might be more to this injury than meets the eye. He's a criminal. He's escaped from prison. We shouldn't be going anywhere near him.'

'Maggie, you're probably right, but he is badly hurt.'

'He's not your brother, Nash. He's not Seb.'

'*Move* it, Maggie!'

'Arggggghhhhhhhhhh!' Leon screamed.

This time, we carried him bodily up the hallway stairs and along the green-carpeted mile towards the Saul-Hudsons' private apartment. Between screams, we learned that the thing which had attacked him in the woods had apparently been 'as big as a jaguar'. It had bitten him as he was halfway up the ladder to the Tree House and the lamp he had knocked over was a kerosene one that Dianna had found in the storage sheds and taken up there for him. He'd knocked it over in his struggle to get away.

'Okaaay,' I said, thinking it was strange that the Beast hadn't taken his foot off completely. 'That must have been your blood we found then,' I said. 'On the ladder and on the snow.'

Leon was still shivering. I vaguely remembered from Brownies that shivering was a good sign. 'I didn't mean to…burn it down,' he said through gritted teeth.

'That's all right,' said Maggie, 'we can just add arsonist to your list of skills. Under murderer and burglar. And rapist.'

'I'm not…a…rapist.'

'There's still time.'

'Maggie, stop it,' I said.

'Oh come on, Nash. What, have you got the murderer kink as well now? You don't honestly buy that story, do you?'

Nobody answered her. She gave up arguing and folded her arms in exasperation. As it turned out, no, I *didn't* quite buy his story, though at that moment I couldn't figure out why.

Finally, at the last stage, Dianna left to start unlocking the doors and we managed to heave him inside the Saul-Hudsons' massive Vettriano-decorated bedroom, manoeuvring him clumsily up onto the frilly-silk king size bed.

'Aaaarrrrghhhhhhhh, Jesus!' Leon wailed again. 'Knock me out, just knock me out!'

'God, he's in so much pain,' cried Dianna, shaking almost as much as her brother.

'How can you tell?' said Maggie, arms annoyingly folded.

Clarice returned with a big pile of blankets. She plonked them on the end of the bed as I started removing Leon's clothes. 'Uh, do you need any help doing that, Nash?' she said.

'Clarice, there's a time and a place,' said Maggie.

Clarice went to say something, but I jumped in. 'Ignore her. Yes, we need to get his coat and jumper off and get some warm clothes on him. See what Mr Saul-Hudson's got in the wardrobe.'

'Aaaaaarrgghhh!' Leon seethed, as I gently tried to remove his jeans, careful not to touch the bite. It was no use. Every tug on the denim produced a blood-curdling yell from the patient so in the end I gave up. I rooted through the drawers of a large white dressing table for scissors, and found some hairdressing ones.

Clarice yelped as though she could feel everything he could. 'Is there anything we can give him in Sickbay, Nash? To help with the pain?'

'Paracetamol—that's about it,' I said.

'What about anaesthetic?'

'I doubt they keep any anaesthetic on school property.'
*Snip snip snip.*

Leon screamed like a banshee as I finally reached the end of his leg and fully revealed his wound to the world.

There was a ring of small but deep incisions, as though something's sharp teeth had clenched around his leg, all gaping open and bleeding. In one of the wounds, I saw bone. My brother had once gashed his thigh on some barbed wire when we'd been playing in a field behind our house and I'd fainted when I saw it. But Seb knew exactly what to do. He talked me through it.

This looked like a big animal bite, but it was no animal bite I'd ever seen. The puncture wounds were so thin, oozing crimson red.

Clarice's hand leapt to her mouth. 'What the hell is that?' Her breathing got shallower and shallower until she was sort of scream-crying, right in my ear.

Tabby was still standing at my side. 'I think the monster did that,' she said. She was completely unfussed, unlike Clarice and Dianna, who were verging on hysterics.

Tabby was too bright to be told otherwise and believe it, so I said nothing. 'Clarice, go to Sickbay and get me the first aid box from the window, please.' I clocked the kettle by the bed. 'Dianna, boil that kettle, will you? There's a measuring jug on the bath. We need to get the boiled water tepid and wash the wound.'

'How are we going to do that?' she asked.

'Uh…a washing-up bowl. See if there's one in the kitchenette, next door. We'll rest his leg on it and run the warm water onto it to try to flush out any infection.'

She set to work, unplugging and taking the kettle into the bathroom. I took one of the sheets from the extra pile by Leon's pillow and started tearing it up. Clarice came back in with the first aid kit, but, when I opened it, the box was empty.

'Go back and look again, Clarice. I need dressings, antiseptic wipes and saline solution.'

'Arghhh!' Leon groaned. His pain seemed to be getting worse.

'I'm sorry, I'm sorry,' she fluttered.

'It's okay,' I said. 'Just bring me back the things and we can start cleaning him up, all right?'

Dianna returned with the kettle and plugged it back in to boil it. Regan then appeared with a bag of ice. She stopped at the foot of the bed. She couldn't take her eyes off the bite. 'Was it a big animal? Like a big cat, only with a pointier head and teeth like knife blades?'

Leon nodded, his face strained. 'I only saw it for a second.'

'You actually saw it?' said Regan, clearly in awe.

'When I got inside the Tree House, I looked down. It was jumping up. It jumped…about s-s-s-six f-f-f-feet in the air. It almost had my face off.'

'Liar,' said Maggie, but no one was paying any attention. Everyone else was either busy or in pain.

'Did it have these mottled markings on it? Like a jaguar but you'd have to be really looking at it and really close to see them?'

'Uh, I don't know. Ow! Watch it! It just looked b-b-b-black to me. With r-r-red eyes.'

'Red eyes,' Regan gasped. 'So the legend *is* true then, that it has red eyes when it hunts.'

'Yeah,' said Leon.

I looked at him. He looked at me and stared me out until I looked away.

My hands were covered in blood again, just as they had been the previous night. 'Did you see…anything else when you were trying to get here? Anyone in the snow?'

'Like who?' The kettle clicked beside him on the nightstand and Dianna filled a plastic measuring jug with hot water.

'A woman. Our matron. She went missing last night. She must be out there somewhere.'

He shook his head, breathing like he was giving birth now. 'You think it g-g-got her?'

Dianna started crying again, messy and unashamed.

'We don't know. We don't know anything for sure. It's okay,' I told her.

'N-n-n-no, it's not.' Leon sweated and seethed in his sickbed like the girl from *The Exorcist*. 'None of you are safe here. You've got to get your p-p-p-p-parents to come and get you. That th-th-th-thing is out there. Look what it's done to me.'

'Why do you think we're all here in the first place?' I said. 'We're all waiting for our parents. The phone isn't working because of the storm. None of us can get home.'

'Call the police,' he begged. 'I don't care if they t-t-take me back.'

'We don't have a phone,' I repeated. 'None of us do. We're all stuck here.'

Leon flopped his head back on the pillow.

Clarice returned, this time with actual medical supplies. Unclicking it, I laid everything out on the bed beside Leon's leg. I gently propped up his foot on the bottom bed board and began swabbing the wound with a saline wipe. He let out the most ear-piercing scream yet.

'Oh screw this,' said Maggie, and left the room.

'Maggie? Where are you going?' I called out to her. She called something back, but I couldn't hear it over Leon's screams.

'She wasn't doing anything anyway,' said Regan, appearing in the doorway, as though from a puff of smoke.

'Have you left Tabby down there with that soup on?' I said.

'No, I did it in the microwave. I'm keeping it warm under a plate.'

'Oh. Good. Thanks.'

Dianna and Clarice dressed the shivering patient in a warm shirt and Argyll cardigan, though Leon took a brief break from his agonies to tell them he wouldn't wear the golf trousers they'd picked out 'under any cock-sucking circumstances'.

Tabby appeared at my elbow and tugged on my jumper sleeve. 'Brody is having his lunch.'

'Good girl.'

'What happened to the man?'

'He's hurt his leg. We have to look after him.'

'Did the monster hurt him?'

'Uh, no, no, Tabs, don't worry. He just…fell over.'

'We've got to…get out of here,' said Leon again, his sweaty face whiter than the sheets he was lying on. 'That thing's out there. It'll get in.'

'It's okay, it's okay.' Dianna tried her best to soothe him.

At that moment, Maggie reappeared, this time with a half-empty bottle in each hand.

'What the hell's that?' said Clarice.

'Alcohol.'

'Where did you get it?' said Dianna sniffily.

'Next door. Keys to their lounge are on that bunch. I brought whiskey and voddy but there's loads more in there. Thank God for Mr Saul-H and his failed stint in rehab, eh?'

'Trust you,' Dianna snipped. 'Long as you're enjoying yourself, nothing else matters, does it, Maggie?'

'Actually, I got them for Laughing Boy there,' she said, walking towards the bed. 'You said you needed anaesthetic.' She nodded at the whiskey. '*Vive la* France. If he's pissed enough, maybe he'll stop screaming.'

'You can't give a hypothermic person alcohol, Maggie. That's stupid.' Regan left the room.

'More stupid than inviting a murderer into a girls' school for first aid and light refreshments?'

Leon sat up and Maggie threw him the whiskey bottle. He caught it in one hand and fumbled to get the lid off. Once he'd unscrewed the cap, he began guzzling faster than an infant at a full teat. Then Maggie began rooting through the bedside drawers as though her life depended on it.

'What are you doing?' said Clarice.

'Looking for handcuffs. These old pervs must have a set or two hanging around up here.'

'You're not handcuffing him, Maggie,' said Dianna, slamming the right-hand drawer shut just as Maggie's fingers left it.

'Put it this way,' said Maggie, 'either you find something to handcuff him to the bedposts with or I call the police right now and tell them just who's come for dinner. Your choice.'

They all looked at me, even Leon. I said nothing.

'Do it,' he seethed. 'I don't care. As long as I'm in here. Away from that thing.'

'Do it,' I said, and at once they all joined the search. Even Dianna, with some trepidation, began opening more drawers and wardrobes.

'It's okay,' I said. 'I know where to look.'

'Where?' said Maggie.

I went to the door at the back of the room and unlocked it. 'Brown wardrobe. Key's on the top behind some Sellotape.'

Maggie, Dianna and Clarice all looked at each other then, one after the other, went into the Aladdin's cave I'd just opened up for them—a dressing room, ostensibly, but also the room where the Saul-Hudsons kept all their most strictly private 'stuff'. It wasn't long before the screams came.

'What the hell is all this stuff?'

'Oh. My. God!' Maggie shrieked. 'It's a total kink fest! Like where Ann Summers went to die!'

I laughed. 'Just bring the fluffy pink handcuffs. Nothing else.'

# 20
## Daughters of Darkness

Regan had gone to check the phone in the Saul-Hudsons' apartment. It wasn't working in there either.

Dianna and I stayed with Leon until we had settled him in his clean, dry clothes and dressed his leg. He'd fallen asleep with his head resting against his empty whiskey bottle. On closer inspection, once all the blood had been washed away, his leg wound didn't look as bad as I'd first thought.

Maggie and Clarice had bonded over the Saul-Hudsons' wardrobe and its Narnian wonderland of perversity. Clarice had stolen a pair of stripper heels and a red feather boa and Maggie had taken a shine to a French maid's outfit and stilettos. She said she would prepare dinner that night, seeing as she was in character: a picnic tea in the common room. She and I hadn't really talked since we'd brought Leon in. I didn't think he was a threat but Maggie was still convinced he had burned down the Tree House and injured himself on purpose, and that he had something to do with Matron's disappearance. She only shut up about it when I agreed on the handcuffs and locking him in the Saul-Hudsons' bedroom. Worse still, she'd then gone down to the staffroom to find our confiscated phones, but the phone box was empty. We had no idea what Matron had done with them either.

We had crisps, cakes, biscuits and, to be healthy, a tin of peaches in syrup. Clarice stuck with low-fat yoghurt and fruit. Dianna took a plate up to Leon and ate hers with him. The rest of us ate off paper plates on our laps in the common room. The rest of the school, including our dorm, was freezing. The boiler hadn't packed up so we still had hot water, but it was a big school to heat and even though the radiators were on full blast, and the fire was roaring, it was still distinctly fridgy. We were all bundled up in double jumpers, tights and Ugg boots. Regan took over lighting the fire in the inglenook, keeping it stoked with logs from the limited pile.

A Christmas tree sat in the corner of the room, its lights twinkling like a piss-take. The sight of it cheered none of us. On the floor underneath lay some presents, all wrapped up by Tabby's class at the end of term.

'Can we open the presents?' she kept asking, shaking them and stroking their silken bows.

'No, Tabs, just leave them where they are, okay? Just for now.' She went back to her place on her beanbag and sucked Babbitt's ear, occasionally feeding him the odd Quaver or crust of bread.

For a long time, we talked rubbish, with conversations

ranging from 'how you can't get pregnant if you wipe yourself with a spunky towel'—instigated by Maggie—to how
Clarice couldn't eat smoked salmon because it reminded
her of a porn magazine she found under her mum and dad's
bed when she was five to 'Who shot JFK?' to which none
of us knew the answer. Regan took the hint as soon as the
conversation nosedived into crudity and set Tabby up on a
beanbag in front of the TV with *Mrs Doubtfire* and a pair
of headphones slightly too big for her head.

'Is it true that if you lick yoghurt lids you get Alzheimer's?'
asked Clarice, staring down at the lid of her Weight Watch-
ers pineapple yoghurt.

'I shouldn't think it would matter in your case,' said Maggie, breaking a Mini Roll in half and stuffing both sides in
her mouth at once.

'Shut up, Maggie.'

'Shut up, Clarice.'

Snipping at each other was becoming the norm. We were
all annoyed and frustrated and scared at having absolutely
no contact with the outside world, but talking about it didn't
make a blind bit of difference. So we didn't. We just allowed
our elephant in the room to double in size.

'Well, here we are then,' sighed Maggie, flinging her
last crust onto the fire. 'Bit like the Spice Girls, aren't
we? We've got Tiny Spice—' looking at Tabby '—Bossy
Spice—' me '—Weird Spice—' Regan '—Slaggy Spice—'
Clarice '—and Dianna's Hysterical Spice.'

'What does that make you then, Maggie?'

'Awesome Spice, of course,' she replied, crossing her
feet on the arm of the chair and fidgeting with the hem of
her maid's skirt.

'I'm beginning to understand why the Saul-Hudsons went

away this Christmas,' said Regan, nibbling the edge of a slice of malt loaf pasted with butter.

'I bet they knew something like this was going to happen,' said Clarice.

'She couldn't have known any of *this* would happen,' said Maggie.

'Couldn't she?' said Clarice. 'I wouldn't put it past her to leave us all here as bait.'

'Why would she?' I asked, more fractiously than I meant to. 'Talk sense.'

I pushed my plate away and rested my chin on my hand. I had an overwhelming feeling of wanting to give up. Scratching my neck, I felt warm rocks beneath my fingertips: the Howlite necklace Charlie had given me while we were at the Gorge. How long ago was that now? Hours? Days? We'd had such a wonderful time. Where had it all gone? It had all been sucked down into the sewer of what had happened since. Half of me wanted the phone to magically start working again, for our mobiles to just appear in a bag in a corner of the room, so I could get help, find out what was going on in the outside world—maybe even phone Charlie and make some attempt to explain. But half of me was glad it was still dead. Because then I'd have to answer the call that I knew was just waiting for me, ready to pounce like a beast in long grass.

'Merry Christmas, everybody,' said Maggie, raising her plastic cup of Tizer. 'Are we having fun yet? Wonder if Santa will come on a snow plough this year.'

An eerie silence followed. I stared around the room at the battered boxes of board games on the shelves, our pitiful collection of DVDs and unwatchable videos, cracked computer monitors gathering dust along the counter on the back wall, the pots of faded felt-tips. 'Maybe we should try the computers again?'

'I've tried,' said Maggie. 'If I can't crack the code, none of you losers are going to be able to.'

'When's Mum and Dad coming?' asked Tabby suddenly, headphones around her neck. She was stroking Brody's tummy on the hearth.

'Soon,' I said. I couldn't bring myself to say more.

'Don't say that,' said Clarice. 'No, Tabs, they're not coming—there's too much snow. Neither's Santa.'

Maggie was incensed. 'Shut your face, Clarice, you odious runt.'

'There's no point lying to her,' said Clarice.

'Jesus, insensitive much? Hitler could take lessons from you.'

Tabby went back over to the Christmas tree and picked up a present. She looked at me. I looked at her. She put it down again and went back over to Maggie, starting to whimper.

'Don't worry, Tabs. Your mum and dad'll be here soon, tooled to the teeth with bayonets and assault rifles. That'll be good, won't it?'

Tabby nodded. I went to say something about swearing around Tabby but closed my mouth before the words came out. What was the point? She was probably going to see and hear far worse before the week was out.

'They won't be tooled up, though, will they?' said Clarice. 'Soldiers aren't allowed to take their guns home with them.'

'Shame,' said Maggie, picking her teeth with her fingernail. 'I could find just the spot for a couple of bullets right now.'

'Har bloody har.'

I was starting to feel the full force of my overtiredness.

I'd had adrenalin pumping through me all day long, from finding the burning Tree House to discovering Leon. Not to mention the thing that had caused Leon's leg injury. That was a whole other level of worry my brain couldn't engage with. Natural chemicals had kept me going and thinking and running and doing all day, but now I was depleted. I needed my fluffy duck-feather pillow. I was just afraid of my dreams…

The door opened and everyone immediately sat up as Dianna came in.

'How is he?' asked Regan.

'Drunk,' she replied, rubbing her eyes. 'Asleep. I'll stay with him tonight, so no one else needs to worry. I'll lock us in the apartment.' She looked at Maggie and sat down at the end of the table. 'He's so pale.'

'Can I do anything for him, Dianna?' said Clarice, coming to the table.

Maggie laughed. 'What did you have in mind, Clarice?' I shushed her, throwing a look in Tabby's direction.

'No, I don't think anybody can do anything more,' said Dianna. 'Can we, Nash?'

I shook my head again. 'No, I can't think of anything. But we need help. We can't just keep dosing him up with booze and changing his bandages. He's been bitten. It could get infected. He could need a tetanus shot.'

Tabby interrupted, being very careful not to look at me. 'Dianna, can I open the presents, please? It's nearly Christmas.'

Dianna frowned. 'What? What presents?'

'These,' she said, going over to the Christmas tree and picking up two of the boxes.

'Why are you asking me?'

'Because you're Head Girl,' said Maggie, as flat as a bath mat. 'Aren't you?'

Dianna took one of the boxes and shook it. 'There's nothing in them. They're just for effect. They're not real.'

'Oh pleeease,' said Tabby. 'Please, Dianna.'

'No, they're for *effect*, Tabby!' Throwing both the presents back towards the Christmas tree, Dianna made a hasty, doorknob-fumbling exit. As the slam echoed, Tabby came running back to Maggie for comfort.

'Why do you do it?' said Clarice, glaring at Maggie. 'You know she's fragile.'

'What? What did I say? I didn't say anything!'

We all fell silent again. But I knew what each of us was thinking about. The bite. What Leon had said attacked him. We had a witness now. None of us could deny it.

'It was probably a wildcat. They get them around here,' said Clarice, her nose turned up and away from Maggie, as though she stank.

'Oh, I forgot you present *Countryfile* in your spare time, don't you?'

Regan stood up. Until now she'd been sitting on the footstool to the side of the crackling fire, nibbling corners of sandwiches and eating crisps around the edges, not saying much of anything. 'It was the Beast. The Beast bit him. I bet it's killed Matron too.'

'Shut. Up,' said Clarice. 'You don't know anything.'

'You saw the blood on Nash's hands last night. The blood on Chief Brody. The bite on Leon's leg. It's certain now. It's out there.'

The lights all around us flickered and outside the wind howled and whistled against the window. It was almost worse with the curtains drawn than it had been when it was daylight and we could see the trees blowing outside. Now it was just a noise in the dark night. It could have been anything.

'Nash, talk some sense, please,' said Clarice. 'You don't think it's the actual, real, mythical Beast...do you?'

'It's December twenty-second,' said Maggie, quietly for her.

'Yes,' I said.

'And, we know that no one's coming until Christmas Eve at the earliest.'

'No,' I said.

'So if we don't find those phones, or get the main phone working, then we're gonna be stuck here for at least two more days.'

'Yes.'

'Unless any of us ventures outside to get help...then we're stuck. Aren't we?'

'Assuming they'll be able to get here in two days,' said a voice. Regan, again.

We all knew what she meant. We'd checked the weather reports on the touch-and-go reception of Mrs Saul-Hudson's bedroom TV several times, but it was patchy and scratchy at best. Thick snow on the ground, more storms expected in the south. Planes grounded. Airports in chaos. Postal deliveries stranded. Millions without power.

'What if it keeps snowing over Christmas?' said Clarice, staring out of the bay window at the pitch-black sky and frittering of snow, just beginning to fall.

'It never snows all over Christmas,' said Maggie.

'And man-eating big cats don't exist, according to you,' Regan snipped back. 'I can go out and get help. I'm not afraid of it.'

Maggie looked at her. 'The nearest phone is in Bathory village, over two miles away, that's assuming the phone mast isn't down there and all. Just walking in this weather would be suicidal, but to do it with Baby Baskerville on the loose is idiotic. I'm not turning myself into a YO! Sushi conveyor belt for anyone. Call me Little Miss Unadventurous if you like.'

'No one expected you to suddenly grow a pair, Maggie, don't worry,' said Clarice.

'Uh, excuse me?'

'CAN YOU BOTH JUST STOP ARGUING? JUST FOR FIVE MINUTES?' I shouted. I sounded like one of the PE mistresses shouting at us for not jumping high enough in netball, but I couldn't help it. I had no patience left. We were all staring into an abyss of hopelessness and fear. And the abyss was wetting its pants and laughing at us. 'All you do is argue! I'm sick of it. I'm so sick of it! We need *practical suggestions*.'

'We *have* no practical suggestions,' said Maggie. 'That's why we're arguing.'

'It's all we can do,' Clarice said with a shrug.

'No, it's not,' I said, getting to my feet.

A brief silence was followed with an actual, factual suggestion from Clarice. 'Shall I go and have another look for the phones? Dianna's left the keys, look.' The bunch was lying on the table. 'I could try the staff toilets. And Mrs Saul-Hudson's office or something.'

'Yeah,' I said.

'We've got four days' worth of food, at least, in the larder,' said Maggie. We were all looking at her, as though we expected her to make a joke, but she wasn't joking for once. She was offering practical feedback on our situation.

'It's all pretty ropey stuff now, there's nothing fresh, but we can live on it, as long as we're careful.'

'And there's water in the taps,' said Clarice. 'As long as the pipes don't freeze. We have weapons in the PE cupboard, we have lockable doors…just in case.'

I had a feeling Maggie's practicality wouldn't last long. 'What's the point of locking the doors?' she said. 'There's the small matter of the escaped murderer on the Headmistress's bed. Don't forget to add him to our list of assets.' She got up off her beanbag and barged past Clarice, into the barely lit corridor. Tabby followed her out, the ever-present Babbitt dangling from her belt.

I stood up. 'We can get through this.' I followed Clarice and Brody through the door and, as I turned out the common room light, I felt Regan's hand on my arm, holding me back.

'Clarice, could you let Brody out for me, please?' I asked her and she took his collar, without argument. I turned to Regan.

'I mean it, Nash,' she said. 'If we can't find the phones, I'll go out there. I'll go and get help. I'm not afraid of it. I'm not afraid of anything.'

'You haven't seen it, though, Regan. It's huge. It's real.'

'I lost both my grandmothers last year. Cancer,' she said. 'One after the other. There's nothing worse than losing someone you love. That's the worst monster in the world.'

I didn't know what to say. 'Regan…'

'I'm not afraid of the Beast. Not like Maggie is. Come with me,' she said.

I followed her up the corridor towards the Reference Library, her second home.

'Regan, I really need to get some sleep. I think you should too.'

'No, wait,' she said, as animated as someone who'd just

had fourteen hours' sleep. She located *Myths and Legends of Small Town England* from the History shelves and carried it to the central reading table, opening it at a page folded down. 'Look at this article. It's from an old history of Bathory and the surrounding villages and fields. There is an old law of the school, laid down in 1858, that "whosoever captures the Beast shall inherit Bathory Manor and its environs". What do you think about that?'

I sighed. 'I think it's nonsense. Look, I don't know what that thing is out there, Regan, but I know it's not hundreds of years old. That's impossible.'

'Yes, but who's to say there isn't more than one?' she said, her eyes wild with excitement. 'The latest in a long line of beasts roaming these parts? When the old Duke and Duchess lived here, they kept big cats in the Birdcage. They called it that so their visitors would be more shocked when they brought out the Beasts. They kept all sorts of things. Lions and tigers—'

'And bears?' I smiled.

'Yes!' she exclaimed. 'Bears and jaguars and panthers. Loads of them. But they kept escaping because the Duke didn't reinforce the Birdcage well enough. It's more than likely that a jaglion, or several of them, exists in these parts. That they kept inbreeding, and—'

'Yeah, okay, maybe it is that. Or a wildcat or something,' I said. She turned the page and revealed a picture that froze my blood. A black beast. With orange eyes. Pointed ears. Glaring at me. 'That's…a jaglion, is it?'

Regan nodded. 'That's what I think the Beast is. I've done a lot of reading on it. I've found a lot of things in those woods—that spine I showed you, animal skulls, bones. It's killed people, Nash. It could kill us. Imagine, if I killed the

Beast, I'd save the school. I'd become a hero. My father might even allow me home more than once a year.'

I reached down and closed the book on the table. A puff of dust flew out from its pages. 'We'll talk more about it in the morning. Come on, we need to get some sleep.'

'I'll sleep when I'm dead,' she said, leaving the book on the table. She threw me the briefest look on her way out of the room, the same look she'd given me when we'd gone to look at the spine in the woods. Her eyes were as dead as a shark's.

# 21
## The Omen

'*Father Christmas doesn't even exist,*' I told him.

'*He does. Where do you think all the presents come from?*'

'*Mum and Dad.*'

'*No, they come from Santa.*'

'*Why is Mum's handwriting on them then? Why do some of them say "To Seb love from Mummy and Daddy" and some say "To Nash love from Mummy and Daddy"?*'

'*Yeah,* those *ones come from Mum and Dad, but the rest of them come from Santa.*'

'*Are you sure?*'

'*Yeah. I'm your big brother. I'm always sure.*'

Some people had gone to town with Christmas lights that year, for charity. We'd taken a walk down our road, in our pyjamas, coats and boots, to walk the dog and see the houses all lit up. We put the coins our mum had given us in the charity buckets and watched illuminated reindeer and dancing snowmen and little Father Christmases climbing up ladders. The issue of the real Father Christmas's existence had been niggling me all day and I couldn't get a straight answer out of Mum or Dad. I knew Seb would always tell me the truth, though. He explained everything to me. Why things happened. What things meant. And that day I wanted to believe he was telling me the truth.

'*Can we sneak out when Mum and Dad are in bed, and eat the mince pie and milk?*'

'*Don't we always?*'

'*Can we have pancakes in the morning?*'

'*Yep.*'

'*Seb?*'

'*Yeah?*'

'*Are you sure Father Christmas is really real?*'

'*Yes, Natasha, I'm sure.*' He always called me Natasha when I was nagging.

'*Seb?*'

'*What?*'

'*Can we always do this on Christmas Eve?*'

'*Yeah, 'course we can.*'

'*Even when you're married and have a wife?*'

'*Yeah.*'

'*Are you sure?*'

'*I'm your big brother, of course I'm sure.*'

Seb said that all the time, about everything. I never really believed him, though, until that night. Because as we were walking home, I heard a noise.

A magical noise.

Looking back now, aged sixteen, I realise it could have been someone's TV, or someone with a party hat on, walking back from the pub, but I swear it wasn't. I was only eight years old at the time, but I know what I heard.

I heard jingle bells. Crossing the sky. Just for about ten seconds, maybe fifteen.

That was Santa. That was Christmas. That was truth— me and Seb, in our pyjamas and coats, walking home to spend Christmas with our family, me happy and safe in the knowledge that whatever my brother told me was the absolute truth. I never doubted Seb again.

Until I'd got that phone call. It was all I could think about as I constantly entered and left sleep. I don't know what time it was when I heard the noise.

We all heard it this time.

I sat up, bolt upright in my bed, and heard it again, loud and clear, right outside the window.

A growl.

'What the hell,' said Maggie, flinging back her covers and running to the window to rip the curtains apart. Tabby and Clarice got out of bed too.

But not Regan. Regan stayed asleep.

We all stood at the window, bed-headed and bleary-eyed, frightened and confused. Tabby was cuddling Babbitt and shaking, and I stroked her back.

'Nash, we've got to get out of here,' said Maggie. 'That thing is stalking the building every night.'

'I know, I know,' I said. My brain was fogging up thickly. I couldn't think what to do.

'Is there any remote chance there's a gun in the school?' said Clarice, getting her dressing gown and Ugg boots on.

'Yeah,' said Maggie. 'We're taking GCSE Automatic Weapons next year, didn't you know?'

'You know what I mean. Anything we could use to kill it, or frighten it off, even?'

'No,' said Maggie. 'This is a girls' school. In England. We're not even allowed dressing gown cords.'

'We're in the middle of farming country. Surely there's a shotgun or two on the premises?'

'Well, if there are, I wouldn't know where to find them,' I said, going to the wardrobe to fetch my dressing gown.

'What are you doing, Nash?'

I didn't really know what I was doing. I just had to do something. 'Going to look,' I said, shoving my feet into my boots.

'No, don't go out there,' said Clarice. 'You're insane!'

'No, I'm not,' I replied, walking to Regan's bed and tugging back the duvet to reveal three pillows, end to end, along the middle of her bed. 'But I know who is.'


We stood at the front door—me, Maggie and Clarice. Dianna must have heard us as pretty soon we heard the unlocking of a door up the main stairs and down she came, blearing-eyed and dressing-gowned, from the Saul-Hudsons' apartment.

'What is it?' she whispered.

'We don't know,' said Clarice. 'We're just going to see.'

Tabby waited on the bottom step of the main staircase, Brody by her side.

'On three, I'm going to open the door, okay?' I told them, hands clutching the Chubb lock and the doorknob below it. 'Don't make any sudden movements or noises.'

Maggie stood behind me, brandishing a carving knife

she'd got from the kitchen and bouncing on the balls of her feet.

'What if it's not Regan? What if Regan's in the loo or something?' said Clarice, her torch beam shaking in her gloved grip. 'What if it's…' She looked directly at Dianna.

Dianna looked at me, then at Maggie, then back at Clarice. 'It's not Leon, okay? He's asleep upstairs. He's in no fit state to walk, let alone prowl the grounds. Anyway, he knows he's not allowed out of the bedroom.'

'Yeah, well, I ain't taking any chances,' said Maggie, adjusting her grip on the carving knife and bouncing on the balls of her feet, her dressing gown flapping open to reveal her Snoopy pyjamas. She bit on the flat edge of the knife blade between her lips while she double-knotted it. 'Go on, Nash. Open it.'

I turned the Chubb and twisted the doorknob. All at once, a huge breath of freezing cold air and snow blew into the Hall. Tabby clutched Brody's neck as the four of us stepped out into the dark night.

There on the doorstep was a large black lump.

Clarice screamed. Dianna ran back inside. Maggie bashed into me in her haste to see what it was. I shone my torch down onto it.

A dead sheep.

'I'm going to be sick,' Clarice said behind her hand, following Dianna indoors.

Maggie shone her torch all around to see if anyone was out there, if anyone was going to own up to the present they had left for us. But there was no one.

'Okay, this is just weird now,' she said, crunching out into the snow as her torch swept as far as the beam would allow. 'There's not even any footprints.'

'It's still snowing,' I said, bending down to take a closer look at the sheep. It was a young one, not much more than a lamb. 'Poor thing.'

'There's nothing out there,' said Maggie, returning from the darkness to join me on the porch. 'What's going on, Nash? This is starting to freak me right out.'

The sheep's head was red with blood. I gently poked at it, and it almost came away from the rest of its body. 'It doesn't look injured anywhere else,' I said. 'It's got puncture wounds here and here on its neck. See?'

Just then, we both caught sight of another light coming up the drive. A single beam, shuddery and moving, like someone jogging with a torch in their hand. We didn't take our eyes from it as it came ever closer. Then a figure emerged from the blackness, stopping dead in its tracks when it saw us on the porch.

Regan.

'Why weren't you in bed?' Maggie, our resident Bad Cop, asked again, circling Regan like a shark as she sat at the end of the first table in the Refectory.

'How long had you been outside? You must be freezing,' said Good Cop Dianna, sitting on the edge of the table.

'It's you, isn't it?' said Clarice. 'The Beast of Bathory?'

'Hardly,' said Regan, folding her arms.

'Was it you the other night, and all?' asked Maggie. 'Making all those noises me and Nash heard outside the window?'

'You heard noises?' said Dianna.

'Yeah. Scuffling noises. And weird throaty purrs, all round the school.'

Regan shrugged.

'You need to start talking,' I told her.

Regan smiled, which none of us could read. 'I was try-ing to lure it,' she said finally.

'What do you mean, lure it?' said Maggie.

'Lure it in. I was going to lure it in and catch it. And kill it.'

'Lure it into the school?' shrieked Dianna.

Regan shrugged again. 'If need be, yes. I could have handled it.'

Maggie laughed. 'I'd like to see a seven-stone weakling like you up against a six hundred pound wildcat. *How* were you planning to kill it? Force your head down its throat until it choked?'

'No,' she said calmly. 'I would have trapped it in the kitchen and killed it in there. With one of the javelins or a knife.'

Maggie looked at me. 'Whose turn is it next to put all our lives in danger? Dianna's had a go, now this freak. Do you wanna have a stab, Nash?' Then she stopped short, like a thought had just occurred to her. 'Hang on—*how* were you luring it in? Did you kill that sheep?'

'No, of course I didn't,' she said, taking off her glasses to clean them on the hem of her nightshirt. 'I told you out-side, that's nothing to do with me. I was at the back of the school and walked around to the top of the drive. The sheep wasn't there when I went out.'

Silence.

'So *how* were you luring it?' Maggie asked again.

'Meat,' she replied.

'What meat?'

'Turkey mostly. And some stewing steak I found in the fridge. And half a joint of beef I found in the freezer a few days ago.'

'*You* stole the turkeys?' cried Maggie. 'Just so you could go out and play Hello Kitty Wanna Bite Me every night? I got put in the Chiller for that!'

'I didn't mean for that to happen,' said Regan, putting her glasses back on and clasping her hands in her lap. 'Look, none of this actually matters anyway. It won't come anywhere near me, with or without meat. You're quite safe. I haven't even seen it.'

I bent down to her level and looked at her. 'Regan, who put the sheep on the doorstep?'

'I don't *know*,' she shouted at me. 'It's nothing to do with me!'

'Maybe it's safe to go outside—if Regan's been doing it every night?' said Clarice. 'Maybe tomorrow we could try to get somewhere. To get help?'

'Maybe,' said Dianna. 'But what about the sheep?'

We all looked at Regan again. Her parting had gone frizzy from wearing a woolly hat and her plaits were coming unravelled. 'The Beast must have left it there. I swear I didn't.'

'Why would it leave it on the doorstep?' said Maggie.

'Cats leave their kill on doorsteps for a reason. It's trying to teach us.'

'Teach us what?' said Maggie, folding her arms but keeping her carving knife solidly gripped in one fist.

'How to hunt,' she replied.

# 22
## Possession

After a lengthy interrogation, we had only established one thing—it was Regan making the 'luring' noises in the night. So desperate was she to find and kill the Beast, just to stand out and be counted at Bathory, she'd been going outside, night after night, after we'd all gone to sleep, trying to catch it. Luring it with tidbits and stolen meat from the school freezers. The thing I didn't get though was the dead sheep. I believed her when she said she hadn't killed it and put it there. And she'd said it wasn't there when she'd first gone out. So who *had* put it there? Was she right; was it trying to teach us in some way? Or was it trying to threaten us? And if so, what would it put there next?

I had a dream in the night that the phone was working. I dreamed I heard it ringing and its ring echoed all the way up Long Corridor. At first light, I was up and washed and dressed and rushing down Main Stairs to check it.

But it was still dead.

Then I heard a noise in the kitchens, a knocking noise. I went to investigate, but everything was still—no one about and everything was as it should be. Leftover cakes and crisps under cling-filmed paper plates on the big metal table, Brody lying down in one of the utility rooms. He looked up at me and his tail started wagging, knocking against the side of his big red plastic bed.

'That was you, was it?' I said to him, crouching down beside to ruffle his head. 'You're a pretty useless guard dog.'

Brody got up, stretched out both his back legs and shook himself awake. He walked over to the back door and sat down, looking up at the handle. I rolled up the blind and looked out. There was white as far as the eye could see, right across the formal garden and the tennis courts and fields beyond. An eerie, glacial world, clear of any moving signs of malice. I still didn't want to open the door.

'Can't you cross your legs or something?' I looked at his brown china water bowl—it was completely empty. 'Evidently not. Okay, go on then,' I said, pulling both bolts across on the back door. I watched Brody walk across the Great Plat, the sunken garden area reserved for bedding plants, walkways and rills. He left his footprints behind him, sniffed around, cocked his leg. Unconcerned. Good enough for me.

I refilled his bowls, then hotfooted it back upstairs to the Saul-Hudsons' apartment, where Dianna was sitting up on the bed next to Leon.

'Hi,' I said quietly, poking my head around the door.

The TV flickered quietly in the corner. 'Hi,' she said. She didn't look as though she had slept a wink.

'Any news?' I said, creeping in to stand at the foot of the bed. I watched Leon's chest, going up, going down. His breathing seemed more settled than it had been yesterday.

'Worst snowstorm yet in the South-west expected to-night,' she said, switching it off with the remote. 'Planes still grounded at all the airports. A couple of them have re-opened in Scotland and the North-east, but traffic is still bad on the motorways and motorists are being advised only to make journeys if they're absolutely essential.' She was saying it like a newsreader. She must have been watching the hourly forecasts all night long.

'I meant Leon, actually, but that's good to know too.'

'Oh,' she said, looking at him. 'I don't know. He doesn't seem as pale.'

'It's cold in here,' I said. 'Didn't the radiators come on at six?'

She shook her head, cuddling herself for warmth. 'Maybe the boiler's packed up now as well as the phone?'

'We'll have to get the plug-in radiators out of the store-room if it has. Did you sleep?'

She scrunched her nose. 'Fits and starts. Is Regan up yet?'

'I don't know and I don't give a toss,' I said. 'Maggie was ready to throw her out the dorm window when we got back upstairs last night.'

'Can't believe she thought she could catch it.'

'Tell me about it.'

Dianna edged herself off the bed. 'I'm going to get him some toast for when he wakes up. Do you want anything?'

'No thanks,' I said, sitting down in her place as she left

the room. I'd just opened Mrs Saul-Hudson's bedside drawer
to have a cheeky nose about when I heard a voice behind me.

'There's no Viagra. I've looked.'

Leon's eyes were open and his head was turned to me,
but still lolling heavy on the pillow.

'I wasn't looking for Viagra,' I said, my cheeks heating
up. 'Anyway, that's in their bathroom cabinet, top shelf.'

'What are you, their resident spy?'

'More like a slave. Did you sleep okay?'

'Ish,' he croaked, with a cough. He manoeuvred himself
up to more of a sitting position. 'What day is it? Christ my
head's thumping.'

Clearly, he had a hangover. 'The twenty-third. Happy
Christmas Eve Eve,' I said.

'Yeah, yeah.' Dianna had given him one of Mr Saul-
Hudson's clean shirts to wear, the buttons open right to the
waist. I started unpeeling the night bandage from his ankle.
His wound had started to scab over. 'I need to change this,
okay?'

He nodded and sat up, easing himself back to sit against
the headboard, his shirt opening a little more. I went and
got the one remaining bandage out of the first aid box.

'You're good at this,' he told me. 'You should be a nurse.'

I squinted at the wound on his ankle. 'It looks better
today.'

'Doesn't feel it. Ahh!' he said, as his wound was once
again exposed to the air.

'It's stopped bleeding. Clotting nicely.'

'Cool. Is the phone back on yet?'

'No,' I said, winding the new bandage around his foot.
'We're just waiting for someone to come. We daren't go out
there with the You-Know-What about.'

''Course, yeah.'

'Do you want the TV on?'

'Yeah, in a bit,' he said, staring at the blank white wall ahead. 'When the phone does come back on, you'll call the police, won't you?'

I tucked in the end of the bandage so it was neat and tidy. 'I don't know.'

'You'll have to. I can't stop you. If I'd known what escaping had in store for me, I'd have stayed in the clink.' I smiled. 'You're cracking-looking, you know.'

I felt myself blush and quickly set to work tidying away the first aid box. He watched me.

'There's no need to blush. Accept it. You're gorgeous.'

'All done,' I announced firmly, scooping up the dirty bandages and dumping them in the wicker basket at the side of the bed. Then I scurried to the en suite to wash my hands.

When I came back, he had settled back down onto his pillow and his eyes were closing.

'I'll come back later and see how you're doing.'

'No, stay here,' he said, his eyes closing. 'Talk to me.'

'About what?'

'Anything you like. Tell me what Di gets up to when I'm not around.'

I couldn't stop looking at his face. His bare chest. He looked wonderful in bed, like a jaguar reclining on a thick branch at the zoo. 'I shouldn't gossip about her.'

'Yeah, you should.'

I went back to the bed and sat down on the edge. 'How come she has a different accent to you? You're Northern and she talks like—'

'Royalty?'

'Yes.'

'Cos she puts it on,' he said. 'She's from Manchester, same as me. We've never been alike. Mum sent her here to get her away from me. From my influence.' He rolled his eyes.

Every chance I got to look at his body when he wasn't looking at me, I took it. I couldn't help it. He was like a scab I couldn't stop picking. I knew it wouldn't do me any good and would probably cause me pain in the long run but I just had to. Then he caught me looking. I snapped my eyes away, as though I'd just seen something incredibly interesting in Mrs Saul-Hudson's chintzy print curtains.

He reached for his glass of water on the side table and took a swig.

'So...Clarice?' I said, pulling at a feather in the eider-down bedspread.

He sighed. 'Don't remind me.'

I laughed. 'I don't need to ask what you saw in her.'

'Gimme a break. I've been banged up for two years. If something like that's on a plate, you don't stop to ask who the chef is.'

'Gross.'

'Wish it'd been you,' he said.

This time I went bright red. I could almost hear my blood pumping, so hot had he made me for him, without any ef-fort at all.

'But I get the impression you'd be a harder fish to fry, wouldn't you? You'd make me work for it. I like that in a girl.'

Just the sight of him, lying there, half naked, injured, was enough to make me giddy. It hadn't been this strong with Charlie, but then maybe it was the bad boy should-have-been-a-rock-star thing he had going on. I'd never believed it before, but maybe there *was* something about a guy who was the polar opposite of you. Like a painful tooth you have to keep prodding to see how much it hurts. It's irresistible.

A thought occurred. I wasn't sure whether it was Maggie's constant paranoia that Leon was a bad lot or my own subconscious, but maybe he was flirting with me for a reason. Maybe he wanted something from me. Once a con, always a con. But what was he after?

'Read me a story,' he said. 'Or just…whassit…paraphrase. Summarise. Something you memorised once. Just to get me off to sleep again.'

The only book I knew off by heart was *The Grinch Who Stole Christmas*. Seb always read it to me at this time of year when we were younger. I'd like to have said it was a biblical tract or some Pablo Neruda poetry or something equally meaningful or literary, but it wasn't any of those things. But it meant the world to me and I wanted to share it. Jailbird or not, he was in too much of a weakened state to try anything at the moment.

So I began. He seemed to enjoy it. His eyes were closed, but he smiled, like I used to smile. 'Keep going.' His eyelids began to flutter, and pretty soon he was snoring. I'd just got to the bit where the Grinch was 'grinchishly humming' when I heard footsteps out on the landing.

Dianna came in with a plate piled high with buttered toast and jam.

'That's the last of the bread. I couldn't find any more in the freezer,' she announced, placing it beside her brother on the nightstand. She looked at him. 'Is he still asleep?'

'Yeah. He was pretty knackered.'

Apropos of nothing, she started to cry again.

'I'm sorry,' she said. 'I'm so tired. Every time I closed my eyes I see that…thing. What if it gets in here, Nash? What if it's got Regan's scent now?'

'It won't get in here.'

'You don't know that. I'm scared.'

'I know.'

'Leon could die!'

'He won't. He just needs a couple of days to get his strength back. Look, he's breathing evenly,' I said, going round to Leon's side of the bed and feeling his neck. 'And I changed his bandage. It looks better today.'

'Does it?' she said eagerly. 'Really?'

'Yes. His pulse is fairly strong too. Why don't you go and grab some sleep? They'll all be awake now so you can have the dorm to yourself. You'll feel much better.'

She shook her head. 'I really used to resent you,' she said, sitting next to me on the edge of the bed. 'You're always winning medals and prizes at Speech Day and stuff. Always in with the Saul-Hudsons. You have so much power and influence in this school. And look at me. Just a wannabe. I just wanted something for my mum to be proud of… I feel awful.'

'Let's forget it, shall we?'

'No, I can't forget it. I'm a useless Head Girl. I'm a useless sister. I've done nothing to help this situation at all, nothing.'

'Yeah, you are pretty useless,' I said, smiling.

She looked at me. She sort of smiled, sort of didn't.

'Look, stop beating yourself up, Dianna. I wanted to be powerful too. That's why I wanted Head Girl. To feel powerful. To feel like I'd done something here. We're all in the same boat.'

Her voice dropped. 'I'm going to turn him in,' she said quietly.

'What?'

'As soon as the phones come back on. At least in prison he'll be safe. I don't want my brother to die.' She sniffed. 'I know I said some bad things about him to you, but I do love him really.'

'I think that's the right thing to do,' I said. 'I don't know how much longer we can hold out here. I mean, his ankle looks okay, but I don't know about his appendix wound. If he was in hospital when he escaped, he probably should be back there.'

'And the food's going down at a rate of knots. We're going to have to start rationing.'

'Yeah, that's a good idea,' I said. 'See? Now you're thinking practically.' I never thought me and Dianna would be having a conversation like this. I'd resented her for so long for trying to piggyback onto my role at Bathory, but here we were. Civil. Friendly. Understanding. No frills. No pretence. No problems. It was quite out of the ordinary.

Then Dianna's face suddenly creased up.

'Oh, Nash, I'm sorry. I'm so sorry. I was just so jealous of you.' More tears dripped down her face in quick succession. 'And you were siding with Maggie over everything and I just… I don't know why I did it. I'm sorry, I took it. I don't think you'll ever forgive me.'

'Took what?'

'I was there when it came. It was a few days ago—the last time we saw the postman.'

'What do you mean? What did you take?' I snapped back from her like she'd electrocuted me. 'What, Dianna?'

She reached underneath the pillow behind her and pulled

out a crumpled, creased and folded envelope. Addressed to me.

In Seb's handwriting.

I could hear them all in the bedroom as I sat on the third step up on Main Stairs. They were tearing into Dianna, all chipping in, even Regan, who never normally said anything unless she had to. Clearly, she was glad someone else was taking the heat.

'You're a freak. An actual freak. There was no good reason in the world for you taking that letter, Dianna!' That was Maggie.

'I know, I know.' More sobbing.

'It's well weird. Why did you do it?' Clarice.

In between sobs, I gleaned that she'd taken it so that she could have it for herself—something else I couldn't have. It was her job to give out the post, but no one ever thanked her for it. So she took a little something for herself. My letter.

'Piss-poor, Dianna.' Maggie again.

'I kept trying to give it to her, but every time I went to, I chickened out. And more and more time passed and it got to the point where I couldn't give it to her because it meant it was such a big deal. So I didn't.'

'This could be her last ever contact with her brother and you read it before she did!'

'It's so bad, Dianna.' Regan this time.

'I know. I know. I'm so sorry.'

'How long have you had it?' Regan again.

'She will never, ever forgive you for this. Never.' Maggie again.

Dianna ran out of the room, sobbing her heart out. She ran down the stairs, stopping when she came to my step. She was behind me, just for a moment, silent. Then she ran to the bottom, across Main Hall, and out into the kitchen corridor.

All was silent. All was still. I took the letter out of the envelope. Along with it fell a wood-carved pencil and a single coffee bean.

*Dear Natasha Emily Staley,*

*This is from our visit to a local township today. Nicest people ever! The pencil was made by an old woman who works outside her house and sells them to tourists and the coffee bean is, well, a coffee bean. Best coffee I ever had, from one of the local cafés. Seriously, you've never had coffee like it! Also tried plantain for first time, this thing called a* Tres Leches *cake (yeah I had three of them, so sue me) and this drink called a* lulada. *I can feel the weight going on my hips, darling, but we're walking loads too so it probably levels out.*

*We're going to Bogota tomorrow, which I'm told is the murder capital of South America. So that'll be nice...I'll try and pick you up a pencil there too.*

*Hope UR okay and school ain't getting you down too much. I guess the Head Girl thing's coming up pretty soon, isn't it? If you don't get it, they're morons who don't know what's good for them. And don't be afraid to tell them that either. Stake your claim. It's about time they put some faith in you. Gnash your teeth once in a while, my little Gnasher. It's like I'm always saying—you've got to toughen up.*

*Can't wait for Christmas: our walk around the block, pancakes in the morning and a laugh at Dad trying to carve the turkey and watch* The Santa Clause

*at the same time. Oh and presents and stockings and
all that shit too.
See you soon, Sissy Woo.
Lotza love Sebastian Matthew Staley, The One, and
Only XXX*

I went back to the dorm and lay on my bed. I stayed
there for hours, reading the letter, stroking it like it was
the most precious jewel, and smelling the coffee bean. And
the handmade pencil with Colombia's motto written on it
*Libertad y Orden*. Freedom and Order. I tried to smell Seb
on the letter but I couldn't. I just smelled paper. And Dianna's peach deodorant.

*See you soon.*

*See you soon.*

*See you soon.*

*Murder capital of South America. Murder capital of
South America. Murder capital of South America. Murder
capital of South America. Murder capital of South America.*

I believed it now. The phone call had sowed the seed. This
had only made it blossom in my head like a black rose. He
wasn't coming back. I wasn't going to see him again. I had
to face that now.

My brother was dead. It was the first time I'd really felt
it, even without knowing for sure. I could see my parents,
there at the British Embassy in Colombia, making plans to
bring his body back to England. My mother inconsolable;
my dad's face like it was when Nanna died, drawn and
pale and tear-stained, like I'd never seen him before. Both
of them broken.

We'd have to plan a funeral, like we'd planned Nan's.
We'd have that disgusting fat man from the funeral parlour

come to visit us again, and sit at our dining table and eat our cake and drink our tea, and promise us 'the utmost respect at this most distressing time' and we'd have to look through that horrific catalogue of flowers and caskets and pick the right one. And we'd have to choose hymns and a reading, even though Seb never set foot inside a church, and then some vicar who'd never even met Seb would get up and talk about him like they were friends from way back. Yuck.

And we'd have to choose songs to play at the service, even though I knew the only song Seb would have wanted was 'Killing in the Name' by Rage Against the Machine and no way would Mum want that. She'd probably choose some hymn and then there'd be a big argument.

I could see it all, in my head, like a bad dream coming true.

And pain. There was so much pain inside me. And there was nothing I could do to stop it. I just felt angry. And sad. And then so angry. And then so sad again. It came in waves.

My heart thudded like an underground train. I thought about going downstairs and walking out into that snow and giving myself to the Beast. Calling for it. Waiting for it. Not even putting up a fight.

*COME AND GET ME! I'M READY FOR YOU. TAKE ME! KILL ME!*

But I didn't even have the will to do that. I just wanted to hug my letter and hold the pencil against my cheek, smell the coffee bean on my pillow and never open my eyes.

Now I kept seeing the dead sheep behind my eyelids, lying cold on the doorstep. Its dirty wool. Its red throat. Its dull, dead eyes. Seb's dull, dead eyes.

Lamb to the slaughter.

Lamb to the slaughter.

Slaughter to the lamb.

I didn't hear the door open, didn't hear Tabby crossing the floor. Not until I felt her lying beside me and her arms around my waist. I turned round and hugged her back.

'All right, Mousey?' I sniffed, resting my chin on top of her head. 'Where did you spring from? The Hidey Hole?'

I felt her nod. 'I was in the Fiction Library. Are you coming down for dinner? Regan's cooking it.'

'Joy,' I muttered. She was back in the fold then. 'What are we having?'

'Cheese pie and chocolate cake with mint Angel Delight. I made the Angel Delight.'

'Wow, did you?' I said. 'Who made the cheese pie?'

'Clarice peeled the potatoes and I helped to grate the cheese. And Maggie's doing the washing-up. She told Clarice off for grating too much cheese and they had an argument.'

'Did they?'

She nodded. 'Yeah, and it was loud. Maggie pulled Clarice's hair.'

'Oh dear,' I said.

'And Regan walked Brody for you.'

'She walked him?' I said, pocketing the coffee bean and the pencil—all I had left of Seb.

'Yeah, but Regan didn't see the monster when she walked him. She said I should call you for dinner.'

'Okay,' I said, manoeuvring myself off the bed. 'What did Dianna do?'

'I don't know,' she said. 'I haven't seen her.'

I looked at her. 'Why, has she been up in Leon's room?'

She shook her head. 'I don't know. She was a bit sad.

Maggie said she was useless and then called her a rude word and she went out the door and didn't come back.'

'Out? Out where?'

'She ran off. Can I have two lots of chocolate cake, Nash?'

Then we both heard it: travelling from the kitchens along the corridor, through the open door of Main Hall, up the staircase and into our dormitory. The sound of one person's horrific scream.

Maggie's.

# 23
## Let the Right One In

'It attacked me...th-th-the Beast!'

Maggie was curled into a ball against the fridge door when I rushed into the kitchen with Tabby. Apparently, she'd been emptying the dustpan outside the back door when something big and brown and hairy had lunged at her and growled.

'What did it look like?' I bent down to her.

'What do you mean, what did it look like? What do you *think* it looked like, a pickled onion? It looked like a bloody massive hairy wolf!' She was shaking hard.

I smoothed her hair gently. 'A wolf?'

'Yes, a wolf. You know, brown hairy things with sharp fangs. Scares the crap out of little pigs and kids in red coats?'

Clarice ran in.

Regan piped up, 'The Beast is supposed to be cat-like. Like a big black panther, or a sabre tooth tiger. It's definitely not a wolf.'

'How many times have you seen it, Regan?' Maggie shouted, getting to her feet. 'It was brown and it had big pointed ears and huge teeth and yellow eyes and... urghhhhhh! It was disgusting.'

Clarice was biting her pink nails in the doorway. They were all stumpy. 'Did it hurt you? Are you hurt or—'

'No, no, I was back inside before it came any closer. I just saw this horrible head and then I ran in and bolted the back door.'

I could smell alcohol on Maggie's breath as she spoke. I went to the window and climbed up on the rung below the sink to look. Everything outside was white, as usual, as far as I could see. The formal terrace was there, with its snowed-over flower beds, bare bushes and frozen fountain. All lay undisturbed. No fangs, no fur. No nothing.

I climbed down and faced them again. 'It's not there now. There's nothing there.'

I saw the cheese pie on the side, steaming slightly and browned perfectly on top. It looked almost appetising. 'Let's eat.'

'Never mind the sodding cheese pie,' said Maggie, visibly sweating now with stress. 'Nash, this situation is getting more and more fucked up and it needs to get UN-fucked right now.'

Tabby went over to Maggie and clutched her hand. I beckoned Regan and Clarice to follow into the corridor.

'How much has Maggie had to drink?' I asked.

'I don't know,' said Regan. 'She went to check on Leon about an hour ago and they were drinking then.'

'Who was drinking?'

'Maggie and Clarice.'

I looked at Clarice. 'How much has she had to drink?'

She shrugged. 'A bit. A lot. I don't know. I wasn't keeping tabs.'

'Where's Dianna?'

'I don't know. She was pretty upset about your letter. Everyone was so angry with her that she ran off.'

'Did she go outside?'

'I don't know. I think so.'

I felt a deep stab of guilt, despite Dianna's crappy behaviour. What if the Beast already had her scent?

Regan whispered, 'The booze cabinet's nearly empty too. Do you think… Do you think Maggie might have imagined the Beast?'

'No, I don't think she imagined it, she gave too much of a description. And I don't think she's lying; she's too shaken up. But she said it looked like a wolf, not a cat. That goes against everything we've heard so far from Leon and the myth book. And…'

They both stared at me. Neither of them was going to speak, so I had to.

'…it's not what I saw that night in netball.'

Regan's mouth opened wide and her face grew about a foot in length. 'So you *did* see it! I knew it, I knew you saw it!'

'Keep your voice down. I don't want to frighten Tabby.'

Clarice started biting her other hand, which had even less fingernails. 'So you've definitely seen it? What, recently?'

'About a week ago, I think. I don't know. But it didn't come anywhere near me and it didn't look like a wolf.'

Regan's face was full of alarm. Her glasses steamed up. 'This is bad, isn't it?'

'I've no idea *what* this is,' I said. I caught my breath. Call it bravado or a death wish, but I just wanted to see it for myself now. I wanted to scare it away. I wanted to do something; something other than just being afraid. 'I'm going to go out. And take a look round.'

'Are you mad?' said Clarice. 'Why would you do that? Why would you go outside when clearly something horrible is out there, waiting to attack you?'

I shrugged and looked at Regan.

'I'll get the javelins,' she said.


Regan and I suited ourselves up in jumpers and coats and snuck out the side door to the kitchen so that nobody would stop us from going. Not that anybody would have. Maggie was still too traumatised, Tabby was too young, Clarice thought we were nuts and Dianna had gone AWOL.

I slowly turned the knob and we stepped out into the clawing cold air. The whiteness was still startling, but we could pick out landmarks on the horizon—hedges, fences, walls, follies.

Regan stepped forward and peered around the corner in both directions. 'Clear.' I joined her on the path of the formal terrace. Looking down, I saw she had two small spray cans in her grasp. One was a half-empty Dove 48h, the other was a travel-sized Elnett Super Hold, almost full. She'd taken them both from the Saul-Hudsons' en suite.

'Thought you could spray it in its eyes or something if it gets too close,' she said, handing me the Dove one.

'Thanks, Regan.' I took the can from her and stuffed it in my coat pocket.

Snow crunched beneath our boots as we walked, slowly and determined, our breath clouding as we breathed. Every sound was a threat.

Something wasn't right. I couldn't put my finger on what, but there was a charge in the atmosphere. It wasn't just me and Regan outside. There was something else out here too.

My heart thrummed painfully as we rounded the building, making our way down the steps towards the formal gardens and the Great Plat on the west side of the school.

*'You need anger and you need fear. You'll think better,'* I heard in my head.

Seb's voice. Karate on the rug. *Always teach not by words but by example. Only a true attack has a true defence.*

He was always telling me that fear was a good thing to keep you on your toes. I never believed him. I still didn't. Regan didn't look scared at all. The javelin was grasped in her left hand, her eyes ahead, always searching. Waiting. I remembered what she'd said about her grandmothers. She wasn't afraid of the Beast. The Beast was the cancer. The Beast was her fear. The Beast was how people saw her at the school.

It was everything she wanted to get rid of.

'It's got much colder, hasn't it?' Her breath was a cloud in her face.

'Yeah. The barometer in the Hall read six below.'

'I've got a hole in my glove.'

'I've got a hole in my tights.'

I laughed, even though it wasn't funny. Regan smiled.

All was still and unthreatening as far as the eye could see. The ponds were frozen in the Ladies Garden and the Rotunda, and nothing had disturbed the places where little white piles of snow had settled on tree branches, hedges and the tops of walls. A choir of frosty crocuses hung with bowed heads to our left. Not a sound came. No birdsong even. Everything the same.

Until I looked down.

I nudged Regan, and she followed my line of sight to the pathway beneath our feet, leading up some slate steps to the formal garden and borders, which the kitchen window overlooked. There were footprints—small and semi-circular, like they'd been made by hooves—dotted in a straight line towards the steps, up the steps, and beyond.

We followed them.

'Why would they be hoof prints, Nash?'

'I don't know,' I whispered, steadying my javelin in my fist.

'What the hell has two hooves?'

'I don't know,' I said again, quietly, as we followed the line of prints towards the kitchen window. 'Mr Tumnus? The devil?'

Suddenly Regan's eyes widened and she thrust her javelin directly forward, missing my face by inches. I gasped and ducked away just in time.

She screamed. I screamed. Her target screamed, diving to one side as the javelin flew past its head and stuck solidly into a holly bush. The Beast was a man. A man with a navy-blue Bath University hoody on and Nike high-tops and jeans. A man with a wolf's head.

Quickly, I pulled out the little can of hairspray, pressing the nozzle right in the wolf's face. I kept it there until it started speaking.

'What the hell are you doing? Stop. Get off me!' said the thing beneath the wolf-head, launching into a coughing fit. Two pink hands fumbled to rip off the head, and there before us stood a sweaty, red-faced Charlie, breathless and annoyed, his blond hair sticking to his forehead. I stopped spraying and threw the can into the hedge.

'Oh my God, you scared the crap out of us!' I shouted, hitting him squarely in the arm.

'What? What the hell are you two on? You just nearly kebabbed me!'

'We thought you were the Beast!' Regan ran to retrieve her javelin from the bush.

'The Beast?' he laughed. 'It was supposed to be a joke.'

'It was you at the back door? You attacked Maggie?'

'Yeah.' He smiled. 'I actually came in peace. I brought the mince pies missing from your order the other day.' He pointed to a white carrier bag sitting in the flower border, containing five boxes of iced mince pies. It was almost invisible amid the snow. 'I put a free box in for the inconvenience. The wolf mask was an afterthought, really.'

I was ripped apart by feelings of anger that he'd done something so idiotic after everything we'd been through and happiness that he was here and he had forgiven me for running off from our date the other day. I wanted to kiss him and hug him and punch him all in one go.

'Were those your footprints in the snow?' said Regan.

'Where?'

'On the path between the borders.'

'Oh, yeah. Probably.'

'They look like hoof prints.'

'I was on my toes. I saw Maggie in the window and I was trying not to make a noise.'

'You freak!' I shouted at him. 'Do you have any idea what's happened to us?'

'Oh, come on, it was a joke,' he said, gesturing towards

the limp wolf mask in his hand. 'S'good, isn't it? I saw it at the fancy dress shop in Bathory Gorge the other day and I went back and got it. You shoulda seen Maggie's face when I scared her at the back door. It was classic. I got her good and proper that time.'

'She was terrified, Charlie,' I told him. 'We all were. You've gone too far this time.'

'Oh come on,' he said, willing us to smile and see the funny side. Neither of us did.

'No,' I told him. 'Things have changed now. Pranks are over.'

'We're in big trouble,' added Regan.

'What do you mean?' he asked. 'And why's there a dead sheep in your driveway?'


We went into the kitchen and told him all about it, behind the safety of our locked main door. We were all starving hungry and ate up both the cheese pie and the mince pies Charlie had brought us as we told him everything. About Matron. About Leon. About the menacing blizzard that had kept us awake night after night. About the phones. About the blood. With repeat choruses of 'It's a bloody nightmare,' and a close group harmony of 'What are we going to *do*, Charlie?'

'Hmm,' he said eventually, when all the nuts of information had been gathered. 'Hmm,' he said again. And 'Hmm,' he said, once more.

'So you've not got any bright ideas either then?' said Maggie. Tabby climbed up onto the draining board, Babbitt ear in mouth, so she could sit beside her.

'No. Well, we're gonna have to get you lot out of here, aren't we? I'll use my phone to call the police. That would be a start.' He patted his pockets, like a best man pretending to have forgotten the ring at the crucial moment.

Except Charlie wasn't pretending.

My heart dropped like a stone. 'Don't tell me.'

'I left my phone at home. It's charging. I thought I'd only be an hour.'

I shook my head. 'I don't believe it.'

'Why did you walk here?' said Maggie, accusing him with her tone. 'We could have used your car to go and get someone.'

'I thought if you saw my car coming up the drive, my cover would be blown.' He nodded towards the wolf mask, lying on the kitchen table. 'Plus, the roads round here are pretty dicey at the moment. It snowed again last night. It's better to walk when it's like this.'

'Maybe we could risk walking then?' said Regan, still clutching her javelin like a Roman sentry. 'It's still quite light.'

'But it'll be dark soon,' said Clarice. 'That's when It comes. I'm not risking my life.'

'Well, look,' said Maggie, extricating herself from Tabby's hug and smacking both hands decisively onto the metal table, which wobbled where the wheels weren't braked. 'The school minibus is here, right? He can drive us all out of here and we'll go to the police station at Toppan. Or at least the nearest phone box.'

'Charlie just said the roads were dicey,' said Regan, giving her the most withering look of her collection.

'Yeah, but we could risk it,' said Clarice, backing Maggie up on something for the first time ever.

'I dunno,' said Charlie, biting his thumbnail. 'I don't feel confident about taking all of you at once. I say I go alone, or take one of you so you can tell the police the whole story.'

I looked at him. 'I don't think any of us should go out there. Leon was attacked, Charlie. I've seen the teeth marks on his leg. You haven't.'

Tabby was looking at me, still cross-legged on the draining board, sucking the life out of Babbitt's ear. I felt awful for admitting the truth in front of her now, but times were changing and she was here dealing with them as much as we were. 'I've seen it. A few times actually. It's a huge catlike thing. And it has yellow eyes. I don't know if it's got Matron or Dianna but if it hasn't then where the hell are they both?'

Clarice frowned. 'Hang on, Leon said it had red eyes. It attacked him, it was *on* him and he said it had red eyes. I heard him say that. Didn't you?'

'Yeah,' I said. 'I heard him say that. But it has yellow eyes. It definitely has yellow eyes.'

'Which means…' said Maggie.

'That he's lying,' finished Regan.

Charlie fiddled with his friendship bands under his cuff and stared right at me. His eyebrows rose and his eyes swivelled to the ceiling, then back to me.

'Leon?' said Regan.

Charlie nodded. 'I'd say *he's* the reason your matron and your friend are missing.'

Tabby reached for the wolf mask and put it on her head. She looked at me and I couldn't help but smile. Maggie looked away. I told Tabby to take it off again.

'What do you suggest we do?' said Regan, twisting the javelin round and round in her grip.

'Is he handcuffed?' asked Charlie.

'No,' I said. 'He sleeps all the time anyway. I don't think he's a threat.'

'It can't be him,' said Clarice. 'I know him.'

'Yeah, she knows him intimately,' said Maggie. Clarice threw her a look. 'No, I wasn't taking the piss. You know him better than any of us.'

'What, so you're agreeing with me?'

'Yeah.'

'Oh.'

'You don't think it's him?' I said.

'Of course it's him,' said Charlie bluntly. 'You can't afford to be this naive any more, guys. We've got to do something before he wakes up.'

'I could lock the apartments. Keep him in there,' suggested Maggie.

'Yeah, good idea,' said Charlie.

'But he's not dangerous. He can barely walk,' I said, stopping Charlie as he went towards the back door.

'Nash, when did you meet this person?'

'Yesterday,' I told him. 'But—'

'Have you got a crush on him or something?'

'What?' I laughed. 'Charlie for God's sake…'

'Why else are you defending him. Hot, is he?'

'Really hot,' said Clarice.

'Shut up, Clarice,' I snipped. 'Charlie you're being ridiculous, I just don't think—'

'Why are you blushing?' He was jealous. He was actually jealous.

'Charlie, stop it.'

'You insisted on bringing him indoors, you just told me that. You've undressed him and bandaged his wound. You like him, admit it.'

Just when my petrol tank of excuses had completely burnt out, salvation came in the form of the last person I'd ever expect to speak up for Leon.

Maggie.

'It's not like that at all,' she said, stepping forward. 'You've got it arse backwards. I told Nash to bring him inside. I thought he was dying. And yeah, I fancied him. I told Nash we needed to help him. Kindred spirit and all that.'

'You wanted him in here?' Charlie confirmed.

'Yeah. Nash had nothing to do with it.'

Charlie looked from Maggie to me, expecting one of our masks to break. But they didn't. We held strong. 'How stupid can you get?' he said, looking straight at Maggie. 'You let your hormones do the thinking on this one, for sure.' He laughed at her. 'Well I guess it's a bloody good thing that I arrived in time, isn't it? Before he murdered you all in your beds.'

'Keep your voice down,' said Regan. 'He's sleeping.'

'But once he gets wind that we suspect him, it could be a different story. Okay, how about a couple of us get the bus moving, say me and Maggie, and you stay here and look after the others, and pretend to Leon like we've just gone to the phone box in the village. Don't say we're going to get the police or anything or he could get testy.'

'I don't think he's that bothered, actually,' said Clarice. 'He told me he'd rather go back to prison than stay outside in the cold.'

'Someone said we should lock his door. We should go and do that now,' Regan suggested.

'I'll do it,' said Clarice and Regan threw her the keys.

'I'm coming with you two to the bus,' I said to Charlie

and Maggie. 'It's snowed in and the wheels are going to need digging out.'

'All right,' said Charlie. 'You're the boss.'

'Come on,' I said, plucking my gloves from my coat pocket and putting them on again. 'Me and Maggie can do the digging. You can try the engine. Tabby needs to stay here.'

'Awww,' she whined. 'I want to stay with you, Nash.'

'No, Tabs, you've got to stay here and look after the Chief, all right? He needs you, go on.' Head bowed, Tabby marched off into the utility room to find the aforementioned Newfie.

'Regan, you look after Tabs.'

'Okay,' she said.

Wrenching open the door of the store cupboard, I found the panel of spare key bunches hung up just inside. I located the one for the bus. 'Might need these then.'

'Great,' said Charlie, catching them as I tossed them over to him. 'So me, Maggie and Nash will go and get help.'

Clarice, Regan and Tabby all looked back at us and stared.

'I tell you what,' I said to Tabby, 'why don't you go and find a nice board game to play in the common room and maybe Clarice and Regan will play it with you? I think there's Junior Scrabble in there. And Mousetrap. Okay?'

Tabby nodded. Regan half smiled. Clarice looked like she'd cheerfully have stabbed me straight through the heart.

# 24
## Resident Evil

'We'll never dig it out of that,' said Maggie.

'We've got to try,' said Charlie.

The three of us stood in front of the huge white mound of snow covering the smaller of our two school minibuses, parked up on the lawn on the right-hand side of the school.

'It's getting darker by the second,' I said.

We started digging out the wheels one by one, using a couple of fallen roof slates Maggie found by a drain. We were careful to shift the snow to the side of the bus, rather than in front of it, pushing great drifts of it from the windows and mirrors as we went. It took an age.

'Surely there's a shovel about somewhere?' puffed Maggie. 'My hands are getting corpsy doing this.'

'They'll all be in the gardening shed which Mr McReady locks in the holidays.'

'Damn.'

'Front wheels are clear,' Charlie eventually called out from the front and we heard the driver's door click open. 'I'll get in and warm her up.'

I joined Maggie at her back wheel and began helping her with my broken gloved hands. Once we were done with the back, we made a start on clearing the path directly in front of the bus.

'Why's it getting so dark? It's only about four o'clock, innit?' said Maggie.

I shovelled the snow as hard and as fast as I could. 'We'll do it. Just keep digging.'

'Think we'll get out of here in time?'

'Nope,' I said. All of a sudden, a quick wet splat of snow came at my face. When I looked up, Maggie was grinning at me.

'What was that for?' I said.

'You had your Bitchy Focus Face on,' she replied.

I smiled. 'That's cos my face is trying to focus. Bitch,' I said, flinging a small handful at her, catching her right on the back of her neck.

'Ooh, you...*mange la merde*!' She winced, wiping her neck with her gloved hand. 'Why isn't this mother-humping bus moving yet?' she said. 'Charlie? I don't hear the roar of the engine,' she called out.

There was no reply.

Maggie threw me a look and then we both stood up and walked around to the front to find out what was the matter.

The air inside the bus felt even more freezing than it was

outside. The driver's door was open. Charlie was just sitting there, staring at the steering wheel.

'What is it?' I asked him.

He looked at me. 'It won't start.'

'What do you mean?'

He turned the key in the ignition on the steering wheel stem. The bus didn't make a single sound. Not even a click.

'Try it again,' said Maggie.

He did. And again. And again. And again. It just clicked. Then it started to tick over.

On the seventh attempt, it spluttered.

On the eighth attempt, it coughed.

'Do it again, come on, it's doing something!' said Maggie, more urgently this time.

Next time he turned the key, the bus spluttered *and* coughed. But it didn't come to life.

'Come on,' he muttered and turned the key again.

This time, the bus spluttered, coughed and wheezed painfully, like an old man with a chest infection. But still it didn't come to life.

'It's making different noises every time. I think we just need to keep trying,' I said.

Charlie sat back in the driver's seat and stared through the windscreen. 'I don't think this is gonna happen, girls.'

Maggie looked down at the wheels. 'Turn the key again and press the accelerator.'

'It's not gonna help,' he said.

'Just do it,' she ordered, and Charlie reluctantly released the handbrake, turned the key again, muttering about how he was probably flooding the engine, and stepped on the accelerator pedal.

This time, the engine hacked into life, roaring up as Char-

lie pressed the pedal down further and further until it settled
and chugged happily on its spot.

'Yes!' shrieked Maggie as she and Charlie high-fived.
The wheels started spinning at the front, but the bus was
still going nowhere.

'It's stuck,' said Maggie. 'There's no what's-it-called on
the wheels.'

I remembered Seb's car getting stuck in the snow last
Christmas. He'd got some old boards and two tea trays out
of the garage and put them under the wheels so they had
something to grip to. 'Traction,' I said, looking down at the
front right wheel spinning for all it was worth in the sod-
den, muddy mush of icy grass.

'Yeah, that's it. It's because it's parked on the lawn. The
snow's made it all boggy,' said Charlie, continuing to roar
the engine. 'We need something underneath the tyres so
they can grip. Something flat.'

'There'll be something in the storage sheds,' I said. 'Scenery and signs from the plays. I know there are. I tidied up
in there a few days ago. I can put my hand right on them.'

'Good thinking,' said Charlie. 'You're not just a pretty
face, then?' He winked.

'I'm lots of things,' I said, smiling back at him.

Maggie grimaced. 'Shall I prepare the altar or are we
gonna get our arses in gear at some point?'

'I'll get the boards,' I announced, and started off across
the lawn towards the formal garden gate.

As I walked, Seb was on my mind again. Once, in some
bad snow at home, we couldn't get his car out of the driveway. He'd told me to get the wooden boards from the garage that we'd written 'Garage Sale' on in the summer, and

we put them under the front wheels. We were on our way in no time.

The only problem was the storage sheds were at the back of the school. I had to go around the other side of the building, across the Great Plat, through the Chinese Gate, across the Orangery lawn and down into the Pig Yard to get there. It was some distance, even without our present urgency.

The icy wind bit my face as my feet chomped and tramped through the thick snow carpet. I pulled up my hood, feeling the immediate warmth of its sheepskin lining and fake fur trim. I pushed my hands into my deep coat pockets and felt for the fruit knife Maggie had given me. Fat lot of good a fruit knife was going to be if I *did* encounter the Beast of Bathory. To do any real damage, I'd have to be close enough for it to bite my head off. But the fact that the knife was there, in my pocket, sharp and ready, made me feel safer anyway.

The night was beginning to draw in as I walked across the Great Plat and through the ornate black Chinese Gate onto the Orangery lawn, surrounded by trees stripped bare of their leaves and clawing at the sky with ferociously sharp branches. I was a sitting duck for an attack, I knew it. A lone, easy target under an ever-darkening sky, with nothing to defend myself but an ancient fruit knife and a pair of teeth chattering so hard they felt like they could shatter at any moment.

But nothing did attack me as I bypassed the tennis courts and entered the Pig Yard where the first storage shed stood. The Pig Yard was called that because pigs used to be kept there during the Second World War, when the school was self-sufficient and reared its own animals. The pigs were long gone though. All the sheds housed now were broken lawnmowers, out-of-tune pianos, ping-pong tables, summer parasols, old play scenery that was too big for the Chiller and the maintenance man's tools. It didn't take me long to find what I was looking for—I'd tidied them behind a broken, warped piano the previous week. We'd had to paint signs for the school production of *Calamity Jane* a couple of years ago and three of them—'The Golden Garter', 'Wells & Fargo Illinois' and 'One Night Only: Adelaide Adams' were resting up against the back wall, next to some big bags full of old costumes and boxes of kerosene lamps, one of which Dianna must have given to Leon to light the Tree House. I reached across and got two of the boards. Then, with an effort, I managed to climb across some broken tables and badminton equipment, get my fingers to the third and pull it out.

'Gotcha,' I said triumphantly. A hidden window at the back rattled in the ever-strengthening wind, and it startled me, just for a second.

I couldn't find any more boards, so I started climbing back towards the front of the shed. The door blew wide open and banged shut. I hurried to it before it banged again and shut it firmly behind me. Outside, all was silent. The birds had stopped.

And there it was. No warning. No sudden movement. Just standing there, a little way up the path towards Edward's Pond. I froze. There was no denying it this time. It was large and proud and very real.

The Beast.

I still couldn't move, even as it sniffed the air around its head, even as I watched its breath clouds, slow and steady, vaporising into the evening sky. Even as its tail swished and its paws padded silently across the ground towards me. It was enormous. This was bigger than any tiger I'd ever seen in the zoo. I made absolutely no movement. I tried not to look directly into its eyes, but that was impossible. I wanted to stare at it. Its eyes were unspeakably beautiful, the brightest clearest orange. It seemed utterly unfazed by my appearance.

It suddenly arched its neck and yawned, its giant teeth emerging from its mouth. It licked over them, and started to step towards me. I still didn't move. I clutched the three wooden boards against my body and stood there, as still as a signpost. It didn't move fast at all. It wasn't in attack mode; I knew it. I knew it wouldn't pounce on me. It just walked closer, ever closer, until it was only a couple of metres away.

*Sniff sniff sniff.*

It smelled the snowy ground. I studied its fur, as black as coal in places yet in others mottled and spotted like a tortoiseshell cat. Its eyes, so orange and startling. It came closer still, until I could hear its paws on the snow. It sniffed around the ground where I stood. It sniffed over my boots. I still didn't move, although I could hear my own breath getting faster and faster. Its jaws didn't gnash. It was beautiful and serene, and when it lifted its head, I could feel its breath on my neck like a dream.

Now it was in front of me. I could have reached out and touched it, held its giant head between my hands, but I still didn't move a muscle—only my eyes, which darted back and forth, trying to take all of it in. As it came closer still, I closed them completely and waited. I couldn't outrun it now even if I wanted to. So I waited. And waited. And felt the soft brush of warm fur on my face for an instant, before I opened my eyes again and looked into nothingness. The Beast's tail swished off in the other direction. It looked back at me once, as though it had forgotten to tell me something, before it sniffed the air again and continued, disappearing eventually into the thick green of the evergreen trees.

And that was when I saw it.

Sticking out of the grass verge, right where the Beast had been standing, was a hand. A pale, white hand.

Even as I walked towards it, I willed it to be just a pale branch. Twigs sticking out of the snow that looked like spindly fingers. I hoped and I hoped and I hoped.

But, as I reached it, I knew for certain there was only one thing it could be.

The Beast had disturbed the snow around her. Uncovered her hand, her snow-filled eye sockets. My hope died and became sick reality.

Matron.

But the Beast hadn't killed her. He couldn't have. I could see it, the second I looked down: around her neck lay a cherry-red necklace of frozen blood. Her throat had been slit from ear to ear.

# 25
## The Silence of the Lambs

I dropped the boards I'd been carrying. My hands leapt to my mouth, as though I was going to vomit, but nothing came out. I just gagged. I'd never understood what 'shocked to the core' meant until now. Until I saw Matron there on the frozen ground, the snow banked up around her. I couldn't blink. I couldn't cry. I could only feel the creeping horror of what I was seeing: her right leg tucked behind the left, her right arm stuck up against the snow, fingers stretched and solid. Her claw-like hand. The crude blood choker around her throat. The tiny pile of snow that had collected over her face, but was now brushed aside.

The Beast had dug her out of the snow and licked her face. It had not bitten her anywhere, or tried to eat what was left. It was like it was showing me where she was. Showing me it hadn't killed her. That meant—someone else had.

I don't know how long I stood there, working things out. *Think logically. Stress makes you stupid.*

Matron had been murdered, and not by the Beast.

That left...

Leon.

The thought struck me like a fist in the face. He'd been out in the woods the night Matron went missing. He was the only one of us who'd killed before. Plus, I'd never really bought his story about the Beast attacking him. A human couldn't survive such an attack from a big cat, certainly not a cat the size of the Beast. Why had I believed him? Why had I let him in?

A terrific pang of dread enveloped me like a lead cape. 'Oh my God.'

He was injured, that was why. He could have been dying. He could have frozen to death out here. But he was inside. Charlie was right. Maggie had been right too. Thank God he'd overruled me and locked him in. I was the only one who hadn't wanted to lock his door. How could I have got him so wrong? Charlie had been right about that too, I did fancy him. I just didn't want to admit it, as though it was a dirty secret. He was going to kill all of us. He was going to slit our throats. What kind of would-be Head Girl was I, letting that happen?

My options narrowed and came into horrifically clear focus. I had to get back to the school and warn everyone we had a madman in the building. We'd have to make a run for it. He was locked in; Clarice said she was going to do that, I was sure she did, so at least that was something we had in our favour. But what if he'd woken up and realised we all knew?

As the last scrap of daylight left the sky, I realised I had no torch. I couldn't go back into the dark sheds to look for a weapon—I'd have to make do with the poxy fruit knife in my pocket. I picked up the boards again and ran back through the gates to the Orangery lawn, back up to the formal gardens. Then I walked. If he was looking out, I didn't want him to think anything was up.

*Don't draw attention to yourself. Knowledge is power. He doesn't know what you know. Use it as a weapon.*

Even though my breathing was short and fast and my heart pounded painfully, I walked slowly back across the driveway with the boards, towards where the bus was parked, trying to look calm, as though nothing had happened. But I couldn't see Charlie or Maggie. I leant the boards against the front wheel and tried the handle. Locked.

I went round to the driver's side and tried the handle there. That was locked too. When I looked down, the tyre was flat. So was the back one. They'd both been slashed. And there on the snow by the deflated back tyre were six little red spots.

My breathing grew shallower still. The more I looked the more blood spots I could see. On the bright white snow. On the melted patches where the ground was trying hard to be seen again. A fresh long red drip down the side of the white bus.

'Oh, Jesus.'

I ached inside for Maggie and Charlie. Leon must have waited for me to leave and then taken both of them.

I had nothing to lose now. I had to get inside the school. *He might know you've seen the blood. Be careful.*

I tried the handle on the front door.

Locked.

I moved along to the common room bay window, which we sometimes left open if we were airing the rugs.

Locked.

I moved round to the west wing, where the kitchen was and tried the door. Both ground floor windows were too high for me to climb up to. Everything was locked down tight. Solid. Jammed. I couldn't see or hear anything from inside. God knows what could have been going on.

And then I remembered the other night, when we were looking for Tabby and how the Chiller was the very last room we tried. And how I'd got in.

Basement window. The faulty catch.

*You need a torch.*

I moved back round to the east wing, where the bus was parked, picked up one of the slates which Maggie had been using to dig out the wheels, and smashed the front window, grabbing the torch off the front passenger seat. Then I headed for the basement steps at the back of the school.

*Keep your wits about you. Keep turning. Speed and surprise.*

My hands were shaking furiously and I couldn't control my breathing.

*Once you're inside, turn off your torch.*

I pulled out the window with the faulty catch, placed my torch inside on the ledge and squeezed my way in through the gap. Once inside, I took a quick look around and turned off the torch, closing the window behind me. The intense darkness of the basement was like having my eyes closed. I felt my way through, remembering roughly where objects had been. Old desks. Piles of chairs. Scenery. Once I tripped and fell forwards over some old cardboard mountains we'd used for *The Sound of Music*, but, after I'd righted myself, I could see a chink of light, so I knew I'd reached the point at which the room separated into the passage to the Chiller and the other that led to the bottom of Back Stairs, and up to the rest of the school.

I risked a flash of torchlight.

On.

Nothing. No one. A scuttling, squeaking sound.

Then a deafening crash, right behind me.

A stack of chairs had toppled to the floor: I'd dislodged them when I fell. I waited, my hand over my mouth, for a heart-paining minute to pass, in case anything else moved behind me. In case anyone came to see what the noise was.

Nothing.

I flashed the torch on again for a second, then crept along the tunnel until I reached the stairs. At the bottom of the door, there was a thin line of light. Feeling in my pocket for the fruit knife, I gripped the handle, holding the blade out in front of me. Then I tiptoed up the stone steps.

I listened at the door. There was no noise but the tiny whistle of a draught.

*Make a plan. Where are you going, once you're out? Be prepared.*

The library. I'll head for a Hidey, I thought. Leon won't know about the Hideys. I'll be safe in there.

*Assess the situation. Keep yourself safe before helping your friends.*

Ever so carefully, I tried the door handle.

*Speed and surprise.*

I yanked the door open and scanned the corridor. The light was on, but all was deafeningly silent and still. Opposite, the staffroom door was shut. A little way along, the Music room and Science lab doors were shut too. The Gym doors were wide open, as were the heavy oak Latin room doors and the frosted ones of the French room.

At the very far end of the corridor, I heard screams.

And then all the lights went out.

I lost my head and panicked. I whipped round, only the glow from the Fire Exit signs above the doors to guide my way. I started to cry, thrusting my knife in every direction I turned.

Footsteps. Distant. Coming closer.

Then a warm hand smashed across my face, and I was bundled bodily into the French room. Behind me, the door was silently shut.

# 26
## Les Diaboliques

The hand stayed there, splayed over my face: thumb against my eyelashes, second finger just below my nose, and the rest of the fingers pressed tightly against my mouth. He held me close to him, so hard I could neither breathe nor struggle.

I knew for a fact I only had seconds to live.

'Don't. Move,' he whispered deep into my ear.

I couldn't even get my mouth open to bite, but I struggled for all I was worth. He just held me tighter, pulling me hard into him, trying to keep me still. Then I got my mouth open and clenched my teeth down into the palm of his hand, hard. The hand didn't move.

Then a shadow passed by out in the corridor.

I stopped biting. I could see the silhouette, moving slowly past the frosted glass. Ever so slowly.

'Little pig, little pig, let me come in,' sang the voice. A man's voice.

I could taste blood in my mouth. Not my blood.

The shadow stopped outside the French room, briefly, then carried on up the corridor.

'Little pig, little pig, let me come in…'

It got steadily more distant until it was far far away.

The hand on my mouth slackened, then pulled away completely. By the light of the low milky moonlight outside the Quad window, I saw I'd bitten hard. My captor slumped down onto a chair behind him, and I finally saw his face.

'Leon,' I whispered.

'Yeah. Who'd you expect?' He winced as he wrapped his palm with a length of toilet roll from his pocket.

'But who…what…'

His eyebrows rose. 'No idea. He just came in, shouting his mouth off.'

'What?'

'Keep down!' he said, sliding off the chair to the floor just as I saw the thing we'd been hiding from through the window, stalking the corridor on the other side of the Quad. The moon glinted on his blond hair.

'No!'

It was Charlie, a carving knife clasped in his fist.

'Come on,' Leon whispered, tugging me down to the carpet and beckoning me towards the corner storage cupboard. Once inside, he pulled the door to so we were hidden, only a sliver of moonlit classroom and one of the frosted doors visible through the gap. The darkness was our friend as much as foe.

His eye stayed trained on the shard of classroom we could see through the gap as he whispered.

'I heard all this screaming downstairs. When I got up, I heard someone shout that he had a knife. The one with the glasses, I think.'

'Regan?'

'I went to the corridor outside the bedroom and looked out. That's when I saw Clarice, dead on the stairs. I think she must have been running up to warn me. Have you seen Di?'

'Dianna? No. What the hell…'

'If he hurts her…' He bit down on his bottom lip. Something in his face had changed. I almost didn't recognise him.

Words slowly formed in the glue inside my head, but I didn't need to speak. Leon filled in all the blanks for me in his low, barely audible undertone.

'Do you know him?' He winced, gripping his side. He was clearly in some pain.

I nodded. 'I… He's Charlie. He's… He was a friend. His dad owns the shop in the village. He came to see us. He was going to start the bus so we could get away. Maggie… Oh my God, Maggie!'

'I didn't see her.'

'She was outside. I was there too. We were digging out the bus so we could drive it to the police station.'

'All right, keep your voice down.'

'Sorry.' I choked down my tears. I concentrated on my breathing. 'I went to get boards for traction. And I found…'

'What?'

'Our matron. In the snow.'

'Dead?'

I nodded.

'Exposure? That beast thing? What was it?'

'She'd had her throat slit.'

He exhaled and for a second I lost his face in the dark-

ness. 'He must be one of those serial killer nutters. He must
have done your mate Maggie outside and all.'

'Don't say it like that,' I snapped at him between sobs.

'I can't sugar-coat it, can I? You didn't see what he did
to Clarice. You need to get your head around what's happening here, Nash. Oh God, where did Dianna go? I haven't
seen her all day.'

'I haven't seen her either.' My entire body trembled and I
suddenly realised how cold I was, despite my tights, regulation pea coat and cardigan underneath. 'I'm going to wake
up any minute and none of this will be real.'

'Nash, look at me,' he said, grabbing my torch and clicking it on briefly. Its golden beam illuminated the cupboard
and he shone it directly over his right hand, clutching his
side. It was red all over. He'd been stabbed.

'He did this to you?'

'Yeah.' He clicked off the torch and the darkness took
over again. 'I don't think it's too deep though. It hurts like
a bitch, but it ain't cut a lung or nothing. I knocked him
down the stairs before he could do any more damage and
then I started running. Well, hobbling—my ankle's still
knackered. The only reason I got away was cos he went
after that Regan kid. She and the little one ran off. I don't
know where they went.'

'Oh God, Tabby!' I was about to burst out of the cupboard, but he grabbed my arm.

'Don't even think about it. You go out there now and
you'll be a butcher's window. You've got to be more canny.
Don't go being a hero, all right? Think of your options.'

It was just what my brother would have said too. In the
dark, it was like he was there with me. I stared at Leon's

hand, his chest heaving up and down as he tried to breathe through the pain. 'Let's get a dressing on that, at least.'

'Don't tell me you've got a first aid box in here and all.'

I stood up, taking the torch from him and shining it on the top of a tall green filing cabinet. There against the wall was a large see-through box. We'd brought in ten of them at the start of term for the school governors' visit. I clicked it open and found a large field dressing.

'Hold this,' I said, giving his good hand the torch. 'Shine it over it for me.'

He did as I asked as I removed his hand to see what I was dealing with. He was right, it wasn't deep, but deep enough. Red and oozing. I tore at his t-shirt, made a large hole and held the padding of the bandage against the wound.

'Mnnnaaarrrghhaargghhh,' he whined, as quietly as he could and started panting like he was in labour.

I pressed it down firmly and began to wrap the bandage around his middle. 'At least it wasn't on the same side as your appendix scar.'

'Yeah. I'm counting my blessings about that one.'

'Keep your hand on that and don't move it. Stay sitting up, okay?'

'This how it's gonna be, huh?' he said, as I shuffled him back against the filing cabinet. 'You my own personal nurse?'

'Seems to be how things are going so far.' I yanked the bandage tight and tied the knot.

He raged his pain through clenched teeth and squeezed his eyes shut.

'Sorry.'

'S'all right,' he said, still doing his Lamaze breathing. 'Is that it?'

'No, I need to bandage your hand as well. Where I bit you.'

'I didn't mind that one so much,' he said.

'Give me your hand.'

'Yes, Nurse.'

I exchanged the patchy red toilet roll tourniquet for a proper one and tidied it up with a small safety pin. 'How's your ankle?'

'Kills.'

I nodded.

'It was a trap,' he said. 'In the woods. A badger trap, I think. I lied to you. It wasn't the Beast.'

I let out a long breath.

'I went out looking for wood and stepped in it. No wild animals involved.'

'Why did you say it was the Beast, then?'

He shook his head. 'I dunno. Seemed right at the time.'

I couldn't believe how well he'd lied. 'You know I thought it sounded weird.'

'You did?'

'Yes. I've seen the Beast, up close. It didn't lay a paw on me.'

'Maybe it had just eaten.' I didn't want to dwell on that.

He heard something outside the door. He peered through again, then pulled back. 'It's all right.'

'You're a bloody good actor, I'll give you that.'

His laugh was pained. 'Dianna told me all about it and about the bloke in the village who got killed and what everyone was saying about the Beast. So when I did it, I thought maybe I could get inside the house if I used that excuse. It looks like a big animal bite though, doesn't it?'

'Yeah, it does.' I thought back. It made sense now. 'That

must have been what our Headmistress meant when she said the grounds man had "taken steps". And why we weren't allowed into the woods over the holidays.' I thought about my monster. The softness of its fur. The way it had showed me Matron's body. The way it had left the dead sheep on the porch for us. It meant us no harm at all. 'There must be loads of traps up there.'

'Yeah, well. There's one less now.'

'So what caused the fire then? Was that a lie too, about the lamp falling over?'

'Kind of. I torched it so you wouldn't send me back there. Dianna said if I had a good reason, you'd let me in. She knows you're soft-hearted. You did a good job, patching me up.'

'We did first aid in Biology. There wasn't a module on "How to Deal With a Knife-Wielding Maniac" though.' I shuffled back on my bottom and leant against the bookshelves.

'I knew guys like him inside. To look at, they're puppy dogs. You wouldn't think they'd have it in 'em. Till you find out what they did. Or till you see 'em when they're off their meds.'

'But he's…Charlie. Okay, I don't know him that well. But he's. He's—'

'The guy you've been flirting with all summer, yeah. Dianna told me. The shop boy. Didn't you have the slightest sense he might be dangerous?'

'No. I had no instincts about him at all. I just thought he was nice.' That was Charlie all over. Nice. Or so I'd thought… 'No, he is nice, he's a good person. He took me out. He always gives us sell-by pies and sweets and stuff.'

'He was clever, then. Reeled you all in.'

'I just don't believe it. I don't believe he's capable of it. He's sweet and funny and—'

'A killer. At heart, at base, he's a killer. He likes killing things. All the rest is decoration. You didn't see his face when he was sticking that thing in my ribs.' He winced with the pain, as though it had just reminded him. 'He *enjoys* this. This is the side of himself he chooses to listen to. He's Jekyll and Hyde.'

I remembered the pill bottle in the glovebox of his car. 'He's on some medication. For his asthma, I thought.'

'What, pills?'

'Yeah. He had to go to the doctor and get them changed because they weren't working. Long name. Something with trip in it.'

'Triptarangurzine?'

'Oh my God, yes, I think that's it. How did you know that? Are you asthmatic too?'

'They're not asthma pills. They're antipsychotics.'

'Psychotic?'

'As in psycho.'

'How do you know that?'

'Loads of blokes in the nick are on 'em for mood swings. We call 'em the trippers, cos they're always spaced out and their drugs all begin with "trip". The pills are supposed to lessen their aggression, dull part of their brain. Some of 'em are on doses so heavy they wander round like extras from *The Walking Dead*.'

I squeezed my eyes shut. 'He killed that guy in the village. He killed those tourists. I went on a date with him.'

Leon's brow was sweaty. I could see it in the crack of light coming through the door.

A door slammed hard in the distance.

'Well, I only saw him kill Clarice, but it makes sense for him to have offed the rest.' He moved his hand away from his belly bandage, checking his wound. The blood had stained the whiteness.

'Keep your hand pressed hard against it,' I reminded him.

'All right.'

'Clarice is dead?'

'Yeah.'

'Are you sure?'

'Yes, Nash. He slit her throat.'

'I…I can't believe…'

'Start believing, Nash,' said Leon. 'We don't have the luxury of time to get our heads around all this.'

More pieces were slowly starting to fall into place. Things Charlie did that day at the Gorge. Really shouting at those virtual aliens on Castle Mars. His hands shaking. His maniacal driving, at top speed on ice and all over the road. At that moment, I felt a choking sensation around my neck, and remembered—the Howlite necklace he'd given me. I yanked it off and flung it away from me, so that it clattered against the broken whiteboard.

'What was that?'

'A present. From him.' I couldn't bear to think about it, much less wear it.

'He had you good and proper, didn't he?'

'He did not,' I snapped. 'We'd only just started seeing each other. Could being on those pills make you, I don't know, lose control of stuff?'

'Yeah, definitely.'

'In what sort of ways?'

'I dunno, I'm not a doctor.' He sounded irascible, like he was just drifting off to sleep. 'The blokes in the nick get the shakes sometimes and find it hard to concentrate on really basic stuff. I know that's a side effect. Apart from that, I haven't got a clue.'

The dirt under his fingernails. Maggie always said it was blood.

'Oh my God. Oh my God.'

'God's busy right now, Nash. Let's think of a plan, yeah?'

'We've got to get to them. We've got to get to Regan and Tabby and Maggie and...'

'And do what?' said Leon, more wearily than ever. 'What the hell can we do? I can't move any more, Nash. I don't know how I even got here without collapsing.'

'I've got a knife.' I showed him the tiny fruit knife from my pocket.

He laughed and stopped, wincing. 'That doesn't look like it'd skin an apple, let alone do anything worse.'

'What about Tabby?'

'She's just going to have to take her chances. We can't do anything. We've got no other weapons. Nobody's coming, Nash. We're on our own.'

*There's always a way. Always.*

'No,' I said. 'We can't just sit and wait for him to come. I'm not doing that. I'm not dying in a French cupboard. And neither are you.'

'What then? I'm not going anywhere. I can't even walk properly, let alone go chasing round after that bag of Brazils with a blunt blade.'

'There's got to be something we can do.'

'Well, I can't do anything—look at me. What if we wait in here for him, then jump out and surprise him? Tie him up?'

'What with?'

'I dunno.' He checked the coast was clear through the gap

before flicking the torch on again to assess the high metal bookshelves around us. I stood up to look in the plastic storage boxes, but all I could see were ancient French dictionaries, copies of the Tricolore textbooks, rolled-up posters for *parfums*, *huile d'olive*, Le Tour de France, Air France and Le Folies Bergère. On other shelves there were see-through boxes of plastic French foodstuffs—*croque monsieurs*, croissants and strings of garlic and folded French flags. In others there were just rolls of craft paper, more textbooks, a broken whiteboard, a redundant blackboard and a whole load of stationery waiting to be used.

'What are we going to do, dry-wipe marker him to death?' he snorted. 'Oww.'

'I don't know,' I said, brain buzzing like a beehive. I sat back down. 'You've killed people before.'

'Hardly *people*,' he winced. 'A man.'

'But how do you do it? How do you…you know, stick it in?'

He breathed a long, hot breath. 'I didn't have a plan when I did what I did. I did it cos I had no choice. You don't know your own strength until you have no alternative but to use it.'

*Don't give up. Whatever you do, just don't give up.*

I wasn't sure about asking, but I did, before I could stop myself. 'How did it feel afterwards? When you'd killed him?'

'What, to finally kill the one man who'd been making my life a misery since I was seventeen? I threw up. I panicked and threw up. Once you do something like that, it changes you somehow. It made me kind of give up on everything, once I'd taken a life.'

I thought I was going to be sick too. I had the rivers in my mouth.

'But this is different, Nash. It's kill or be killed. There's no other option now.'

'I can't do it. I'll have to make a run for it.'

'Run where?'

'To get help. I know it's safe outside now. The Beast won't go for me.'

'It's suicide. It's pitch dark now and there's no street lights round here. Not to mention the three feet of snow you'd have to traipse through. You said yourself the nearest help is two miles away. You'll never make it.'

'The Beast will protect me,' I muttered.

'What?'

'Nothing.'

'However quick you are, he's a lot quicker.'

'I've got to do something.'

'Nash, you're dealing with a psychopath. At the moment, he is capable of anything. Literally anything. If he finds you, he won't stop to make conversation. He won't see you as his girlfriend. He will stab you. Don't go thinking you can find his sensitive side.'

'I'm not stupid,' I hissed. 'But I still have to go.'

I stood back up and moved the door an inch wider. That's when we heard the newest round of screams. My chest heaved. They were young screams. And from the echo, I knew where they were coming from.

'That was Tabby,' I said. 'She's run into the gym. I've got to find her.'

'Nash, for fuc— Just be careful, all right? Don't be the hero.'

'I will. I mean, I won't.' I held my fruit knife out in front of me. If Charlie was going to kill Tabby, he was going to have to kill me first.

*Use your anger. Believe in yourself. Act quickly and decisively. Trust your instincts.*

'Stay here,' I told him. He nodded. He was shivering. I undid my pea coat and carefully put it over him, despite his protests that he was all right and it was a girl's coat. 'Just shut up and wear it. And stay here.'

I stepped out of the storage cupboard, checking for noises or movements in the corridor through the window on the other side of the Quad. The lights were back on in the corridor. There was no sign of Charlie, though.

'Nash. Nash!' came a harsh whisper from the cupboard. A hand reached out from under the coat with something clasped inside it. A lighter.

'Maybe you can use this, I don't know,' said Leon.

'Thanks,' I said, putting it in my pocket.

He nodded, then slowly closed the door behind him.

Back out in the corridor, there was another noise: a laugh. A hysterical, tinkling sound like summer bells. I poked my head through the gap in the door and listened again. Charlie was laughing. Like he'd won something. It was a victorious chuckle.

He'd found Tabby.

# 27
## The Descent

I could hear him teasing her now. After every teasing little taunt, he would laugh, as though he could barely hold it in. The sound made me shake as I followed his voice.

'What makes you think I'm going to hurt you? I'm not going to hurt you. I just want to ask you something. Come here, it's okay. Look, I've got your rabbit.'

Past the Art room. Past the CDT room. The voice grew louder still.

'Come and get your rabbit,' it sang. 'Come on, I'm giving it to you, look. Here he is. Don't you want him?'

Past the House noticeboards I crept, until I reached the double doors of the gym. They were wide open.

'I don't wanna hurt you. Come on, come out.'

Slowly, I peered around the door. He was standing there

in the middle of the stage, his back turned, the knife still in his hand. He'd taken off his hoody and had on just a light blue t-shirt and jeans now. And he was talking to the bulging curtains in the wings. Babbitt was hanging from his belt, tethered at the neck.

'Look, he's here. He's right here. You've got to come and get him though. He wants you. Look, he's sad.'

Now Charlie was getting tired of waiting.

'I've called you, and you haven't come. I'm getting angry now. You come out here NOW or I swear the bunny gets it. I'm gonna do it. I'm gonna cut his head off.'

He yanked the toy rabbit from his belt and held it up, squeezing its face with one hand.

*Think two steps ahead of him. Where will you go when you make your move?*

'You ready? I'm gonna cut off his head RIGHT NOW.'

She didn't appear. Maybe she was gone. Maybe she was just too afraid. Charlie's fury intensified.

'Come out here NOW. You're only making this worse for yourself in the long run, you little squib.'

Suddenly, he started slashing at the curtains, over and over again. If they'd been alive, he would have drowned in the blood. He started yanking them down, pulling them off their runners, throwing them over the stage.

Then I saw a face, peering out at me. Regan. She wasn't on the stage or behind the curtains. She was on the gym floor, under the piano, peering at me beneath the dust sheet, directly across from where I stood outside the double doors. I saw the shining tip of her javelin on the floor beside her. Charlie still had his back turned to me.

I signed, *Are you OK*?

*Yes*, she nodded.

*Where's Tabby?* I asked her.

*In the dorms,* she mouthed. *He thinks that's me behind there.*

My chest almost collapsed in relief. I mouthed the words *Don't move.* Then held my finger to my mouth to say, *Don't make a sound*, and then made more gestures until she got what I meant.

She nodded again.

I'd worked out where I needed to go next. It was a stupid plan, but it was the only one I had. I had to get to the kitchens.

*Three, two, one.* 'RUN!' I shouted.

Regan darted out from beneath the piano sheet, just as Charlie disappeared into the tattered black curtains on the stage. She was halfway across the gym when he reappeared and yelled:

'OI! YOU LITTLE BITCH. COME HERE!'

By the time he'd sprinted across the stage, jumped to the floor and hurled his knife at her, she was through the double doors and we were slamming them closed together, wedging them shut with the strong steel javelin threaded through the handles.

Fuelled by adrenalin and something else I couldn't explain, I saw mist at the edges of my eyes and yelled at his face through the glass, 'COME AND FUCKING GET US, CHARLIE!' His heaving breath fogged up the window. He didn't look like the Charlie I knew any more. His eyes were dark and determined and he banged on the door like the room was on fire. Regan and I ran back down the corridor, furious bangs and shouts and threats echoing after us all the way.

'Where are we going?' puffed Regan as we ran, her cheeks streaked with tears.

'Kitchens,' I puffed back, pumping my arms for all I was worth. 'You're sure Tabby wasn't in the gym?'

'No, I told her to go up to the dorms and hide. I had Babbitt so I threw him on the stage when he was coming to distract him.'

'Good thinking, Regan.'

As we turned the corner into the long corridor towards the front of the school, we heard the sound of breaking glass. Then there were heavier, rubber-soled footsteps *pad pad padding* behind us, but far enough away that we had a good head start. Adrenalin made us pelt down those corridors faster than either of us had run in our lives. We pumped our arms and sliced our legs, *one-two one-two one-two*, and didn't stop pumping until we came to the first dividing door. Regan kicked away the wedge at the bottom, I slammed it shut and slid the bolt across.

His silhouette was still coming at us. He'd just rounded the corner.

'Come on,' I panted. We picked up the pace again, driving our legs like pistons all the way to the next internal door.

Behind us came the clattering sounds of a doorknob being furiously jiggled. More banging, more breaking glass. By this time, we'd locked the next dividing door and were on our way to the kitchens. We bolted the kitchen door shut, knowing it was made of thick oak and had no glass in it, so we were safe. For now.

'What do we do?' she heaved.

'Look for something, anything, to fight him with. Knives. A rolling pin, anything.'

There was a drawer full of knives at our disposal. A cupboard full of oven cleaner, bleach and washing powder. We couldn't link any of them with something useful and the knives all looked smaller than Charlie's. I grabbed the oven cleaner.

Now he was outside the kitchen door. *Bang bang bang.*

Regan was panicking. 'I can't fight him, Nash. I can't.' She threw down a thick-bladed carving knife and it tinkled to the floor. 'I just can't. I'd rather hide.'

*Use any means necessary. Stress makes you stupid. Think.*

'Okay. Get out the back, or something. Just keep out of the way.'

Regan disappeared behind me as I rootled in the knife drawer. When I looked back, she was gone.

The door *bang bang bang banged* again as Charlie kicked at it, and my hands shook so much I dropped the bread knife I'd found. A black shape moved into the kitchen from the utility room. Chief Brody had just woken up, stirred from his bed by all the banging. It was a relief to see him. He cocked his head to one side, sniffed the air, looked at the door as it *pulsed* and *pulsed* and *pulsed* from the other side. He yawned. Then he sloped off back to his bed.

'Thanks, Chief.' I almost laughed, sweat dripping into my eyes.

The *bang bang banging* continued until all of a sudden the bolt splintered away, and the door flung open and bounced off the side of the fridge. I backed away from the knife drawer. There he was, his wet blond hair dangling in his eyes like pondweed. He had one of the large fire extinguishers in his hand from Long Corridor. He dropped it with a loud *clang* on the hardwood floor. The only thing between us was the large metal table.

*Any means necessary.*

I grabbed the oven cleaner spray and held it out in front of me, not taking my eyes from Charlie for one second, even to blink.

He smiled. He was sweating too, and there were blood spatters all over his blue t-shirt. He glanced at the oven cleaner can. 'What you gonna do with that? Clean me?' He looked like he was on the verge of laughing. 'I'm too dirty to clean.'

*Don't connect with him. Don't look him in the eyes. He wants to own you.*

'What's the matter? Are you afraid, Nash?'

'No. I'm not afraid,' I lied. I didn't even want him saying my name.

He started moving around the table. I moved the other way. He quick-changed to the other direction, and so did I.

'Come on, you know me,' he said.

'No. I don't,' I said, trying to stamp out the quiver in my voice.

'I'm Charlie. I'm your boyfriend. I know what's best for you. This is for the best. He wants you. All of you.'

'Who does?'

'My beast. I have to feed him or else he'll go away. He can't do that. We need him here. Think what will happen if the Beast goes away. No one will come here any more.' Babbitt was dangling from his belt, tethered with one of his friendship bands.

My arm was locked in front of me, the oven cleaner still clutched in my hand. 'You kill people and feed them to the Beast?'

'No, I don't. It's the Beast that kills 'em. They're not dead when I take them to him.'

As he got closer and moved into the light more, I could see his nose was bleeding and going purple on one side of his face. He'd been punched or kicked or something. Maggie, I thought. Maggie would have fought him for her life.

'*You're* the only beast around here,' I said. 'That thing's just a wildcat. You kill people and you hope he'll eat the evidence.'

'Well, yeah,' he laughed, wiping his bleeding nose with the wrist of his knife hand, painting a long smear along the bare skin of his arm. 'It's worked till now.' His knife glinted.

He did another quick change around the table, and I swerved away until I was as far from him as I could be.

'Come here. Stop running. You know you can't outrun me. I'm just too damn quick for you. It's pointless.'

I shuddered, remembering him saying the exact same thing at the arcades.

'You killed Matron.'

He bit his bottom lip and nodded at me, like he was a naughty little boy afraid of being told off. 'You didn't find her, did you?'

He sounded like we were back in the shop and he was asking if I'd found the Coco Pops next to the Rice Krispies. 'Yeah. I found her.'

'Knew it hadn't snowed enough. Should have covered her up more.'

'The wildcat took me to her body. It dug her out.'

He laughed a bit. Then he stopped laughing, like someone had pulled out his plug. 'That's a lie.'

'No it's not. I saw the Beast. I've seen it. Up close. It took me to her.'

'If you'd seen it, you'd be dead too.' He made a quick dart to the left. As I went right, he banged his free hand down on the metal table. 'Do you know, I'm just starting to get the teeniest bit bored of this. You really are wasting your time trying to fight me.'

*Don't let any of it go in. They're empty words. That's all. Keep moving. You're as strong as him. Stronger.*

'How come I'm here then? Alive?'

'Not for much longer,' he said, lunging round to my side again. We went round and round the mulberry bush a few more times, and every time he thought he was getting close enough, he would slash out with the knife.

Then a strange thing happened: I lost my fear. Just lost it, like snow turning to melt water. And I started to goad him.

'I'm going to survive you and I'm going to win.'

'Nash, you CAN'T win. You stupid, STUPID little girl. Don't even THINK you're better than me and the Beast. We are SO much stronger than you will ever be.'

'You lost your mum,' I said. 'I lost my brother. We're not so different.'

'I'M DIFFERENT,' he roared. 'You don't know what I can do, Nash. The power I have in these hands.'

The final time round the table was the fastest. In one quick motion, I yanked the top off the oven cleaner and sprayed it as close to his face as I could get.

He sneezed, like a dog, then laughed. 'That wasn't nice, was it?' I backed off. 'I'm going to take my time with you, Nash.'

'I'm going to tell them what you did. I'm going to live through this and I'm going to tell them all exactly what you are. That wildcat isn't going to get the blame any more. You need to be locked up.'

'Says the girl who's been harbouring a convicted killer.'

Suddenly, there was another noise, behind him. We broke

our stare for just a second and he followed my eyes to where it had come from. The oven.

He looked back at me. 'Where did that other girl go? The one with the plaits?'

I swallowed, tasting iron in my spit. 'She left.'

He looked down to the oven again. 'Are you sure?'

'Yes.' I locked my gaze with his.

He reached down and held the central knob on the front of the oven. 'So if I turned up this dial, that wouldn't worry you?'

I swallowed again. I couldn't catch my breath. 'It's me you're after, Charlie. You need to come and get me.' I started round the table again, but this time he stayed where he was. I moved back. He turned up the dial.

'How long does it take to get to temperature?' he said, turning the dial again, more and more, until it was at maximum, and holding the door closed with his foot. 'Think I might stay here for a bit. Let things warm up.'

A hollow, muffled scream came from inside the oven. I had to move. I had to think. I had to get him away.

'I don't think the Beast minds whether his food's hot or cold. He might like to try something different for a change. What do you think?' He twisted the knife in front of him, to the left, to the right, to the left, to the right, as though urging me to make a choice—let him stab me or Regan would die. 'Oh, Nash?' he called. 'Nash, time's running out. I need an answer.'

I had to move now. I had to think harder. But nothing was coming. Nothing was helping. *There's always a way.*

Then the little yellow fire symbol on the can caught my eye.

Charlie moved then. He switched directions round the

table and came right at me. I fumbled in my pocket for Leon's lighter and flicked the switch on the squirt of oven cleaner. It didn't light. I dodged Charlie and tried again at the same time. On the third attempt, just as he was almost on top of me, I got the flame in the line of the spray and a thick, flaming torrent burst from the spout, right into Charlie's face.

'AAAARRRRRGGGHHHHHHH!' he screamed, dropping his knife and raising both his arms over his face to shield himself.

'Regan, RUN!'

The oven door burst open and Regan scrambled out onto the floor in a mess of arms and legs. Still holding my makeshift flame-thrower in front of me as a warning shield, I walked backwards towards the kitchen door, now hanging from its hinges. With my right foot, I flicked up the brake on the table island and kicked it towards him, pinning his body against the sinks. I flicked the brake back up so it was locked, holding him there, then I made my escape.

'Regan, go and get help,' I ordered her. 'Back door. Just run. Get as far away from here as you can.'

Oven cleaner and lighter still clutched tightly in my hands, I sprinted, barely any breath left, back down the corridor with no thought to where I was going. I could still hear Charlie screaming behind me.

'You're DEAD. Bitch, you hear me, you are a DEAD. GIRL. WALKING.'

His words were following, echoing, closing in. I could keep running, but where would I run to?

The dorms. It had to be the dorms. I knew my way around the school—right now, that was the only thing on my side. I sprinted up the stairs, two steps at a time, and fled along the corridor. Our dorm-room door was closed. Now I heard him coming up the stairs, shouting and screeching after me.

'Where are you, bitch? I'm gonna have you!'

Without thinking, halfway along the landing, I ducked into the airing cupboard and silently closed the door.

Footsteps along the corridor. My skin was alive with prickles. In the close confines of the airing cupboard, my breathlessness sounded so loud and obvious. I covered my mouth with a small pile of pillowcases. He was creeping about. I could see his shadow through the slats in the cupboard door.

'Just come out, will you?' said Charlie's voice, closer than ever now. He was right outside. 'This is getting really boring.'

Did he know I was in here? Would he try the door?

I heard the rattle of a doorknob, but it wasn't the airing cupboard knob. It was one across the corridor. Prefect Dorm Two. The handle rattled louder. There was a thump. He was kicking it. Harder.

'Come on, Natasha, you know I'll get in eventually.'

No way would he open it. The doors up here were too heavy and thick. Except my airing cupboard door; he could have kicked that one in, easily. It was thin. It had slats. And I was right there on the other side of it. I had to get further inside, back behind the boiler. I scrabbled my way back through the piles of blankets and sheets and tablecloths. Once I was ensconced behind the boiler, I piled everything up around me. It was a mess. But at least I was hidden.

*Bang bang bang.* He was at my door now. The handle rattled. A wide band of light flooded in. He was inches away now. Sniffing the air, as though he could smell me. I could smell him. I could smell BO and the vague scent of burnt hair.

'Nash?' His voice was softer now. I cupped my mouth with my hand again to swallow my breathing. 'Nash. I don't know what I'm doing. I need you. Help me. I love you.'

I couldn't move. I couldn't breathe. I didn't know if my heart was still beating. Then all of a sudden his voice seemed to sing out:

'I'm gonna cut your head off when I find you, Natasha. I swear to God. I'm gonna take my time with you. You're going to feel everything.'

My body froze at the sound of his unnaturally matter-of-fact voice. A door slammed and his footsteps pumped back along the corridor. I let out my breath into a stack of clean gym socks.

I still had the can of oven cleaner and the lighter in my pocket, but the can felt empty. I needed something else. I clicked on the little light pull to ignite the small bulb and looked around me. There was nothing but sheets and blankets and spare uniform piles as far as the eye could see. The shelving units groaned under the weight of it all. I spotted one thing, the only thing that might come in useful, on the second shelf up. A small box of biological washing powder. I reached up and took it, snatching up a large handful into my cardigan pocket. It would have to do for now. I had to get out of there. I had to find Tabby and Maggie. I had to get help.

I clicked off the light and silently opened the airing cupboard door, closing it carefully behind me and checking the corridor, up and down. No sign of anyone. I was completely on my own. I started quickly back down the landing, one hand in my pocket the whole way. I could smell him. I could smell his burning hair.

The smell disappeared at the top of the staircase, which meant he had gone downstairs. I jiggled the knob on the door marked 'PRIVATE', which took me along to the Saul-Hudsons' apartments and the front staircase. I could see the front door.

But between me and freedom were the stairs. And a body lying there. Like a butterfly Charlie had crushed beneath his shoe.

Clarice Hoon. Her blood was all up the wall. Unlike Matron, her eyes were closed. I knelt down beside her head and robotically felt for her pulse, just to be sure. No movement. No breath. Her skin was cold. Many a time I'd wished Clarice would just disappear. Now I'd have given anything for her to wake up. She looked quite beautiful. A painted lady.

A bang in the corridor to the kitchens. I sprang to my feet. He was coming. He would find me. I couldn't make it up the stairs, and I couldn't get out through the front door without a key. I was trapped. He would see me and kill me and I would die there, next to Clarice.

And then I had a thought.

'Clarice,' I said, and in a flash I knew where to go. I had just enough time to get down the remaining stairs and into Mrs Saul-Hudson's office, closing the door behind me. I could bolt it from the inside too—so I did. I looked around. Untidy shelves. Papers all over the desk, in large messy stacks. I'd told Clarice to lock all the windows the night Matron went missing, but I knew beyond doubt she wouldn't have gone in the Headmistress's office. No way would she have voluntarily gone in there. I climbed across the desk and jumped down the other side, leaning across to lift up the pane. It flew up like a bride's dress and a rush of cold air greeted my face from outside.

'Thank you, thank you, thank you,' I muttered, clambering out just as the door to the office began to *bang bang bang*.

I closed the window behind me. I didn't have a clue where I was going or what I was doing. I just knew I had to run, fight and keep fighting until someone came. Anyone came. Someone would come, eventually. I had to believe it.

But then the voice returned—the one I thought had left me.

*There's nowhere else to run. You have to hide.*

I was running past the Reference Library window. The Hidey. I could get to the Hidey behind the encyclopedias. If the window was open, I could get to it in time. Charlie didn't know they were there.

I climbed onto the hedge and tried the window, but it was locked tight. Without another thought, I jumped down and grabbed a large pebble from the flower bed, hurling it at the pane, which shattered completely.

'Knowledge is Power' said the sign outside the door. Maybe the books would save me.

But he had heard the breaking glass.

And he was at the door before I'd jumped down from the window.

His face was red and peeling from the fire, his blond hair burnt at the fringe and smoke-blackened. I held the can up again, threatening him with it.

'There you are,' he snarled, stepping closer to me, knowing I was cornered. The Hidey was out of the question now. He'd follow me in, and then I would die in complete darkness. I fumbled into my left pocket for the oven cleaner. I pressed down on the squirt and lit the flame again, holding it in front of me like before.

'Don't come near me or I'll light you up again,' I warned through ragged breaths.

'I don't care,' he said. He closed the door behind him and walked towards me. 'I'm going to slice you into ribbons.'

The flame burned and roared in front of me like a dragon's breath—and suddenly burnt out. Now I had nothing. I shook the can. Empty. I threw it at him. He batted it away with his free hand like he was swatting a butterfly. My hand dived into my left pocket for the washing powder. I threw it at him. It completely missed. His knife hand rose.

I threw the lighter at him. It missed. Still he kept coming. Then I went for the books. Encyclopedias. Big heavy dictionaries and atlases. Book after book after book after book I launched at him. Overarm. Underarm. Over my shoulder. I threw with all my might.

*Go down fighting.*

Some bounced straight off his body. Some he batted away. Some he slashed at with the knife in mid-air. One hit him square in the face. But still he kept coming and coming at me, until he was on me and the knife was raised and his free hand was on my shoulder to steady me as—

'GET BACK FROM HER, YOU BASTARD,' shouted a voice behind us. He whipped his head round and found Maggie standing there, as if appearing from a puff of smoke, a javelin raised in her fist, pointed straight at his face. She'd emerged from the Hidey.

There was no warning. Charlie faced her, stepped forward with his knife raised, and with one quick movement Maggie plunged the javelin deep into his thigh.

'AARRGGHHH—JESUS!' he cried, backing off.

Maggie steadied herself against the bookcase as he writhed in agony, wrenching the spear from his leg and flinging it across the room towards the door. 'How's that for a prank, bitch?' she yelled at him.

I didn't even have time for relief. Charlie was on his feet again before I could say a word. As straight as he could manage, he raised his knife again and dived at Maggie, sticking it straight into her belly as far as it would go. I heard the dull thump of it going in.

The sound of my own scream petrified me to the spot.

She made a gurning noise as he stabbed her. She didn't scream. It was like the knife had zipped up her breath and forced it back inside her throat. She slid down the bookcase and hit the floor hard on her bottom. The knife stuck out of her stomach, buried up to the hilt.

Then Charlie turned back to me, his red face contorted in pain, and grabbed me by the neck. His grip was so tight.

*Go for the vulnerable parts of the body. Throat.*

I punched out at his Adam's apple. He coughed and drew away. I tried to scurry away, but he grabbed my hair and pulled me face down to the floor. He was on my back.

*Headbutt.*

I jerked my head back as hard as I could. As it made contact with his face, he yelped and I struggled free, just for a second. But I couldn't get my footing on the polished floor, and then he was back, turning me to face him, lying on top of me, all his weight pressed against me.

'You'll enjoy this, I promise,' he whispered.

*Eyes.*

I pressed my thumb against his eyeball until I felt the soft jelly give under my touch.

'Arghhh!'

*Nose. Up to the nose with the heel of your hand.*

I grabbed and yanked and punched what I could. But it was no use. He got his hands around my neck again and again and held me down.

*Knee him in his crotch.*

I couldn't get to it. I couldn't move my legs at all. He had me pinned.

*Hit him. Bite him. Pinch him. Grab him. Slap him. Don't. Ever. Stop.*

He pulled my head up and brought it back down, hard, to the floor. Again and again, squeezing the breath from my throat at the same time. I could feel myself slipping away, no breath coming, an iron grip around my throat. Something dug into my leg. I was dying.

'I really fancy you,' he said, his voice sounding almost as strangled as mine. 'We could still have some fun, though you won't have much say in it.'

All my breath had left me. I couldn't contend. I was disappearing down a well and had no strength left. Nothing to fight for.

'You struggle too much, Nash. Look on the bright side. You can join your brother now, can't you? He's dead, now, Nash. Remember, he told you he wasn't going to make it.'

It was *him*. On the phone. Pretending.

Not Seb. Charlie.

Something was digging hard into my leg.

Seb hadn't phoned. That hadn't happened. It was *him*.

I knew what it was now. I got my hand underneath my cardigan to my tunic pocket and fumbled for it. I found it. I pulled it out. The pencil.

Seb not dying. Still hope.

I got it into my fist. Drew it out. Drew it away. Drew it

back. Drove it hard, fast, right into the side of his neck with a glorious squelching punch. I wasn't on target. But it was enough. Deep enough.

His blood spouted straight into my face, into my eyes, my mouth, but the pressure on my neck released and I gasped in as much air in as I could, pushing him back with all my might. He stumbled and fell, scuffling backwards along the blood-soaked rug, half the pencil still jutting out of his neck.

I spat every fluid from my mouth and coughed as I stood up. I walked over to him. I looked down. He was gasping for air. I bent to his level, not looking at his face, and untied Babbitt from his belt. Then I stood up again. His free arm reached out for me, but I slapped it away, pulling my pencil out with a spray of blood and a sickening *pop*. He gasped. I put Babbitt in my tunic pocket and went over to sit beside Maggie. I picked up her hand. She looked at me, scared.

'Jesus, Nash.' Her hand shuddered over the knife sticking from her belly.

'No. Leave it in,' I said. My voice didn't sound like mine.

It was only then that I heard the sirens.

# 28
## Final Destination

It was Tabby who'd saved us.

She had run from Charlie to the Hidey at the back of the gym, and gone straight up to the dorms and she'd stayed there and bided her time until she heard the library window breaking. Then she'd gone back through the Hidey and arrived at Sickbay. It was there, on a shelf on the wall, that she'd found the plastic carrier bag full of our mobile phones, hidden there by Matron. She called the police herself and said the bad man had a knife, told them the address, and they'd come running. They'd all come running.

I don't remember much of what happened between sitting with Maggie in the library and being brought outside. I think I must have blacked out, like I did when I 'attacked' Clarice in the Chapel. How long ago that was now. Some policemen came in, wearing vests and brandishing guns. There were shouts. People talked to me. People talked *at* me. I stayed in my bubble, not really hearing them or feeling them as they poked and prodded and covered my shoulders with a foil blanket. I told them Leon was in the French room cupboard. I definitely told them that. Then they cleared me out of the library.

By the time I got outside, it was early in the morning on Christmas Eve, and there were flashing lights everywhere. Police cars, vans and ambulances met my eyes at every turn. Bustle, noise and scratchy receivers barking orders from every shoulder.

I sat on the back of an ambulance, wrapped in my foil cape and staring at the lights until my eyes stung and watered. Tabby was in the back of another ambulance, sitting next to Brody, who was chewing a stick. Two police officers sat with them. Tabby was cuddling Babbitt and one of the policewomen was reading her a story. I kept looking down at my hands, thinking about what they did. How they'd killed someone. How I'd become a monster to kill another.

Another woman was asking me questions. A policewoman. I hadn't really seen her face. She had short dark hair and talked in a Scottish accent. I didn't know if I was answering her correctly. I was just watching the school. Watching the dusting of snow on the roof beginning to melt away as though it had never been there. Watching the front door as the stretchers were brought out.

First Clarice. I saw her red hair, dangling like a theatre curtain beneath the sheet covering her face.

Then came Leon, sitting up, his hand cuffed to the metal rung under the bed. I stood up.

The Scottish policewoman's voice. 'Nash, come back.

Nash, you need to sit down, you've had a terrible shock.'
I kept walking towards the stretcher. 'You need to stand
aside, please.'

'Leon.'

'Nash,' he said, his face brightening. 'I'm gonna be all
right. Where's Dianna?'

'I don't know, Leon. I don't know.'

'Miss,' said a tall dark policeman, with a beard this time,
'we need to get him to the hospital now.'

I looked at the policeman. 'He saved me. If it wasn't for
him, I'd be dead.'

'All right, all right.'

'No, listen to me,' I said, grabbing the bearded policeman's arm and not letting go. 'You need to take that into ac-
count. I know he escaped, I know he did bad things before,
but here—he did good things here. He didn't hurt anyone
and he saved my life. Please.'

'You just tell that to the lady there then, all right? We'll
make sure it's all noted down. She'll look after you.'

The policeman gently moved me to one side as the bed
continued past me. Leon winked, mouthing *Thanks*, before
closing his eyes and being rolled off towards a ramp at the
back of one of the waiting ambulances. As the bed passed
me, I could have sworn I'd seen a tear fall down the side of
his face to the sheet.

'Nash?' said the Scottish policewoman again. She adjusted the foil cape around my shoulders again. I hadn't
even realised it had come off. 'Let's go back to the ambulance now, okay? The paramedics are waiting to have a
look at your neck.'

'I want to see Maggie.'

'They'll bring her out in a minute. We'll wait for her in the ambulance, shall we? Where it's warm?'

'No,' I said, more firmly. 'I'm waiting here for Maggie.'

'Okay, well—you just keep that cape around you then.'

Two ambulances started down the driveway and police milled around in the empty spaces they'd left. Making calls. Talking about the news crews. Setting up caution tape. I looked at the white school minibus. Some cops were already marking where blood had been found. I heard two of them mention 'the boy in the library' and 'twenty-seven separate wounds', but I didn't make the connection then. Other policemen were taking an empty stretcher down the path to the Orangery lawn where I'd told them I'd found Matron. I looked back to the front door. Waiting for Maggie.

'Will you at least let them clean your face?' said the Scottish voice again.

'What's wrong with my face?' I said, not taking my eyes off the front door.

'Well, it's a little bit messy. Let's just go and do that, shall we?'

I let her guide me back to the ambulance where a paramedic was waiting with some sort of medical wet wipe. I caught sight of my face in the wing mirror. My entire head was covered in dry blood. My blue eyes stared out. My vision went, momentarily, as a giant wet wipe was smeared across my face. The wipe came away red but the paramedic hid it quickly in a plastic bag and fished out another one, doing the same again.

'Where has all that blood come from?' I heard my voice say. 'Did he get me?'

'No,' said the woman. 'This is his blood. Okay, if you

just sit down there, my love, so we can take a look at you.
That's it, thank you.'

'His blood?'

The other paramedic started checking all round my neck.
I felt it then. The soreness. The searing pain in my throat
and my collarbone. It killed.

'Oww.'

'It's okay, you've just got a bit of bruising there. Nothing serious.'

'Nothing serious,' I repeated. It still didn't sound like my
voice. I'd forgotten what I was meant to sound like.

I heard a rattling and a gaggle of people came out of the
front door, followed by the next stretcher. Maggie.

I shook off the two paramedics and rushed towards her.
I couldn't see her for people—she was shrouded in policemen and women and ambulance crews. I couldn't see if the
sheet covered her face or not. I barged my way through the
throng of bodies, and then I saw her face. Her brown eyes—
open, beautifully alive.

'All right, Nasher the Flasher?' she said, her voice
scratchy and one eye closed. 'Nice necklace.'

She meant the purple choker where Charlie's hands had
tried to squeeze the life from my body just an hour before.
I put my hand to my throat and winced in pain again. It
was then that I looked down her body and saw the hilt of
Charlie's knife sticking out of her belly, a cluster of blood-
soaked wadding all around it. My own stomach turned over
at the sight.

'You did it, Nash. You slew the dragon. *Tu est…mag-
nifique*.' She felt around at her side for my hand and I
grabbed it and held it tightly.

'We slew the dragon,' I said.

'No, I didn't get close. I missed him. You went to town on the bastard. He looks like Swiss cheese in there.' Her voice was getting weaker. She groaned with the effort of talking.

*Twenty seven separate wounds*, I kept thinking. I wanted to know what she meant, but she was fading. 'You got him, Maggie. You got him.'

The bed didn't stop moving so we couldn't talk properly. I walked alongside her. 'We didn't watch *Con Air*,' she mumbled.

'Another time,' I told her. 'I'll find out which hospital they're taking you to and I'll bring it in for us to watch there. Okay?'

She nodded. 'I'd like that.'

'Are you going to be all right?'

'Yeah. I'll survive. Worse luck for Saul-Hudson, eh? Back in this dump next term. Well, might take a bit longer, I dunno.' She winced. 'I'm all right. They got good drugs, you should get some. Nice.' Her eyes started to close.

'Maggie…' I tailed off, then started again. 'You're a true friend.'

She started laughing. Really laughing. And then crying, from the pain the laughter was causing. 'Aww, sorry, that just sounded so wet.'

I tugged her hair gently. 'Oi you, I was trying to have a moment there.'

'Let's get two of those naff necklaces from Argos. "BFFs Forevs".' Her eyes closed again.

I tried to laugh. We'd arrived at the ramp of the ambulance. 'I'll see you soon, okay?'

She nodded. Though her eyes were watery, no tears escaped. Typical Maggie. The stretcher started to move again, up the ramp and away she went. Once again, I was guided

back to my ambulance, where the paramedic was still waiting with his wipe.

Then the Scottish policewoman, whose name, I learned,
was Krissy, asked me questions. Loads of questions. I told
her everything I could, from the beginning. I told her how
I'd found Matron. How Dianna had kept Seb's letter from
me and how everyone had shouted at her and she'd disappeared. How Charlie was on some antipsychotic drugs. I
told them what he'd told me—how he had killed them all.
The man in the village. The two tourists in the summer.
Matron. Clarice. Probably Dianna too. How he left them
in the forest for the Beast to eat.

'What about Clarice's and Matron's families?'

'Someone's informing them,' said the policewoman. She
had told me her name but I'd forgotten it already. Krissy,
that was it.

'My parents are abroad, but they were due back today. I
know their mobiles…'

'We'll call them, don't worry. We'll call them all. You
just concentrate on yourself right now, okay? Let's get you
sorted.'

Another tinkling in the distance. The wheels of the last
stretcher.

Charlie. A white sheet over his face.

I stayed sitting as they wheeled him straight up into another ambulance and slammed the doors.

'You're the hero, don't forget that.'

'Huh?' I said, snapping out of my daze and looking at the
policewoman's face. 'I'm not a hero. I'm a killer.'

'You saved your friends' lives. You saved your own.'

I didn't even feel the cold when my foil cape slipped off
my shoulders again and Krissy had to put it back on. Her

radio crackled on her shoulder and she spoke into it. I heard the words 'body' and 'lane'.

I knew it was Dianna.

'They've found her, haven't they?' I said. She didn't answer.

'Okay, Sarge. I'll let them know.' She looked at me. 'Yeah. In one of the lanes about two miles away from here in Bathory village. In a phone box.'

'She was going for help. I know she was. Charlie must have seen her on the way here. We had an argument. I said she was useless.'

The policewoman took a long deep breath and blew out a cloud of bemusement. 'My colleagues are searching Bathory Basics in the village. I've had word that a man's body has been found in the upstairs flat.'

My eyes banged shut and my heart truly sank inside me. 'His dad.'

She leaned into me. I could smell her perfume—the same as our Geography teacher wore. 'You saved four people's lives today, including your own. Don't you forget that. I've got to inform my colleagues, okay? I'll be back in a tick.'

Four people's lives? Tabby, Leon, Maggie and…Regan. 'Regan,' I said aloud. 'I left her in the kitchen when I…'

'Nash, I'm here,' came a voice behind me and I looked to see Regan standing to the side of the ambulance, beaming as though I'd just called her up to collect a prize. She didn't have a scratch on her.

'Oh my God,' I said, and gathered her in for a hug. 'Are you okay?'

'I'm fine. I'm fine. I saw it, Nash! I saw the—'

'Don't say it,' I said. I led her away from the ambulance so we were out of earshot of the two paramedics. 'Where?'

'Through the kitchen window. When I escaped the oven, I ran for the woods and that's when I saw it. I followed it, up through the Landscape Gardens and up to the Birdcage. It led me to safety, Nash. The Beast saved me!'

'You saved yourself,' I told her. 'Listen, don't tell the police about it.'

'Why not? They'll want to know where I went, won't they?'

'Yes, but leave that bit out. Just say you ran and hid. If they go looking for it, they might try to capture it or kill it. We wouldn't want that to happen, would we? Not now that we know it doesn't mean us any harm. Okay?'

She seemed sad, but she nodded. 'It's just something we know about.'

'Yeah. Just you and me.'

'It means I won't be the hero for finding it though.'

'We have to protect it, Regan. It'll be our…'

'Secret?' she suggested.

'No, I don't like secrets,' I said. 'It'll just be ours. Okay?'

She grinned widely. It looked strange on her face, but not unpretty. 'Okay. What's wrong with your neck?'

I couldn't even feel there was anything wrong with my neck, until I swallowed and then I felt it. Jesus, did I feel it. I went to the back of my ambulance again and wrapped the foil cape around me. Both the paramedics were at the front of the ambulance. The man was talking into the radio by the steering wheel. The woman was fiddling about inside her medical bag. I looked through the windscreen. Dawn was breaking on the horizon. Something was breaking in me too. I kept thinking back to him, lying there on the library floor.

The blood spurting from his neck; a graceful fountain of red.

The sound as I plunged the pencil into his flesh.

The sound as I pulled the pencil back out and watched as his skin closed back around the hole I'd made.

I only remembered stabbing him once. Twenty-seven times? That wasn't me. That *couldn't* have been me.

I only remember watching as the last rattling breaths left his body. And I did nothing but sit there, watching, hoping.

I'd enjoyed it. The power was in my hands. I'd killed him. I'd stabbed him over and over and over and over again. His blood covered my face. Some of it had gone in my mouth. I could still taste him. And I'd sat there and watched him die.

What a monster I had inside me. And I never even knew it.

Another police car, or another ambulance, was coming down the drive. As it got closer, I could see there were no flashing blue lights. Maybe it was Clarice's parents. Or Dianna's mum.

I stood up and went round the side of the ambulance.

The car was getting closer still, but it was so dark I couldn't make out its colour or shape. Just the lights, getting brighter and coming down the drive faster and faster. It parked up hurriedly on the grass verge, just outside the turning circle. I kept on walking towards it. The closer I got, the more details I could make out. Big car. Square lights. Soon I could see the colour of it. Blue.

A blue Volvo Estate.

My dad's car.

'Miss, come back here, miss,' came the Scottish voice, but I kept running towards it. No way was I going to look back. No way was anyone going to stop me from running towards that car.

My dad got out of the driver's seat. My mum got out of the passenger seat, not even closing her door.

'Mum! Dad!'

'Nash!' she screamed. It was her, it was Mum. Dad was running too. He was shouting for me too. I kept running and running towards them, running hard, as though I was being chased again, but this time the only thing chasing me was the need to hold my parents again and have them hold me and tell me everything was okay. Their faces were white and terrified.

'Nashy! Baby, my baby, what's happened?' said Mum, as I ran into her arms and breathed in her familiar scent of Marc Jacobs Daisy and coconut shampoo. Dad grabbed both of us in his wide embrace and squeezed us.

'It's all right, she's all right. We've got her, it's all right.'

'Ow,' I said.

Mum pulled back and cupped my face in her hands, her cheeks streaming with tears. 'What the hell's happened here? Look at you, you're...' She saw my neck. She looked into my eyes. It was like she didn't recognise me for a moment. 'Oh my God, what's he done to you? We heard it on the news coming down...'

'I'll tell you everything—just don't touch my neck, okay?'

They hugged me again, but this time I didn't feel a thing. Because a voice was calling me from somewhere else.

The car. I swallowed, painfully.

'Nash?'

It wasn't in my dreams and it wasn't in my nightmares. He was there. He was real.

Getting out of the back of the car, his foot in plaster,

shaking off the chequered blanket we always slept under. My brother. My Seb.

'Oh my God.'

I barely heard my dad, saying how he'd got lost in some Colombian village, which didn't have a phone signal. How he'd broken his ankle hundreds of miles from a hospital. How these nice villagers took him in and sent a scout to the nearest town to get help. I heard it, but I didn't take it in. When I reached him, and felt him against me and held him in my arms and he held me back, I could feel everything. The pain in my head, my back, all around my neck, my hands, my knees. I cried like rain through the trees. Everything hurt and everything was wonderful, all in one mightily painful punch.

'I kept hearing you in my head, the whole time,' he whispered to me. 'You kept me going.'

I didn't ever want to let go of him.

'You too,' I squeaked.

'What d'you do, burn the joint down?' He laughed, pulling away from me, his eyes wide as he looked around at all the police cars and flashing lights. I looked at him, his face illuminated by the brightness. He was sunburned. He looked older. There were new lines under his eyes. And thinner. His jawline was more obvious. And stubbly like Dad's.

'I missed you so much,' I said, clasping him in again for a hug and squeezing my eyes shut so tightly I saw stars.

When I opened them, I saw the woods beyond him and the rising sun ricocheting back at me from the tree trunks.

He hugged me again. 'Did you get my letter? Did you get the pencil?'

'Yeah.' I sniffed. 'I got the pencil.' And I started crying all over again. And I tasted blood in my mouth again.

'It's all right, it's all right.'

But though I was comforted by his presence, and though I'd always believed everything he said because he was Seb and Seb was my big brother and he was always right, *this* I didn't believe. This didn't feel all right. It didn't feel like this, whatever it was, was over. It felt like he was too late to pull me back this time. Like I had changed. Like something new and dark and monstrous had just been let out of its cage.

'Hey come on,' he said, pulling back and holding my freezing face in his large warm hands and crying like no big brother should. 'It's over. It's finished. We can have Christmas now.'

'Yeah.' I nodded, looking beyond him into the woods again where I just caught sight of it—a large black shadow, slinking slowly away, between the trees and out of sight.

\* \* \* \* \*

## Acknowledgements

Jenny Savill at Andrew Nurnberg Agency for your belief when I needed it most.

Anna Baggaley, Sarah Reader and everyone at Mira Ink for your ceaseless support, editorial advice and general love for my little Monster

All my family, friends and early readers—my sister Penny Skuse, Matthew Snead, Laura Myers, Di Toft, Rachel Leyshon and Barry Cunningham. Thank you for all your advice and encouragement.

Hestercombe House and Gardens—a constant inspiration to me. This time round, Bathory School in the flesh.

Connie Bowler—for your very helpful reminiscences about boarding school life.

Judy Wasdell—for having a dog who habitually sniffs out spines.

All the UKYA book bloggers who follow me on social media and regularly spread the word about my books.

As always, a soundtrack of artists helped me knit and unpick this book every step of the way: Aiden, Alice in Chains, Gabrielle Aplin, Avicii, The Bangles, The Beatles, Birdy, Eminem, 5 Seconds of Summer, Foo Fighters, Frankie Goes to Hollywood, Ellie Goulding, The Heavy, Hole, Keane, Jay-Z, Linkin Park, Marilyn Manson, My Chemical Romance, Nirvana, Paramore, Rage Against the Machine, Royal Blood and Slipknot.

And to anyone who has screwed me over, rejected me or even just mildly pissed me off in the last thirty-odd years—you helped too. A lot.

# THE IRON PRINCE—
# MY NEPHEW—
# BETRAYED US ALL.
# HE KILLED ME.

# THEN I WOKE UP.

Waking after a month on the brink of death,
Ethan Chase is stunned to learn that the Veil that
conceals the fey from human sight was temporarily
torn away, casting the human world into chaos.
In the face of unprecedented evil and unfathomable
power, Ethan's enemies must become his allies, and
the world of the fey will be changed for evermore.

**The long-awaited final book in the
bestselling Iron Fey series**

*Coming soon...*

www.miraink.co.uk